"If you've read any of the ten previous Maggody mysteries, you know what to expect. If not, you're in for a treat."

—*The Advocate* magazine

"Fans of the Maggody series will revel in this entry. . . . Hess does again here what she has done so expertly before: keep a firm hand on outrageous characters whose peccadilloes are worthy of a French farce."

—*Publishers Weekly*

"C'Mon Tours is not highly recommended but this new hilarious episode in the popular Joan Hess series is."

—*Mystery Covers Bookshop News*

"As marvelously giddy as anything in Hess's first ten chronicles of Maggody, with a core of logic as surprising as a Cracker Jack prize."

—*Kirkus Reviews*

Also by Joan Hess

The Maggody Series

Malice in Maggody
Mischief in Maggody
Much Ado in Maggody
Madness in Maggody
Mortal Remains in Maggody
Maggody in Manhattan
O Little Town of Maggody
Martians in Maggody
Miracles in Maggody
The Maggody Militia

The Claire Malloy Series

Strangled Prose
Murder at the Mimosa Inn
Dear Miss Demeanor
A Really Cute Corpse
A Diet to Die For
Roll Over and Play Dead
Death by the Light of the Moon
Poisoned Pins
Tickled to Death
Busy Bodies
Closely Akin to Murder
A Holly, Jolly Murder

Joan Hess

Misery Loves Maggody

POCKET BOOKS
New York London Toronto Sydney Singapore

This book is a work of fiction. Names, characters, places and incidents are products of the author's imagination or are used fictitiously. Any resemblance to actual events or locales or persons, living or dead, is entirely coincidental.

 POCKET BOOKS, a division of Simon & Schuster Inc.
1230 Avenue of the Americas, New York, NY 10020

Copyright © 1998 by Joan Hess

Originally published in hardcover in 1998 by Simon & Schuster Inc.

ISBN: 0-671-01684-9

First Pocket Books printing January 2000

10 9 8 7 6 5 4 3 2 1

POCKET and colophon are registered trademarks of Simon & Schuster Inc.

Cover art by Ben Perini

Printed in the U.S.A.

For Philip D. Hart, Jr.,
who fought the good fight.

ACKNOWLEDGMENTS

I am grateful to the generous help of Lori Ham, Linda Nickle, and Deborah Adams in matters of research. It is rumored that at least one of them has shared a fried peanut butter sandwich with Elvis.

Misery
Loves
Maggody

O N E

"**I just don't know,**" **Ruby Bee was saying as I came across** the dance floor. Due to the twang in her voice, as well as the whine (fruity and full-bodied), all four words were polysyllabic.

The remark was intended for her best friend and co-conspirator, Estelle Oppers, who was perched on her favorite roost at the end of the bar, but I butted in anyway.

"You don't know something?" I said, my eyes wide and my jaw waggling as if I'd received a collect call from the White House. "But I've always assumed that you know everything, Ruby Bee. I am so stunned by the enormity of this revelation that I may faint in this exact spot where Popeye Buchanon tossed his cookies not more than a week ago."

Ruby Bee crossed her arms. "Suit yourself."

I eased onto a stool midway down the bar, where I could inspect the pies under glass domes. "What is it you don't know? How to calculate the circumference of a circle? What really goes on between Raz and his pedigreed sow when the drapes are drawn? Where all the flowers have gone?"

I was being a real pain, but it was so cold and windy that nothing was going on in Maggody. Nothing worthy of my attention as chief of police, that is—as well as the entirety of the department. I'd had a deputy for a while, but he'd lost his mind and murdered the love of his life. In that he was a Buchanon, there hadn't been all that much to lose. Buchanons are scattered across Stump County like scrub pines, and a heritage of dedicated inbreeding has resulted in simian foreheads, squinty yellow eyes, and surly dispositions. If Charles Darwin had encountered the Buchanons, he might well have abandoned his life's work and checked into a monastery.

Estelle arched her carefully drawn eyebrows. "I'll tell you what I don't know—and that's where you got that smart mouth. Sometimes you act like you was raised in a barn."

"Instead of a motel?" I said.

Ruby Bee snatched up a basket of pretzels and set them well out of my reach. "Now listen here, young lady, the Flamingo Motel's a sight better than a trailer out in the Pot O' Gold or a shack up on Cotter's Ridge. Remember all those times I washed your mouth out with soap for using nasty language? You didn't miss Sunday school more than once or twice a year, and only then if you were sick. I worked my fingers to the bone so you could wear nice clothes and—"

"Enough," I said, conceding in hopes I could wheedle a grilled cheese sandwich out of my mother the saint. I knew my chances would be better if I waited until her nostrils quit flaring. Most of the time she comes off as a harmless, grandmotherly sort (if you overlook the pink eyeshadow and unnaturally blond hair), but she's booted many a drunken redneck out of Ruby Bee's Bar

& Grill. One of them required nine stitches in his buttocks, or so the legend goes.

Estelle shot me a suspicious look, then picked up a creased flyer and said, "I realize a hundred and seventy-nine dollars ain't chicken feed, and there'll be some other expenses, but I say we ought to up and do it, Ruby Bee. I disremember when you last set foot out of the county except to go to that flea market on the other side of Hasty." She gestured at the row of empty booths along the wall. "It's not like you'll be losing a lot of business if you close for four days."

"I have plenty of customers at noon and happy hour," Ruby Bee countered coldly. "This time of day's always slow. You don't seem so busy yourself, or you wouldn't be sitting here yammering about a trip."

"A trip?" I said.

"That's right, Miss Snoopy Ears. Estelle and me are thinking about going on this four-day Elvis Presley Pilgrimage. I was always a big fan, you know. I was barely out of pigtails when I heard him on the radio, and I thought I'd died and gone to heaven. That first time he was on *The Ed Sullivan Show*, a dozen of us girls gathered in Jo Ellen's living room to watch. You should have heard the squealing! Jo Ellen's pa said it sounded like the greased-pig contest at the county fair."

Estelle deftly repositioned a bobby pin in her towering red beehive and gave Ruby Bee a sly smile. "I'd have thought you were well out of pigtails by nineteen fifty-six. Weren't you born in—"

"Let me see that," said Ruby Bee, plucking the flyer out of Estelle's hand. "It says on the first day we go to Memphis, get checked into a motel, and have the evening free to eat supper and relax. On the second day, we spend the morning at Graceland and souvenir shops. After lunch, we drive to Tupelo to see Elvis's birthplace, the museum, and a special chapel he had built after he got rich and famous. Isn't that just like him?"

I feigned a sentimental smile. "It sure is. By the way, is there any chance you might fix me a grilled cheese sandwich?"

"Then," she continued, apparently unimpressed with my ploy, "the next day we go to a little town south of Memphis to spend the night. That whole stretch is where they've got all those riverboat casinos, although from what I've heard, they don't exactly float out in the Mississippi River. They just ring 'em with concrete canals and call them that because of some state law about gambling. That evening we're gonna see a show featuring Elvis impersonators. On the fourth day we drive back to Farberville."

"I think it sounds real nice," said Estelle.

I sighed. "I think a grilled cheese sandwich sounds real nice, too."

Ruby Bee looked at me over the top of the flyer. "All you ever think about is food, Arly. You ought should spend more time fixing your hair and putting on makeup and shopping for clothes that show off your figure. That sloppy old sweater isn't gonna attract a man, and you're not getting any younger. You don't want to end up like Perkins's eldest, do you?"

That was one of the stock threats hurled at local juvenile delinquents; I'd heard it all my life, starting on the day I'd filched a dime out of her handbag to buy an ice cream cone at the Dairee Dee-Lishus. Chocolate and vanilla swirl, for the record—or rap sheet.

I slid off the stool. "I guess I'd better go back to the

PD in case someone's preparing to commit a heinous crime that will require all of my courage and cunning to solve. Only this morning the mayor of our quaint village caught a high school girl attempting to shoplift a carton of cigarettes at the supermarket. He wanted to convene a firing squad on the spot, but I convinced him that life imprisonment would be more appropriate."

"Who was it?" asked Estelle.

Ruby Bee smirked. "I'll bet it was Darla Jean McIlhaney. I see her and Heather Riley puffing away like smokestacks every time they go past me in the station wagon."

"Maybe," Estelle said, "but it sure could have been that runty Bodine girl. Lottie has her in home ec and says the girl can't even put bread in a toaster."

I buttoned up my coat and left them to their speculation. I had no doubt they'd have all the sordid details by suppertime, in that the grapevine makes a marked detour through the bar and grill, curls around Ruby Bee's private unit in the motel out back, and then takes off at a brisk clip for Estelle's Hair Fantasies.

No heinous crimes seemed to be in progress as I trudged up the road, my hands jammed in my pockets and my face lowered in an ineffectual attempt to keep grit out of my nose and eyes. The vacant buildings with yellowed newspapers taped across the windows were still vacant, as far as I could tell, and the newspapers were still bragging about the lunar landing. The bench in front of the barbershop was unoccupied. It was too early in the day for brawls at the pool hall, and the inhospitable weather might keep all but the worst of its patrons at home that evening, glued to their televisions. Roy Stiver had closed his antiques shop for the season and retreated to a more civilized climate, and what had briefly been a pawnshop (and before that, a New Age hardware store) was once again a sanctuary for field mice and spiders.

I went into the front room of the red-bricked PD, continued into the back room to pour myself a mug of coffee, and, having done the grand tour, was settled down at my desk with a magazine when the telephone rang. I answered it without enthusiasm.

"Hey, Arly," said Harve Dorfer, the esteemed sheriff of Stump County, "you done with the paperwork on that wreck by the reservoir? It turns out the driver's father is a lobbyist for the poultry industry, and the reporters are swarming like flies on a meadow muffin."

I rocked back in the cane-bottomed chair and regarded the water stains on the ceiling for inspiration. "Yeah, I have, but there's something wrong with my transmission and I need to get it fixed before I drive into Farberville. It's too damn cold to sit and wait for a tow truck."

"Colder'n a witch's tit, but that's not keeping the reporters out of my hair. First thing in the morning?"

"Okay," I muttered. "Anything else going on?"

Harve exhaled wheezily, and I could easily imagine the cigar smoke swirling around his head like exhaust fumes from a bus. By the end of the day, the evil-tempered dispatcher was the only person fearless (or perhaps feckless) enough to enter his office. "Nothing but the usual crap," he said. "Some moron ran over a gas pump in Emmet and damn near flooded the town. A preacher in Scurgeton keeps calling all the time because he's convinced that satanists are sneaking into his church at night. A woman in LaPierre swears her husband's been abducted by international terrorists, but the fellows at the garage where he works are pretty sure he ran off with an eighteen-year-old tramp. Rumors about drugs at a nightclub down past the airport, and a holdup at a convenience store. You're more than welcome to any of them."

"Gee, Harve, I was hoping for something with a little class," I said.

"Like another rash of UFO sightings?" He guffawed at his boundless wit. "Tell ya what, if Bigfoot sticks up a shoe store, I'll give you a call. While you're waiting, write up the damn report and get it to me in the morning."

I mumbled something and hung up, annoyed at his wisecrack. Admittedly, some peculiar things had happened in Maggody since I'd slunk home to pull myself back together after a debilitating divorce from a Madison Avenue hotshot. It had taken me a long time to figure out that while I was studying menus in trendy restaurants, my so-called husband was slipping his office telephone number to waitresses. He may have worn silk ties, but his soul had proved to be strictly polyester.

I'd presumed that nothing could happen in a tatty little town with a population that hovered at seven hundred fifty-five, depending on who was doing time at the state prison at any given moment. Despite everything that had gone on, from the arrival of Hollywood movie stars to a recent invasion of militia wackos, most of the locals still considered the night Hiram's barn burned as the primo focal point of the century.

I reached for the magazine once again, but before I could get to it, the telephone rang. Doubting that it was Ruby Bee calling to say my sandwich was ready, I picked up the receiver.

"Arly, this is Eileen. Have you seen Dahlia?"

Although I most certainly had seen Dahlia (née O'Neill) Buchanon on more occasions than I cared to remember, I opted not to confuse Eileen. She has enough to worry about, what with being the mother of one of Maggody's least bright Buchanons, Kevin, and the mother-in-law of the above-mentioned Dahlia, who's in a class by herself.

"Not lately," I said. "Is she lost?"

"I'm not sure. She asked me to come over after lunch and watch the babies while she went to the supermarket. That was more than three hours ago. The babies are good as gold, but I'm getting worried about where she could be all this time."

"Did you call the supermarket?"

"I talked to Kevin, and he said she hadn't been there. Even if she decided to drive into Farberville to shop, she should've been home by now."

"Maybe you should call Wal-Mart and have her paged. She could have been overwhelmed with the array of disposable diapers and gone into a stupor." I did not add that with Dahlia, it would be hard to tell; her expression is generally that of a deeply baffled bovine.

"I suppose I could do that," Eileen said unhappily. "I know it's silly of me to get upset over this, but you'd think now that Dahlia's a mother, she'd be a sight more responsible. It's hard on her, what with Kevvie Junior fussing half the night, and then Rose Marie waking up the minute she gets him to sleep. I do everything I can to help her out while Kevin's at work, and he's real good with them when he's home, but it's still an awful burden on her."

This was not a topic I wished to explore. "Tell you

what, Eileen, as soon as I finish some paperwork, I'll drive around town and look for her car. She might have gone to the county home to visit her granny, or be working her way through the menu at the Dairee Dee-Lishus."

"Thanks, Arly," Eileen said, sighing. "It's just . . . well, you know how it is."

I replaced the receiver, but without feeling the typical stab of exasperation I seemed to be experiencing these days whenever a local resident intruded with yet another idiotic complaint. Raz Buchanon, for instance, believed he was entitled to police protection whenever the "revenooers" went after his moonshine operation somewhere up on Cotter's Ridge. The reasoning is hard to explain. Hizzoner the Moron wanted me to fix a speeding ticket with the state police. Elsie McMay felt as though her old license plate (circa 1987) made her car legal. Pathetica Buchanon could not understand why she shouldn't sell herbal remedies out of her basement; she did, after all, have a one hundred percent guaranteed cure for prostate cancer, eczema, and vaginal warts.

Take your choice.

Maggody was more than a fly splat on the map. It was a mind-set, and I wasn't sure how much longer I could survive on stimulation that peaked with running a speed trap out by the petrified remains of Purtle's Esso station. An APB for Dahlia would not result in grand drama, since odds were excellent that she'd drag in with a lame story about a sale at Kmart or a two-for-one ice cream sundae special at a café in Farberville.

My efficiency apartment above the antiques store seemed more cramped and less efficient every day. My

mother's most exciting idea to date was to take an Elvis
bus tour. Harve had failed to proffer an investigation
centering on a zillion-dollar Brink's robbery; most of the
cases foisted on me involved stolen dogs, wrecks, and
pitiful domestic disputes in which I wanted to shoot all
parties concerned—innocent, guilty, and the odd bystander—on principle.

I needed a break.

"Honey, you know I go every year," Jim Bob Buchanon
said as he scraped the last of the scalloped potatoes onto
his plate. "The Municipal League meeting in Hot
Springs always gives me ideas how best to oversee our
community."

Mrs. Jim Bob slid her napkin into a plastic ring, then
began to gather up dishes from the table. "So you say,
but it seems to me there's more drinking and partying
than workshops. When have you ever come home with
anything more than a three-day hangover?"

There wasn't much of an answer to that, so Jim Bob
took a final bite and put down his fork. "I was reckoning
I'd leave Thursday and be home Sunday afternoon. I'm
particularly looking forward to the session Saturday on
bonds. Why, we could have us another stoplight in no
time at all."

"Who else on the town council is going?"

"Roy's off in Florida, and I can't see him coming all
the way back for this. Larry Joe sez he can't go on account of Joyce's mother coming to visit. Hobert ain't
been back to town since he was let out on parole. It
looks like I'll have to drive all that way by myself."

Mrs. Jim Bob considered suggesting she could accompany him just so she could watch his face turn as

green as the solitary lima bean on his plate. However, it was not a charitable thought, so she put it aside.

"Brother Verber came by this morning," she said, raising her voice as she ran hot water in the sink. "He wants me to organize a rummage sale at the Assembly Hall. As reluctant as I am to shoulder the responsibility, I owe it to the congregation to make sure it's done properly. I shudder to think about what might happen if Eula Lemoy tries to do it. Her linen closet is a nightmare of mismatched sheets, and her medicine cabinet is overflowing with expired prescriptions, hairpins, bent tweezers, and gunky tubes of ointment. You'd never think from the way she prances around town that she has piles, would you?"

"I never would have thought that for a second," Jim Bob said sincerely. Holding in a belch so's not to give her an excuse to launch into a lecture about unseemly table manners, he stood up. "I think I'll run down to the SuperSaver and finish up some paperwork."

She looked over her shoulder at him. "Is that *all* you're planning to do?"

Despite the fact the oven had been off for quite a while, he felt a sudden dampness in his armpits. Her eyes weren't as yellowish as most of the Buchanons on her side of the family (her legal name being Barbara Ann Buchanon Buchanon), but they were real beady and, at the moment, real shrewd. There wasn't any way she could know about his plans for the weekend, he told himself as he forced a grin. "Someone's got to make sure the store doesn't run short on canned corn while I'm gone. The ladies in the Missionary Society'd whup me when I got back."

"Would they?" she murmured.

He grabbed his jacket and headed for the back door. "I may be there till midnight, checking stock and working on the payroll. No reason for you to wait up, what with your busy day tomorrow getting ready for the rummage sale. Asking you to be in charge is the only smart thing Brother Verber's done since . . ."

Unable to finish the sentence, he shut the door and hurried out to his truck, where a half-pint of bourbon was tucked under the seat. It was the only antidote he knew for the indigestion that invariably accompanied a dose of his wife's self-righteousness.

C'Mon Tours had no walk-in trade, since it was situated in the kitchen of a house in one of the shabbier neighborhoods in Farberville. Pesky zoning regulations made it necessary to use a post office box as an address, and not so much as a discreet brass plaque hung beside the front door of the residence.

Miss Vetchling, who served as president, office manager, secretary, bookkeeper, and receptionist, gloomily thumbed through the folder marked "Elvis." With only six pilgrims lined up, she would barely break even. Certainly there would be no profit after the van rolled back to Farberville and the driver submitted the invoices for gas, motel rooms, and his fee.

She pulled out a calculator and crunched figures. She'd determined the price of the tour based on eight paying customers, and even then would have netted less than five hundred dollars to cover office overhead and unanticipated expenses. The van had more than a hundred thousand miles on the odometer, and had broken down twice on the Gala Azalea Tour to Little Rock. The windshield wipers had quit working on the Cherokee

Spree to Tahlequah the preceding summer; the turn signals had done the same midway to the Branson Bonanza Weekend.

Being self-employed had not proved to be quite as invigorating as Miss Vetchling had hoped. It had seemed so very promising when she came upon the idea of arranging tours for those with modest means yet a thirst to explore the world, to feast their weary, middle-class eyes on the wondrous and even the exotic. Giddy with her own sense of derring-do, she'd used her savings to purchase the van (surely the first of a veritable fleet of sleek silver buses) and placed a small ad in the local newspaper. She'd thumbtacked flyers on bulletin boards outside grocery stores and taped them on utility poles along Thurber Street.

She knew better than to expect to make a profit during the first several months, but it seemed to her that rather than building up a roster of satisfied customers clamoring for the next tour, she was spending entirely too much time writing letters in response to their complaints. It was ridiculous to presume one would be staying in a Hilton when one was paying a pittance. She had never knowingly booked rooms in a dangerous establishment or requested a breakfast buffet of stale muffins and tepid coffee. She'd simply relied on the integrity of her colleagues in the travel industry. It was not her fault that some of them had let her down. How could she have known about dirty sheets, cockroaches, and, in one instance, a thriving drug business conducted in the lobby of the motel? None of her customers had been wounded during the raid. In all honesty, she reflected testily, it might have been the most exciting thing that would ever take place in their pedestrian little lives.

Miss Vetchling shoved a strand of gray hair out of her eyes and studied her calculations, searching for ways to economize. The married couple would share a room, as would the two women from Maggody. This left the male professor and a woman, who dotted the i's in her name with little hearts, in single rooms, unless they perchance struck up a romance on the road to Memphis. Otherwise, they might object to being roommates. Her driver had made it clear that he wouldn't so much as start the engine without the promise of a room to himself.

Perhaps it would be best to cancel the tour, she thought. As loath as she was to acknowledge failure, she was even more loath to spend her last few dollars to subsidize the pilgrimage. She would be obliged to return their money, however, which meant she might not be able to pay the long distance bill at the end of the month. Without a telephone, C'Mon Tours would go nowhere and she'd be back in some dreary office, filing papers for executives who could scarcely recite the alphabet.

A rap on the back door startled her out of her dispirited reverie. She gave herself a second to resume her composure, then gestured at the man on the porch to come into the kitchen.

He was not an imposing figure, but he was vital to her operation. He was several inches shorter than she and moved with an odd scuttle, as if he fancied himself to be a CIA operative approaching a snitch in a smoky Berlin nightclub. Liver spots and moles were sprinkled across his wrinkled brown face, and his eyes were disconcertingly cloudy for someone with a current chauffeur's license. Miss Vetchling was careful never to ride with him.

"Yes, Baggins?" she said.

"I changed the oil like you told me to," he said. "I suppose it'll make it over to Mississippi and back, but it sure as hell ain't going to pass no safety inspection when it's time to renew the plates."

"We'll worry about that at the appropriate time. At the moment, I'm trying to decide whether to cancel the tour. Only six people have signed up."

Baggins sat down across from her and looked at the figures she'd written on a pad. "Gas ain't gonna cost that much, and you're paying insurance even if the van's parked out back."

"That may be true," she conceded, not pleased to be corrected by an employee lacking a high school diploma, even one who was proficient in automotive repairs and maintenance—skills that she suspected had been learned in prison. "That does not affect the cost of motel rooms, however. We require five rooms each night, and I've budgeted forty dollars for each. It comes out to six hundred dollars."

"I got a cousin what lives in Memphis. He might know of someplace cheaper than forty dollars."

She was pondering this when the telephone rang. "C'Mon Tours," she said into the receiver. After a moment, she continued, saying, "It does happen that we've had a cancellation for the Elvis Presley Pilgrimage, dearie. We will be able to accommodate you, but I'm afraid there's an additional charge because of last-minute adjustments. You do realize the price is per person, double occupancy, don't you?"

C'Mon Tours was back in business.

T W O

" **I** was under the impression this was to be an *escorted*
tour," Estelle said as she climbed into the van and
assessed her fellow travelers. It was a mixed bag, but
everybody looked respectable—for the most part, anyway. The two women who'd taken the first double seat
were tacky, gussied up like they were planning to stop
by church on their way to a beer bust. Estelle had never
trusted women that wore fake fur coats, and she could
see right off the bat that no critters on God's green earth
had been sacrificed in the making of theirs.

Baggins stopped studying a map of Memphis long
enough to put on his C'Mon Tours cap. "I'm the escort.
My name's Hector Baggins, but don't go calling me by
my first name."

"You're the one that's gonna lecture us about the important Elvis destinations and tell us fascinating facts
about his life and times?"

"Hush, Estelle," said Ruby Bee as she sank down on
the nearest torn vinyl seat. "The sooner we leave, the
sooner we'll be back."

"She's absolutely correct about the escort," chimed in

a man on the seat in the back. Ruby Bee swiveled her head to glare at him, but she couldn't make out much, since he was wearing a floppy cloth hat and darkly tinted sunglasses. His lips were on the thin side, like Mrs. Jim Bob's. What hair that was visible was jet black and came close to brushing the collar of his khaki jacket, but his voice was not that of some kid fresh out of high school. He sounded more like a politician, although it'd be hard to explain why he'd be traveling in a battered van if he was. She concluded he wasn't.

"Furthermore," he continued, "I have a copy of the brochure, and it implies that an expert in Elvisian folklore will be available to offer insights into—"

"That'd be me," Baggins said, folding the map with professional expertise. "Anything you want to know, you just ask."

"In what year did Colonel Parker buy a controlling interest in Elvis's management contract and for how much?"

Baggins tucked the map behind the sun visor. "The next thing, you'll be asking me about his bowel habits. Sure sounds like somebody could use a laxative."

"I asked a straightforward question," the man retorted.

Baggins grinned. "You ever tried Ex-Lax? May do the trick."

"I beg your pardon!"

"Are we gonna talk about poop for the next four days?" said the woman clad in molting orange fur. "How icky."

There might have been a rebellion in the making had Miss Vetchling not arrived on the scene with a clipboard. She ascertained Ruby Bee's and Estelle's names, asked the man in the back if he was Rex Malanac, and looked at the two women. "Ms. Crate? Yes, thank you. Ms. Zimmerman? Oh dear, if that is a cigarette I see in your hand, you must put it out immediately. Out of concern for others, there will be no smoking permitted on the van. Also, alcoholic beverages are specifically forbidden, as well as the use of vulgar language."

She moved aside to allow a young couple to squeeze past her. "Todd and Taylor Peel? Well, then, it looks as if we're all present and accounted for. Did all of us place our complimentary C'Mon Tours duffel bags in the luggage compartment at the rear of the van? We wouldn't want to find ourselves in Tupelo without our toothbrushes, would we?"

Rather than solicit responses, she beamed at the pilgrims as if they might arrive at the Holy Land sooner or later. "I do so hope you'll appreciate the spirituality of your journey. You have this marvelous opportunity to explore the complexity of Elvis's impact on contemporary culture, his contribution not only to rhythm and blues but also the dawning of rock and—"

"I thought we were supposed to have an escort," Estelle said sullenly. "It seems to me all we have is a driver."

Miss Vetchling's smile slipped but did not fail her. "You weren't planning to walk to Memphis, were you?"

Before anyone could offer an argument, she stepped down and slammed the door of the van. Baggins winked at Estelle in the rearview mirror, turned on the ignition, and coaxed the van into a somewhat jerky departure. Miss Vetchling was waving jauntily as they went around the corner and up Thurber Street.

Ten minutes later they were on the highway that

would take them through the mountains to the interstate, which in turn would take them across the state in
five hours or so to their first goal: Memphis. The next
day they'd drive a hundred miles in a southeasterly direction to Tupelo, Mississippi. Their final destination,
the casino in a town south of Tunica, wasn't more than
thirty miles south of Memphis, but the shortest route
from Tupelo went through towns that prided themselves on perpetual road construction.

Estelle glanced at Ruby Bee, who looked as anxious
as a preacher at the Pearly Gates. "Is something wrong?"
she whispered.

"I'm fine," Ruby Bee said, resting her head against the
window.

"Does anybody *really* care if I have a cigarette?" asked
the woman identified thus far only as Ms. Zimmerman.

"I most vigorously object," said the married woman
seated behind Ruby Bee and Estelle. "Aren't you aware
of the dangers of secondhand smoke?"

"I'll put you on the side of the road if you light up,"
said Baggins. "Miss Vetchling told you the rules before
we left."

"Bunch of crap," muttered Ms. Zimmerman.

Baggins stiffened. "Mind your tongue, missy."

This was not the most promising beginning, Estelle
thought, as she watched cheap motels, gas stations, and
used-car lots fly by. She chewed on her lip for a moment, then decided to take matters in her own hands
and do what it took to make this a "marvelous opportunity." If nothing else, they were all stuck with each other
for the next four days.

"Listen up," she said in the perky voice she imagined
an escort would use. "Let's all introduce ourselves and

say why we came on this trip. I'm Estelle Oppers from Maggody. I'm a licensed cosmetologist and a lifelong Elvis fan. I almost cried my eyes out when he died back in August of nineteen seventy-seven. I remember just like it was yesterday where I was when I heard the news. I was giving Elsie McMay a permanent when my second cousin Charlaine in Magnolia called to tell me. Charlaine was always real thoughtful about passing along things of that nature."

When no one else jumped in, she took a breath and went on. "My friend here is Rubella Belinda Hanks, but you can call her Ruby Bee. She owns a bar and grill in Maggody and makes the fluffiest buttermilk biscuits west of the Mississippi. She was saying just the other day how she remembered when Elvis first appeared on *The Ed Sullivan Show*. I ain't sure any of the rest of you are that old."

"Estelle!" said Ruby Bee. "There's no call to—"

"So let's move on to you," Estelle said, pointing at the woman with curly brown hair, scarlet fingernails, and a thick slathering of pancake makeup. "Tell us all about yourself, honey."

"My name's Cherri Lucinda Crate, and I just love Elvis. I don't want y'all to think I'm some kind of crackpot, but I'm not convinced he's dead. My niece's roommate's boss is positive she saw him in a record store in Minneapolis last fall. She got right smack next to him and—"

"That's ridiculous," said the man in the back. "I'm an expert in the field, and I can assure you that the King is dead. All these conspiracy theories about falsified autopsies and empty coffins are hogwash."

Cherri Lucinda twisted around in her seat. "Who says you're an expert?"

"I do."

She looked at the others for support. "I want to know what makes him such a know-it-all. Like he has a degree in Elvis or something? I happen to know plenty myself. I can tell you the exact day Priscilla arrived in Germany—and what she was wearing when she stepped off the airplane. I can recite Gladys's genealogy back four generations. Just when did the angels come down and anoint this fellow?"

Estelle agreed that this was an interesting question, so she nodded regally at the man in the hat. "Mebbe you should tell us."

"My name is Rex Malanac, and I'm a professor of twentieth-century European literature at Farber College."

Cherri Lucinda cackled. "I told you he didn't have a degree in Elvisology or whatever you call it. All I can say is he'd better not start lecturing us like we're a bunch of snot-nosed college kids. I paid too much money to be bored to tears from here to Tupelo and back."

"I am also a scholar of popular culture," Rex said in a steely voice. "I have presented more than two dozen papers on the impact of Elvis on contemporary social values. I am considered one of the leading authorities in the field."

"Why doncha take a hike across that one?" said Cherri Lucinda as she pointed out the window at an expanse of stubble. "You'll be right at home with all the bullshit in the weeds."

This was not going as Estelle had planned. She cleared her throat and looked at the would-be smoker, who had frizzy blond hair and even more makeup than her companion. "I'm sure we all have something to contribute. What about you?"

"I'm Stormy Zimmerman, and I don't have a blessed thing to contribute. I just decided to come along at the last minute. All I know about Elvis is that he died the same year my brother did. My mother made me sing 'Love Me Tender' at the funeral. I've hated that song ever since."

"That's so sad," said Cherri Lucinda. She pulled a tissue from her purse and carefully blotted the corners of her eyes. "How come you never told me?"

"You never asked." Stormy looked up at Estelle. "Will you please get on with this stupid party game?"

Estelle had been feeling sorry for the gal up until that point. "We're not exactly in a rush, are we? What is it you do for a living?"

"Cherri Lucinda and I are entertainers. What else do you want to know? My ma was an alcoholic and my pa took off when I was ten. I married a truck driver when I was seventeen, but he turned out to be a real bastard and I got divorced two years later. Before I moved to Farberville last fall, I worked in Bossier City. Oh, and I have a butterfly tattooed on my butt."

"Oh, really?" said Rex. "I'm a bit of an amateur lepidopterologist. Ten dollars says I can identify the particular species. I'll give you two-to-one odds."

"In your dreams—or your worst nightmare," she shot back, her hair obscuring her eyes but not her scowl.

Estelle tried again. "How about you two?" she asked the couple in the third seat. "You're married, aren't you?"

The purported husband stared at his purported wife, then slumped down in the seat, exhaled loudly, and closed his eyes. His neck was as thick as a ham and his bulk took up a good deal of the space. His round head and close-set features reminded Estelle of a bowling ball just waiting to be rolled down an alley. The woman, in contrast, was trim, with short, sensible dark hair, a clear complexion, and wire-rimmed glasses that gave her a sober look.

"I'm Taylor," she said, "and this is Todd. I wrote on the form that we're married, but that's not exactly true. We're supposed to have a big wedding this summer in a church in Little Rock, with five hundred guests and a dinner dance at a country club after the ceremony. Todd's mother has been handling all the preparations, since we're both students at Farber College." She looked over her shoulder at Rex. "Todd's third-year law, and I'm a business major, so I guess we've never taken any classes from you."

He shrugged. "One of the prerequisites for my classes is the ability to read and write. From what I've heard, neither is required in your respective fields."

Estelle doubted she could persuade the driver to stop long enough to chuck the smarmy professor off the van. "This wedding sounds real lovely," she said to Taylor.

"I got married in a courthouse," said Stormy. "Afterward, we had a dinner dance at a truck stop just outside Texarkana. The orchestra canceled at the last minute, so we had to feed quarters in the jukebox all night long."

"Yeah, real lovely," Todd said suddenly, opening one eye. "So what the hell are we doing on this shitty van?"

Now it was Taylor's turn to pull out a tissue and dab her eyes. "The thing is," she said in a quavering voice, "my parents were killed in a car wreck when I was a baby. My grandparents, who raised me, died last summer. They left a sizable estate, but there have been problems with probate and until the court sorts them out, I'm virtually penniless. I had to borrow money from the bank to cover tuition this year."

"Give me a break," said Baggins, bearing down on a lump of roadkill in the middle of the lane. "You want to stop at one of these junk shops and buy a violin?"

Estelle glowered at the back of his head. "One more word out of you and I'll call your boss at the first rest stop. Please go on, Taylor—we're all just as interested as we can be."

Taylor blinked earnestly. "It's customary for the bride's family to pay for the wedding and reception. As things are right now, I couldn't afford five hundred hamburgers, much less lobster and steak. Todd's mother insisted that she and Todd's father would pay for everything, but I'm not one to accept charity. I guess you could say we're eloping. I've made arrangements for us to get married in the chapel next to Elvis's birthplace. All of you are invited."

Todd rumbled like a backhoe on a steep incline. "My mother is gonna have a stroke when she finds out. She's already booked the club and the caterers, and is expecting to have an engagement party during spring break."

"She'll survive," Taylor said. "She can use all the money she saves to treat herself to a month at one of those incredibly expensive spas. The pedicurists and masseuses will adore hearing her complain about our treachery."

"I'll hear it for the rest of my life. We've been over this a thousand times. My mother got carried away with her plans, but we don't have to go along with everything. She can cut back on the guest list, and if we get married in the morning, we can do the cake-and-punch thing at the church."

Rex leaned forward and said, "Why don't you invite her to meet us in Tupelo? She can be your flower girl."

"Shut up," snarled Todd, his face turning so red that he, rather than his mother, appeared in imminent danger of a stroke. "Leave my mother out of this—okay?"

Taylor elbowed him hard enough to elicit a grunt. "Why don't you go back to sleep, Todd? You'll feel better when we get to Memphis, and we can have a blast on Beale Street tonight."

"We might as well, 'cause all hell's gonna break loose when we call my mother and tell her we're on a really glamorous honeymoon in friggin' Tupelo. Who wouldn't rather be there than in Hawaii? I can't believe I let you talk me into this."

"Well, then," Estelle said, abandoning any perkiness, "I guess that's it. I think we should all agree to have a fine time."

Cherri Lucinda flicked Baggins's shoulder with one of her talons. "What about you, Mr. Escort? You a big Elvis fan?"

"He's more likely to be a convicted felon," drawled Rex.

The van went into a gut-wrenching swerve before it squealed to a stop on the shoulder of the highway. The driver of the pickup behind them yelled an obscenity as he went past, and his gesture was far from salutary.

Baggins cut off the engine and swiveled around in his seat. "I ain't taking that kind of shit from anybody, sir. I may not have a college degree, but I've been driving for a good forty years. If you got a problem with me, let's step outside and settle it right now."

Cherri Lucinda held up her hands. "Hey, I was just making conversation. There's no reason for everybody to get all hot and bothered, especially with so many miles in front of us. Mr. Malanac, you owe this man an apology. He's a working stiff like the rest of us."

"That's right," said Estelle. She was hoping Ruby Bee and the others would jump in, but everybody was pretending to be more interested in the chicken trucks grinding past. It was right cowardly of them, Estelle thought, and of Ruby Bee in particular. College students and entertainers might not know how to face down bullies, but barkeepers sure did.

She was about to say as much when she noticed Ruby Bee was giving Cherri Lucinda a downright bumfuzzled look, and to make things even more peculiar, Cherri Lucinda was looking toward the back of the van with the exact same expression.

"I apologize," Rex said grandly. "Please drive on."

Once they were back on their way to the interstate, Estelle nudged Ruby Bee and in a low voice, said, "Are you sure you're okay?"

"I wish you'd stop pestering me, Estelle. There's not a single thing wrong—okay? If you ask one more time, I swear I'll get off this van at the first stop and hitchhike home."

"Who's gonna stop for a middle-aged woman carrying a green-and-orange duffel bag? You'd look like a fugitive from a health club."

Estelle thought she was being funny, but it was clear from Ruby Bee's snort that she didn't have the same opinion. There wasn't much to do but sit back and keep her fingers crossed that they'd survive for the next four days without bloodshed.

"Hey, Arly," Kevin said as he came into the PD, "have you seen Dahlia?"

"Yes," I said, finishing the last cold swallow of coffee. I set down the mug, stood up, and began to pull on my coat. "Give me a few days to think about it and I can come up with the precise moment I last saw her. It may have been outside the emergency room before they took her up to the maternity ward. I'll let you know." I slung a wool scarf around my neck and picked up my car key. "I'm in a bit of a rush, Kevin."

"I can see that." He gulped several times, causing his oversized Adam's apple to bobble like a buoy in a squall. "The thing is, Dahlia left right after she got the twins down for a nap, and she hasn't come back. I'm gittin' worried."

"You didn't leave them home alone, did you?"

"I'd sooner kiss Perkins's eldest than do a thing like that. I called my ma and she came over to watch 'em while I went looking for Dahlia. Ma said she called you a few days back, but you dint have any luck."

I hadn't exactly beaten the bushes until dark, but I had kept an eye out for her car as I followed one of the school buses to the county line to make sure everybody stopped when the children scrambled out of the bus. Upholding the law in Maggody usually doesn't require spurts of hand-to-hand combat or manhunts up on Cotter's Ridge. "No, I didn't see her that afternoon."

"What am I gonna do?" he said with a groan. "She ain't been herself since the babies came two months ago. One minute she's cooing and kissing their little toes, and the next she's locked in the bathroom, bleating like a calf left out in the cold. I don't know what to make of it, Arly."

He was so pathetic that I relented. "Sit down," I said, gesturing at the uncomfortable chair I keep for unwanted visitors. Kevin most assuredly fell into that category. "Have you talked to her?"

"I tried, but you know how she can be." He took out a wadded handkerchief and blew his nose. "The doctor sez it ain't unheard of for a new mother to feel kinda blue, 'specially when she's dog-tired all the time. Kevvie Junior and Rose Marie are perfect angels, but they still got to be fed and have their diapers changed and take their baths and—"

"I get the picture," I said. "When Dahlia left, where did she say she was going?"

"She said it weren't any of my business," he said, giving me a bewildered look. "This isn't the first time she's gone off like this. I'm scared that some day she won't come back from wherever she goes, and my sweetpeas will grow up without a ma's love. What'll I tell them when they get older?"

"How often has she been disappearing like this?"

"Two or three times a week. She stays gone all afternoon, then comes home and goes straight to the kitchen to make supper. If I so much as try to give her a peck on the cheek, she threatens to knock me silly with the skillet."

I was mildly intrigued. "Any particular days?"

Kevin screwed up his face as he considered my question. "I reckon not, but never on Sundays. We always have dinner at my ma and pa's and spend the afternoon there. Ma turned my old bedroom into a nursery. Kevvie Junior's crib has a blue blanket and Rose Marie's has a pink one. There's a sampler on the wall that sez—"

"It sounds charming," I said. "Are you sure Dahlia hasn't said anything about where she goes? She's never mentioned a name?"

His jaw dropped, giving me a distasteful view of his stained teeth. "You don't think she's seeing some fellow, do you? She wouldn't do something like that, Arly. We have spats like all married folks, but she ain't the kind to turn her back on her babies and her lovin' husband."

"No, Kevin," I said, trying without success to keep the irritation out of my voice, "that's one thing I most definitely was *not* thinking. It's more likely that she feels the need to get away for a few hours and is doing nothing more than driving around the county."

"Then why's she more ornery than a polecat when she gets home?"

"All I can suggest you do is ask her."

"And git my face squashed with a skillet," he said morosely. "I thought what with you being a trained police officer, you should be able to do something."

I readjusted the scarf. "I can't arrest her unless she's sticking up liquor stores on her afternoons off. I have to leave now. I was supposed to meet someone in Scurgeton five minutes ago."

Kevin thrust out what little chin he had. "You got to promise to talk to her. You can act like you just dropped by to see the babies, then trick her into spillin' the beans. I cain't go on with her being mad at me all evening and rolling over in bed and knocking my hand away if I so much as dare to cuddle up. It ain't healthy."

"All right," I said, "I'll stop by in the morning. You may continue to sit there the rest of the afternoon if it amuses you. Close the door when you leave."

I went out to the car, not at all sure I wouldn't find him there when I got back, snuffling and sniveling as he pictured his three-hundred-pound love goddess in the arms of a swarthy stranger. Kevin's mind, in the rare moments when it's activated, can come up with some damn peculiar ideas.

Scurgeton's population was half that of Maggody's, and its appearance even bleaker. I drove past a couple of trailers and a gas station nearly hidden behind a mountain of tires, found a faded sign that read "Mount Zion Church," and turned down the indicated dirt road. The church, a squat concrete block structure with a flat roof, was a hundred feet from the intersection and ringed on three sides by stark trees. All it needed to perfect its resemblance to a prison was a fence topped with concertina wire.

I parked behind a sedan, buffed my badge with my coat cuff, and tried to simulate the demeanor of a qualified and competent law enforcement agent who was eager to serve the public. Which, at that moment, I was anything but.

The interior of the church was no more inviting than its exterior. The furnishings consisted of metal chairs and a wooden pulpit. One the back wall was a framed depiction of Jesus surrounded by sheep. An elderly man with thin white hair, a beakish nose, and hunched shoulders was pacing behind the pulpit; as I approached, he halted and gave me a suspicious look.

"You are . . . ?" he said.

"Chief of Police Ariel Hanks from Maggody. Sheriff Dorfer asked me to take a statement from you and have a look around."

"You're a woman."

"Is that an observation or an accusation?" I said, wishing I'd brought my gun and at least one bullet.

"I was not expecting a woman. The desecration of my

church is a serious matter. Sheriff Dorfer should have come himself."

He did not add "or at least sent a man," but I could almost see the words hovering above his head. I had a feeling he and I were not going to be bosom buddies by the end of the interview.

I took a notebook and pencil out of my pocket. "And you are . . . ?"

"The Reverend Edwin W. Hitebred. I'm the pastor of the Mount Zion Church, and nothing like this has ever happened in the fifty-seven years I've served the congregation. I really think I'd better call Sheriff Dorfer and insist that he deal with this in person."

"Go right ahead, Reverend, but you won't have much luck catching him. He's dealing with a drug-related shooting in a sleazy nightclub on Tuesday. One guy dead, two critically wounded, DEA agents camped in his office, reporters demanding updates every hour. That's why he asked me to talk to you."

Hitebred's bushy white eyebrows twitched as he studied me for a long moment. "Well then, Chief Hanks, it looks as though you are my cross to bear, although I will not do so gladly. Where do you want to begin?"

"I understand you believe that trespassers have entered the church on several occasions. Is there evidence of this?"

"I would hardly describe these satanists as mere trespassers," he said icily, "and of course I have evidence. Come this way."

He went through a doorway into a small room with a desk, several straight-backed chairs that were apt to be more uncomfortable than the one in my office, and stacks of journals and battered hymnals along the wall.

I waited just inside the doorway while he opened a desk drawer, pulled out a manila envelope, and dumped its contents on his desk.

"Here's your evidence," he said.

I went over to the desk and examined the debris. "A paper clip, a cigarette butt, a pink barrette, three rubber bands, a button, and a piece of chalk. What exactly does this prove?"

"It proves that satanists broke into the church at least four times in the last month. They conducted abhorrent rituals and desecrated the sanctity of the church. I demand that you put a stop to this, Chief Hanks. I want the culprits caught and sent to jail to ponder the wickedness of their deviant beliefs."

I held up my hand. "Let's take this one step at a time, if you don't mind. Just why does this pile of trinkets prove anybody is breaking into the church? Isn't it more likely that members of your congregation dropped these during services?"

"Absolutely not!" he snapped, scraping everything back into the envelope. "I should have known you would fail to grasp the significance of this evidence. When will Sheriff Dorfer have this other business wrapped up?"

My teeth clenched, I moved newspapers off a chair and sat down. "Why don't you explain the significance, Reverend Hitebred? Speak slowly and perhaps I can follow you."

He returned the envelope to a desk drawer and sat down across from me. "My daughter cleans the sanctuary after each service. She sweeps the floors, straightens the chairs, and puts away hymnals. Anything accidentally left behind is placed in a box in the vestibule to be retrieved by the member before the next service. We find eyeglasses, pens, scarves, umbrellas, and Sunday school lessons. The evidence I showed you was not discovered after a service but beforehand, when I was making sure everything was in readiness to offer praise to the Almighty God. Do you attend church, Chief Hanks?"

"This is an official investigation, Reverend Hitebred, and personal remarks are inappropriate. Even if I accept your assertion that the objects were not dropped during or after a service, I still don't see why you think satanists are involved."

He began to drum his fingers on the desk in an uneven cadence. "It's obvious that unauthorized persons have been sneaking into the sanctuary at night. There's nothing worth stealing. I take the cash box and checkbook home with me after each service. Our hymnals are worn and dog-eared from decades of use."

"I still can't make the leap to satanists and rituals. Why not kids with nowhere else to meet?"

"My daughter sets the thermostat at fifty when she leaves. The folding chairs were selected for durability, not comfort. Furthermore, members of the congregation have driven by at odd hours during the night, and no one has noticed a light. A cold, dark building would hardly make a cozy clubhouse, would it?" His fingers quickened their beat. "If not satanists who find twisted satisfaction in defiling the sanctuary, then who?"

I felt as though his fingertips were pounding my temples. "These unauthorized entries could be taking place during the day. Maybe some unfortunate guy's holed up in a shack out in the woods and is taking advantage of your plumbing."

"Our plumbing consists of a sink and a toilet in a shed

out back. We do not waste the contents of the collection plate on luxuries, but on doing God's work."

He may have been boasting about their contempt for worldly pleasures, but he had a point. It may not have been sharp enough to poke through a slice of bread, much less do damage to a hostile cyclops, but I could tell from his condescending smile that we both knew it. Despite the weather, I would have preferred to be at a roadblock with Harve's deputies, stopping vehicles to make sure sinister drug dealers weren't hunkered in the backseat, than to be sitting in the office of the Mount Zion Church in the company of the Reverend Edwin W. Hitebred.

"Okay," I said, "then what about locks? Surely the doors aren't left unlocked for the convenience of stray souls seeking asylum in the bosom of the Lord."

His smile vanished. "That smacks of sacrilege, Chief Hanks. Yes, both doors are kept locked, and my daughter and I have the only keys. If someone wishes to bring in flowers for a holiday service, one of us comes down to open a door. We live only a mile farther down the road, and since I'm retired, I'm always available." He paused, then added, "Unlike Sheriff Dorfer, or so it seems."

"There's nothing he can do," I said, standing up, "but feel free to call him if you find any hobgoblins under your bed."

I would have preferred to exit on a broomstick, but as it was, I just walked out the door.

T H R E E

Estelle poked Ruby Bee as the van started across the bridge that spanned the Mississippi River. "Look," she said excitedly, "you can see the skyline over that way, and the Pyramid over there. Isn't this something?"

Ruby Bee rubbed her grainy eyes. "I suppose so. How much further to the motel?"

"You feeling bad?" asked Cherri Lucinda, reaching over the seat to pat Ruby Bee's knee. "I have some saltines in my purse if you want something to nibble on."

"I'm perfectly fine." Ruby Bee stared out the window at the wide stripe of milky brown water. Traffic down there was a sight less frantic, what with a few barges placidly pushed along by tugboats and a motorboat cutting circles for no apparent reason. In contrast, Baggins seemed to think he was going to win a prize if he got to the far side of the bridge before everybody else in the state of Arkansas. The only thing he deserved was a traffic ticket for speeding or reckless driving, she thought with a frown.

"I've got some antacid tablets," said Estelle.

Ruby Bee turned on her with a glower that could have melted an iceberg, or at least a good-sized ice cube. "How many times do I have to tell you to let me be? Would you feel better if I tap-danced in the aisle? I'm already getting fed up with you, Estelle Oppers, and we ain't even one-fourth of the way through this trip."

"Well, pardon me for being concerned. You can say whatever you want, but you were moaning while you were asleep and right now your face is pale as a sow's belly. Your eyes don't look so good, neither. Do you recall how Two Claude Buchanon's eyes turned all orange after he ate nothing but carrots for three months?"

Ruby Bee resumed staring out the window. Cherri Lucinda looked like she wanted to say something, but she kept her peace as Stormy squeezed her way through the aisle from the back of the van and plopped herself down. Behind them, Todd was snoring, and Taylor was reading a thick paperback book. The professor was humming bits of Elvis tunes; Ruby Bee hoped she wouldn't have to slap him upside the head in the next day or so, but she could see it might happen.

Baggins grunted and cursed under his breath as he battled the late-afternoon traffic. Big stone buildings gave way to less imposing structures, until most everything was real sorry. A discount liquor store sat next to an establishment to cash checks. A club promised naked women, cheap drinks, and no cover charge. Pretty soon they were treated to nothing more than walls splashed with graffiti and vacant lots strewn with broken glass.

"Just where are we going?" demanded Estelle.

"The Starbright Motel," Baggins said, dodging a car filled with raucous teen-aged boys that reeked of trouble in the making. "Five or ten more minutes."

Taylor lifted her eyes from her book. "I assume it's accredited with a nationally established chain."

Baggins braked to allow a couple of drunks to weave across the street. "Elvis himself stayed there before he hit it big. That's why C'Mon Tours chose it. One of you may be lucky enough to stay in the exact room he did back in nineteen fifty-three."

"I'm unfamiliar with that factoid," Rex Malanac said from his seat in the rear.

"Ain't my fault," Baggins countered as he swerved around a bag lady wheeling a cart, slowed down as a police car sped by, and then pulled into a parking lot. "Here we are, folks—the Starbright Motel. It may not look like much, but it's an important site for dedicated Elvis fans. Ain't nobody come to Memphis without stopping here."

"Here?" said Estelle, gawking at the shoddy two-story structure. What once had been a swimming pool was now a pit of cracked concrete that seemed to be nothing more than a garbage dump. Two overweight men in vests, baggy pants, and caps were on the upstairs balcony, waving their arms at each other and mouthing what might well have been, to employ Miss Vetchling's terminology, vulgar language. One of them held a bottle in a brown paper bag. A woman with purple hair came out of a downstairs room and shook her fist at them. One of them pretended to unzip his fly, which sent her scurrying back inside.

"Here?" Taylor echoed.

Rex snickered. "No doubt this was the inspiration for Elvis's first big hit, 'Heartbreak Hotel,' although I should think as many heads have been broken here as hearts." He pushed back his jacket cuff and made a production of studying his wristwatch. "The time is exactly four-seventeen, in case anyone's interested."

"So I owe you twenty bucks," muttered Stormy. "Big fuckin' deal."

Baggins parked in front of the office. "Now listen up," he said, grinning like he'd wangled guest rooms in Graceland, "you came for the Elvis experience, not some sanitized tour. Sure, we could stay at the Holiday Inn or the Ramada, but C'Mon Tours is dedicated to giving you more than that. If everybody'll sit tight, I'll be right back with your room keys." He glanced up at the balcony. "It might not be real wise to get out and stretch your legs just yet. Won't take me but a minute to get us checked in."

Estelle licked her lips, trying to think what a perky escort might say in this situation. "So Elvis stayed here. Isn't that exciting?"

"I'm about to wet my pants," said Cherri Lucinda, "but not from excitement. Do you think this hellhole has indoor plumbing?"

"Of course it does," Estelle said firmly. "Like Baggins said, it's part of the Elvis experience."

Stormy smirked at her. "Are fleas and bedbugs part of it, too? I'll bet we're the first people since nineteen fifty-three to rent rooms by the night. Everybody else does it by the hour or the month."

The other pilgrims were still pondering this when Baggins slid open the van door. "We're all set. I'll get your bags out of the back and give you your room keys. After that, you're on your own till nine o'clock tomorrow morning, when we head for Graceland."

"What about this so-called complimentary breakfast?" asked Estelle.

"You can get coffee and doughnuts in the lobby. If you want something more, there are a couple of restaurants within walking distance. Should be safe at that hour, but you ladies need to mind your purses."

They climbed down out of the van and formed a huddle as Baggins pulled seven identical orange and green duffel bags from a compartment. Storage space being at a premium, each of the travelers had been warned that he or she could take no other luggage, so most of the duffel bags were bulging.

Rex Malanac grabbed his, accepted a key, and hurried toward the end of the building, looking up every so often at the men on the balcony. Todd picked up a bag and, after Taylor hissed at him, a second one and dutifully followed her into a room.

"Hanks?" said Baggins, turning over tags. "Oppers?"

"I'll get 'em," Estelle said. "Come along, Ruby Bee. We'll get settled and have ourselves a nice rest."

"I want to find a drugstore," said Stormy as she lit a skinny brown cigarette and looked at Baggins. "Assuming you can suggest one that won't be robbed two seconds after I walk in the door."

"You should be okay as long as it's light outside. Won't be any gunfire until ten, maybe eleven tonight."

Ruby Bee clutched Estelle's arm. "Let's find our room—okay?"

Estelle took a key from Baggins and hustled Ruby Bee along until they arrived at the door of #12. "Just think of it," she said with as much enthusiasm as she could choke out as she opened the door, "this may be the very room that Elvis slept in."

"He didn't sleep all that well," Ruby Bee said, eyeing the swaybacked double bed. A cobweb hung from the cracked light fixture in the ceiling. Even from the door-way, she could see the dingy porcelain in the bathroom and a wet towel on the floor. "This is awful, Estelle, and what's more, I'm afraid to set foot outside until morning. What are we gonna do about supper?"

Estelle managed a smile. "Oh, it's not so bad. We can put on our pajamas, turn on the TV, and order a pizza. That way, you can be ready for Graceland in the morning. I can hardly wait to see Elvis's house and cars and airplanes! The last time Charlaine was here she bought a tea towel with Elvis's picture and a set of beer mugs depicting Graceland in all the seasons. In the winter, there was snow on the gate, and in the spring—"

"I'm not hungry." Ruby Bee went into the bathroom and locked the door with a loud click.

"Excuse me," said Estelle as she put down their duffel bags. "I don't recollect begging you to come on this trip, Ms. High and Mighty. The Flamingo Motel ain't exactly the Ritz."

"What?" Ruby Bee said from the bathroom. "You say something about the Flamingo?"

"No, I was just looking up the number of a pizza place." She picked up a telephone directory, glumly noted its thickness, and put it down. She wasn't smitten with the notion of walking around after dark in hopes they'd find a cafe, but the cheeseburgers they'd had for lunch at a truck stop wouldn't hold them till morning. Especially not Ruby Bee, who'd taken only a couple of bites before pushing hers aside.

She was still perched on the end of the bed, fretting and gnawing her lip, when she heard a rap on the door. Despite the urge to duck into the closet, she made herself open the door.

Cherri Lucinda fluttered her fingers. "Stormy's insisting we go out so she can buy a few things. Can we bring you and your friend something to eat? She looks mighty wan, like my sister-in-law did just before she was diagnosed with liver cancer. Three months later she was in an urn on the mantel."

"Ruby Bee doesn't have anything wrong with her!" Estelle retorted, then realized she'd spoken too loudly and lowered her voice. "This is sweet of you, though, and we'd dearly appreciate a couple of sandwiches and cans of soda pop. Are you sure it's safe to walk around here?"

"No, but Stormy's going whether or not I do, and I figure two's safer than one. I was gonna ask Todd the Clod to go with us, but I knocked on their door and nobody answered. Same with that professor, although I don't think he could scare off a wino, much less a mugger. About all he could do is recite poetry."

"Come inside so I can get you some money," Estelle said, keeping her fingers crossed that Ruby Bee'd stay in the bathroom for a few more minutes. "You think ten will cover it?"

"Yeah." Cherri Lucinda stopped in front of the mirror and scowled at her reflection. "I can't believe all the gray hairs I'm getting at my age. Didn't you say you're a cosmetologist? Maybe one night you could put on a rinse for me, and trim the split ends while you're at it."

Estelle was going to point out that as a professional, she expected to get paid, but then she thought about the sandwiches and soda pops Cherri Lucinda had offered to fetch. "I don't have my scissors with me. Otherwise, I'd be tickled pink."

"You think I'd look better with bangs?"

"I'm not so sure. Your face is already kinda plump, and bangs tend to—" She stopped as a fist pounded the door. "Oh my gawd, what should we do? What if it's some drug-crazed rapist?"

"Plump?" said Cherri Lucinda.

Ruby Bee poked her head out of the bathroom. "What in tarnation's going on, Estelle? Stop gaping like a widemouthed bass and open the door before whoever it is breaks it down!"

Estelle opened the door. Before she could so much as get out a squeak, Stormy stumbled into the room, shoved her aside, and slammed the door shut. Once she'd locked the deadbolt, she seemed to notice her stunned audience.

"Sorry if I scared you all," she said with a weak laugh that wouldn't have fooled a newborn baby. "I was waiting for Cherri Lucinda out by the van, and all of a sudden . . ."

Estelle felt her knees begin to buckle. "A drug-crazed rapist attacked you? Are you hurt?"

"You'd better sit down," said Cherri Lucinda. "You don't want to faint and bang your head and have to get stitches. When that happened to me, they shaved half my head and I had to wear a wig for three months."

"Poppycock," Ruby Bee muttered as she closed the bathroom door.

Stormy sat on a chair. "Nobody attacked me. I just got real nervous on account of all these lowlifes lurking nearby. Considering what we're paying, you'd think we could stay somewhere halfway decent. I don't care if Elvis was born here, much less spent one night more than forty years ago. It ain't like there's a rack of postcards in the office." She went to the window, peered through the dusty slats of the venetian blind, and after a moment, said, "My imagination must be earning time-and-a-half. There's nobody out there."

Estelle went over to see for herself, nearly tripping over a duffel bag on the floor. Hers and Ruby Bee's were next to the bed where she'd set them earlier. "Whose is this?" she asked.

Stormy picked it up. "Mine. I was afraid to leave it in the room. You never know who might have a key." She looked at Cherri Lucinda. "You ready to go? I'd just as soon not be out there in the combat zone after dark."

"Here's some money," said Estelle. "Any kind of sandwich will be fine, as long as it's not barbecue. Ruby Bee seems to be experiencing a touch of something, and I don't think she needs to be eating anything spicy."

"I heard that!" the accused roared from inside the bathroom.

Cherri Lucinda took the bills from Estelle and unlocked the door. "God willing, we'll be back in half an hour. You might ought to use the chain as well as the deadbolt. Those two guys on the balcony are still hanging around."

As soon as they'd left, Estelle relocked the door and made sure the chain was secured, then moved back to the window to watch their progress across the parking lot. In spite of Stormy's earlier panic and Cherri Lucinda's warning, nobody seemed to be loitering in the vicinity of the van.

"I don't know why I let you badger me into this," Ruby Bee said as she came out of the bathroom. "The Flamingo may not be the fanciest motel in Stump County, but I make sure to scrub the commodes and collect dirty towels off the floor. When we pull back the bedspread, we're likely to find bloodstains. Maybe Elvis died here."

Estelle ordered herself not to so much as glance at the bed. "Everybody knows he died at Graceland. He's buried there, too, so we don't have to worry about his ghost dropping by for a chat long about midnight. Which side do you want?"

"All I want is a place to stretch out for a few minutes. If I had my druthers, it'd be on my own bed in Maggody, but that ain't going to happen for another three nights."

She didn't pull back the bedspread, but instead lay down, folded her hands, and closed her eyes like she was the featured attraction at a funeral. Estelle figured it wouldn't be wise to launch into 'Love Me Tender,' so she sat down on a chair and unzipped her duffel bag. She'd managed to cram in a change of clothes for each day, along with underwear, pajamas, a toothbrush and toothpaste, several combs and hair clips, and a bottle of her preferred brand of shampoo, but there'd been no way to bring foam rollers and her industrial-sized can of hair spray. C'Mon Tours needs a bigger van, she thought tartly as she hung what she could on the single clothes hanger in the closet.

She thought about turning on the television real low, but she couldn't tell if Ruby Bee was asleep or playing possum and waiting for the chance to start complaining again. She finally went back to the window and peeked through the slats, her fingers crossed that Cherri Lucinda and Stormy had found a place nearby and might be on their way back.

She was expecting to see nothing more interesting than the woman with purple hair or maybe the two men from the balcony, so she was a little surprised when a black car pulled into the parking lot, circled the pool like a shark closing in on a swimmer, and stopped right behind the C'Mon Tours van. There were two men in the front seat, both as broad-chested as wrestlers. The driver was hard to make out, but the passenger had a bald head, a nose that was as bumpy as an unpaved road, and puffy lips.

Estelle held her breath, even though she knew darn well they couldn't hear her. If they were getting ready to steal the van, it would be up to her to stop them somehow. Rushing outside to shoo them off didn't seem wise. She'd feel real stupid if she called 911 and then later found out they had checked into the motel and were looking for their room.

She must have made a small noise of frustration because Ruby Bee said, "Now what's wrong? Did Elvis drive up in a Cadillac? Why doncha ask him inside to sit a spell and tell us whereall he's been for the last twenty years?"

"There's a car out there."

"In a parking lot? Goodness gracious, what will these big-city folks think of next?"

Estelle let go of the slat. "What's gotten into you, Rubella Belinda Hanks? I ain't seen you this persnickety since Arly moved up North and married that good-fornothing Yankee peckerwood. You tried my patience back then, and you're doing it now."

Instead of apologizing like she was supposed to, Ruby Bee pulled a pillow over on her face.

Estelle looked back out at the parking lot. The black car hadn't moved and both men were just sitting there like warts on a toad. After what seemed like an eternity—but according to her watch, was more like five minutes—Baggins came limping into view from the direction of the street. He froze for a second, then approached the driver's side of the car and bent down.

Whatever was happening seemed to upset him. He backed away from the car, nearly losing his balance as his heel hit the curb. The driver was the one doing most of the talking; Baggins shook his head a couple of times, then shrugged and said something, although Estelle could see he was less than enthusiastic.

She was wishing she could read lips like her great-aunt Dorita, when she realized the bald man was staring at her, his eyes narrowed and his face stony. She snatched her hand back and dropped to her knees. Her heart was pounding so hard she was afraid it was gonna burst, and for a moment she was sure she was going to pass out on the dirty carpet.

Keeping low, she made it to the bathroom, locked the door, and sat down on the commode until she could get her breath. What a silly goose she was, she scolded herself. For starters, all the man could have seen was the slit in the blinds. There was no way he could have seen her face or even been sure she was watching them. And so what if she had been? The parking lot was nigh onto empty, and the arrival of a car might attract attention from any of the rooms. Or why couldn't she have just been waiting for a pizza to be delivered?

She took a few more deep breaths, splashed some water on her face and wrists, and went out of the bathroom. Ruby Bee had dozed off, if her snoring was to be believed. Just to be on the safe side, Estelle tiptoed around the bed and peeked ever so slyly through the blinds.

The car was gone, as was Baggins. She was wondering

if he'd been kidnapped—and what she should do about it—when she heard female voices approaching the room. She took off the chain, and at the sound of the first tap, twisted the deadbolt, opened the door, and held her finger to her lips.

"Ruby Bee's taking a nap," she whispered, gesturing for them to come inside.

Cherri Lucinda held out a paper bag. "The best we could find was a Git 'N Go. One of the sandwiches is tuna salad, the other roast beef. We got you some chips and a couple of candy bars, too. Your change is in the bottom."

"This is real thoughtful of you," said Estelle.

Stormy leaned against the door, her duffel bag in one hand and a plastic bag in the other. "Can I ask a favor? Cherri Lucinda here said that you offered to do her hair. I've been thinking for a long time that I need a new look. As long as we're stuck here for the evening, would you consider doing something with mine?"

"You're making a big mistake," Cherri Lucinda said as she resumed examining herself in the mirror. "Don't come crying to me when you see what you've done."

"Well?" Stormy said to Estelle. "It beats sitting around listening to gunfire."

Estelle felt like she'd been cornered by a pit bull. This particular pit bull was six inches shorter and most likely thirty years younger, but her eyes had a disturbing gleam and it was hard to guess how she'd react if she didn't get her way. Estelle nodded and said, "I suppose I can give it a try, even though I'm used to my own equipment. What do you want?"

"To be a brunette, for starters," Stormy said as she dumped the contents of the plastic bag on the seat of the chair. "I'll take care of that while you eat, and you can cut my hair afterward."

"You'll be sorry," said Cherri Lucinda, her face inches from the mirror as she explored a blemish on her chin.

Stormy picked up a box with the depiction of a radiant brunette. "So will you if you don't shut up. You should know that when I make up my mind to do something, I do it no matter what. Remember when I told you that I was going to knock the crap out of that bouncer if he touched my tit one more time? I'll bet *he* does."

She went into the bathroom, and seconds later water began to run in the sink. Estelle took out the sandwiches and put them on the bedside table as Ruby Bee woke up and made a selection. "How long have you and Stormy been friends?" she asked Cherri Lucinda.

"Couple of months. Do you honestly think my face is plump?"

"Only in a fetching sort of way. You remind me of one of those actresses who always ends up with the handsome hero," Estelle said tactfully. "Maybe that's why you look kind of familiar. Did you work at Kmart before you became an entertainer?"

"I've worked a lot of places." Cherri Lucinda dangled some curls across her forehead. "So what do you think? Does it make me look like a chipmunk?"

Estelle was casting around for a way to soften her answer when there was a knock on the door. She took a quick peek through the blinds, then opened the door and let Rex Malanac inside. "I suppose you want your hair cut, too," she said irritably. "If I had this much business back home, I'd have hired a limo to take me to Memphis."

In spite of the fact it was dark outside, he was still wearing sunglasses and the canvas hat. "I did not realize I was interrupting what used to be called a hen party when I was in college. I'm in need of some change to use the pay telephone at the corner. I went to the office, but it's locked and the lights are off."

"Can't a college professor figure out how to use the phone in a motel room?" said Cherri Lucinda, making it clear she hadn't forgotten the exchange in the van.

"One cannot make long-distance calls on the room phones," he said. "No doubt the owners of this establishment have been stiffed on many occasions. Is she"— he pointed at the supine form on the bed—"ill or in some sort of distress?"

Ruby Bee's voice was muffled but her tone was unmistakable. "The only thing causing me distress is the procession through this room. You'd think this was one of the rooms in Graceland, what with everybody traipsing in and out like a herd of tourists. I'm surprised I haven't heard cameras clicking."

Estelle took her wallet out of her purse and poured coins onto the corner of the bed. "How much change do you need? I've got what looks to be three dollars' worth."

"That will have to suffice," he said.

Stormy came out of the bathroom, her hair obscured by a terrycloth turban. "What's going on? Are we gonna play poker or something?"

Cherri Lucinda rolled her eyes. "Now there's a swell idea. I'm sure the professor here is a big fan of strip poker. He's probably hoping you'll lose so he can see that butterfly of yours. Ain't that right, Rex?"

"Don't be ridiculous," he said.

Stormy put her hands on her hips. "I'll drop my pants if you'll drop yours."

Ruby Bee groaned loudly. "What does a body have to do to get some peace and quiet around here?"

"Come on, Rex," continued Stormy. "Let's have a little game of show-and-tell."

Cherri Lucinda began to play with the top button of her jeans. "Hey, I've got a mole on my thigh. Can I play, too?"

Estelle stood up. "Cut this out, and I mean it. You all are acting worse than a third-grade Sunday school class. Nobody is taking off anything in this room. Now you either behave or march yourselves right out the door. Go squabble in the parking lot—and try not to get yourselves shot."

Stormy's hands fell to her sides. "It was just a joke. Are you still willing to cut my hair?"

Cherri Lucinda looked at Rex. "Do you think my face is plump?"

He smiled. "No one would accuse you of being emaciated, but you are hardly Rubenesque."

"What's that supposed to mean?" she demanded.

"This is craziness!" said a muffled voice.

Estelle had to agree with that.

F O U R

"**W**hatta you want?" asked Dahlia as she opened the front door. Her puckery frown made me feel as welcome as a bout of the flu.

"I dropped by to see how the babies are doing," I said, frantically trying to remember their names. It had been a tempestuous topic at the bar—they were Buchanons, after all—but most of it had rolled right past me. "Ruby Bee's been telling me how cute they are."

"They're sleeping, and the last thing you wanna do with twins is wake 'em up. I wouldn't so much as tickle their toes if Armageddon commenced to begin across the road."

I reminded myself of my promise to Kevin and nodded sympathetically. "What if I take a quick peek from the bedroom doorway? I'd love to see them, Dahlia."

"All right," she said as she gestured for me to come inside. "But just for a second and keep your voice low. Rose Marie wakes up ever'time a dog barks in the next county. When she starts howling, Kevvie Junior does, too. It's all I kin do not to join right in."

I tiptoed to the bedroom door, ascertained that there

was a blanket-clad bundle in each crib, and eased the door closed. "I sure could use a cup of coffee before I go," I said, "but if you're busy with something else . . . ?"

Dahlia shrugged and headed for the kitchen. "I don't reckon I've got time to learn how to do brain surgery afore lunchtime. There's still coffee in the pot from breakfast. Sit there at the dinette and I'll fetch some for you."

I did as ordered. Dirty dishes were piled beside the sink, and an empty milk carton lay on the floor next to an overflowing trash can. Keeping my hands off the tabletop to avoid contact with what appeared to be petrified grape jelly, I said, "How old are they?"

"Eight weeks, give or take." She took a cup from a cabinet, then set it down and turned around. "What do you really want, Arly?"

What I really wanted was to leave, but I smiled and said, "To see the babies and have a cup of coffee. I should have come by as soon as you came home from the hospital, but I figured you were too busy for visitors."

"That didn't matter to anybody else. After three days, I told Kevin to get his pa's shotgun and stand out on the porch in case the County Extension Club pulled up in a chartered bus. You and Raz must be the only two folks that didn't come calling—not that I'd let him get within spittin' distance of the babies, ornery ol' sumbitch that he is. Ever'time I see him riding around town with that sow in the front seat, it's all I can do not to start throwing rocks."

"You sound as though you're experiencing a lot of stress these days," I murmured, keeping an eye on her in case she yanked open a drawer and whipped out a knife. I doubted that I could disarm her, but I most certainly could outrun her.

She squinted at me. "Have you been talking to Kevin?"

I opted for the truth, but not the whole truth. "We had a brief discussion about the weather when I was in the supermarket this morning. The bar and grill will be closed for three more days, so I'm having to survive on canned soup and peanut-butter sandwiches."

"It's a good thing you ain't married, then. I fix Kevin breakfast and supper, and put his lunch in a bag so he won't waste money at the deli. Lord knows we don't have none to waste. You wouldn't believe the bills that keep coming from the clinic and the hospital. Kevvie Junior got an ear infection, and the medicine alone costs twenty-three dollars. I wash so many diapers that I use up a five-pound box of detergent every week." She had her back to me, but I could see her hands trembling so violently that coffee was sloshing all over the counter. "Before long, we're gonna need another high chair, another car seat, another stroller, twice as much clothes as we'd planned for, and who knows what else. Kevin's putting in twelve hours a day, but he can't work 'round the clock. I'd go plumb out of my mind if I didn't get a break once in a blue moon."

"It'll be yard sale season before too long. Perhaps you can have Eileen baby-sit while you hunt for bargains. She's pretty good about that, isn't she?"

"I reckon," Dahlia said. "We're out of milk, so you'll have to use formula unless you can drink it black."

The idea was slightly more nauseating than gnawing the grape jelly off the tabletop. "Black's fine. How often does Eileen baby-sit for you?"

"Whenever I ask her, mostly. There've been a couple of times when there was something she had to do, like go to the dentist. The other day she took Elsie and Stan to the vet's office in Farberville. Stan got into a fight with a big yeller tomcat and came near gettin' his ear tore off." She set down a cup in front of me. "I read in one of those tabloids that cats can suffocate babies by sucking all the air out of their lungs. You think that's true?"

I had made no measurable progress in determining the nature of Dahlia's mysterious outings. I decided to leave before the babies woke up and I found a particularly leaky one thrust into my arms. I have nothing against babies as a subspecies, but I prefer them at a civilized distance. Needless to say, Ruby Bee is not pleased with my attitude, and swears that she breaks out in hives whenever I admit it.

"That cat business is an old wives' tale," I said as I gulped down some coffee and stood up. "Thanks for letting me see Kevvie Junior and Rose Louise."

"Her name's Rose Marie."

"And an adorable name it is." I hurried back to my car, shivering as the wind sent leaves skittering down the road. As I drove past Raz Buchanon's shack, I caught a glimpse of a glistening pink snout behind a window-pane.

I did not blow a kiss.

The red light on the answering machine was flashing when I went into the PD. It was likely to be someone other than Ruby Bee, who's been known to leave half a dozen messages telling me how much she hates to talk to my "dadburn silly contraption." She and Estelle had left the previous morning on their grand adventure, although she'd sounded rather grumpy about it when she'd come by to leave a schedule and tell me (in mind-numbing detail) how to get hold of her in an emergency. I had a feeling she suspected the first thing I'd do once she was past the city limits sign would be to elope with a backwoods Buchanon like Diesel, who, as far as anybody knew, was still residing in a cave on Cotter's Ridge and biting heads off live squirrels and rabbits.

I hit the rewind button on the machine and sat down, bracing myself for anything from Kevin's nasal whine to the mellifluous baritone of Prince Charming himself. What I heard was Harve's drawl.

"Hey, Arly, I got a whole damn stack of messages from that preacher in Scurgeton. He wasn't real happy with the way you interviewed him. Now I'd never for a second think you might have smarted off with him, 'cause you and I both know you're a proper little lady." He sighed so I could appreciate the depths of his misery. "Thing is, I'm still up to my ass with this drug case. The district attorney put together a task force, and most of 'em are sprawled on the sofas in the break room, eating doughnuts and driving LaBelle so crazy she's gone and locked herself in the restroom. The DEA is having us track down every last customer over the last five years. There's a membership list on account of it being a private club, but you wouldn't believe how much of it is either fake or out of date."

"Yeah, I would," I inserted as I was treated to yet another sigh.

"You go see that preacher and talk some sense into him before I lose my temper and go out there myself. You wouldn't want me to disgrace the dignity of my office, would you?"

The message ended with a burp. The day was not shaping up well. Dahlia was definitely out of sorts, but

I wasn't prepared to keep her under surveillance unless Kevin and Eileen came up with proof, or even a hint, of something multifarious. The Reverend Hitebred needed an exorcist—or sessions with a shrink. There were no chicken-fried steaks, biscuits and gravy, and black-eyed peas in my immediate future.

I was trying to decide what kind of soup to have for lunch when Mrs. Jim Bob came into the PD, closed the door, and sat down across from me as if settling down to knit and purl her way through a beheading. A word of welcome on my part would have been hypocritical, so I merely waited.

Once she'd put her purse by her feet and removed her gloves, she acknowledged me with a sniff and said, "I've come to discuss a date for the rummage sale at the Voice of the Almighty Lord Assembly Hall."

"I'd donate the shirt off my back, but it's the only clean one I've got until I get by the Suds of Fun to run a load," I said. "As for a date, I'm not ready for a relationship just yet."

"I told Jim Bob he was making a big mistake when he hired you. If you don't mind your mouth, you'll find yourself mopping the floor at the Suds of Fun."

"Does this mean you don't want a date after all?" I said with a stricken look. "I can picture us on the swing on your front porch, sipping lemonade as the moon rises over the ridge. Of course we'd better wait until the evenings are warmer and the scent of honeysuckle fills the breeze. I'll bring my kazoo to serenade you."

Mrs. Jim Bob did not appear to share my idyllic fantasy. "You'd better mend your ways if you want to keep your job, missy. Don't think for a second that Jim Bob won't hear about your disrespectful attitude as soon as he gets back from the Municipal League meeting." She smiled grimly, no doubt envisioning my dismissal (with a tar-and-feathering as the grand finale), then said, "I have set the date of the rummage sale for two weeks from Saturday. I'll need you to direct traffic from seven in the morning until midafternoon. I see no reason why we can't use the parking lots at the bank and the old hardware store, as well as the one behind the Assembly Hall."

"Did Queen Elizabeth donate a few choice pieces from the crown jewels?"

"I shall require each family in the congregation to make a substantial donation of clothing and household goods. Eula Lemoy has been assigned to make sure that the sale is listed in the community calendars of the *Starley City Star Shopper* and the *Farberville Gazetteer.* We will have not only quality merchandise for sale, but also sandwiches, hot dogs, cookies, soft drinks, and coffee. Brother Verber and I prayed for guidance, and the Lord has promised tolerable weather and a fine turnout."

"Are you sure the Lord approves of all these financial dealings in a house of worship? Didn't Jesus boot the money changers out of the temple?"

Mrs. Jim Bob raised her eyebrows. "Well, it's good to see that you still remember stories from your Sunday school days, even though everybody knows you became an atheist when you went to live in New York City. I suppose your mother's grateful you didn't become a streetwalker at the same time."

"I've enjoyed chatting with you," I said, "but I need to go hunt for satanists in Scurgeton. If I catch them, I'll confiscate their black candles and pickled newts' eyes for your rummage sale."

"Just mark your calendar," she said as she picked up

her handbag and started toward the door. "I'll expect to see you at seven sharp that morning."

"Don't bet the farm on it," I muttered as the door slammed.

"Is Todd sick?" Estelle asked Taylor as they watched Baggins load the duffel bags into the back of the van. "When I said good morning to him, all he did was growl."

Taylor glanced over her shoulder, then said, "I'm afraid he had too much to drink last night. He kept insisting it was his bachelor party and buying rounds for everybody. When the club closed, an old friend from Little Rock had to help me carry him out to a cab."

Baggins slammed down the compartment door. "You ladies enjoy your complimentary breakfast?"

Estelle glared at him. "As much as anyone would enjoy stale doughnuts and lukewarm coffee. Elvis didn't stay in any cheap motels in Tupelo, did he?"

Taylor pointed her finger at Baggins. "If we're forced to spend another night in a place like this, Todd and I will sue C'Mon Tours in small claims court and demand a full refund."

"You do that," said Baggins, who'd heard variations of the sentiment on every trip. "Y'all be aiming to stand here much longer?"

Estelle and Taylor climbed into the van. Todd was sprawled across the last seat, his face pressed against the upholstery. Cherri Lucinda and Stormy were in the seat in front of him, and in front of them, Ruby Bee and Rex sat in stony silence.

"Everybody seems a mite glum," whispered Estelle as she and Taylor took the first seat.

"Maybe the sirens kept them awake last night," Taylor

said, thumping the back of Baggins's seat in case he hadn't heard her.

If he had, he ignored her. "Here's the schedule for the day," he said loudly. "We should be at Graceland Plaza in fifteen minutes. You can take the full tour or any part of it you choose, visit the gift shop, and eat lunch in one of the restaurants. We'll meet back at the van at noon and leave right away for Tupelo."

"Are you going to stay with the van while we're at Graceland?" asked Stormy.

He looked up at the rearview mirror, then turned around and gaped at her. "What'd you do to your hair, woman? It looks like you stuck your head in a bucket of pitch."

"How would you like to have that stick shift crammed up your nose?" she countered.

Estelle managed to stop short of smacking him. "I happen to think it looks real cute."

"But it's all shaggy like it was hacked off with a dull pocketknife," said Baggins, his eyes still wide with horror.

Stormy held up a fist. "You want to meet me in front of the van and repeat that?"

"Don't change how it looks," Baggins mumbled as he started the engine.

The van pulled out of the Starbright Motel parking lot. Estelle considered suggesting that they sing Elvis songs to get in a jolly mood, but she had a feeling it wouldn't sit well. Ruby Bee had seemed a bit better when she woke up, and had even choked down a doughnut. For the moment, anyway, her eyes were open and she seemed to be taking an interest in the storefronts and buildings they passed.

Even though the sky was overcast, the professor was

wearing his hat and sunglasses. He was acting kind of squirmy, Estelle thought as she watched him in the mirror, what with the way he kept stealing looks out the back window like he was worried that a police car would pull them over. Yesterday she wouldn't have been surprised, but for now Baggins was driving in a mannersome fashion.

Estelle patted Taylor's knee. "I guess you're starting to get fluttery. What kind of arrangements did you make with the folks at the chapel in Tupelo?"

"Nothing much. One of the ladies who works at the museum offered to pick up a small bouquet for me to hold, and a justice of the peace will be there to take us through the vows. I'm really upset with Todd. If he doesn't start feeling better, we may end up with a funeral instead of a wedding." She pulled off her glasses and cleaned them with a tissue, then put them back on and gave Estelle a wan smile. "Do you think I'm doing the right thing to insist we get married this way? I don't want Todd's mother to hate me because of it."

"There's no point in worrying about it now," Estelle said briskly. "Once she calms down, you can explain how you eloped because you didn't want to spend their money—even though it sounds like they have plenty of it."

"Todd's father is a senior partner in one of those law firms with so many names that the receptionist nearly hyperventilates every time she answers the telephone. If Todd succeeds in putting himself through law school and passes the bar, he'll be given a position at the firm."

"He has to pay his own way through school?"

Taylor began to twist the tissue in her lap. "He got into some trouble when he was an undergrad. His father saw to it that the charges were dropped, but then told Todd he was on his own until he graduated from law school."

"Serious trouble?"

"Not *that* serious. Something about a stripper claiming she was pushed around at a frat party. Todd assured me that he was an innocent bystander who got dragged into it because of his family name. His grandfather was lieutenant governor, and a great-uncle was on the state supreme court."

"Is that so?" said Estelle, more intrigued by the here and now. "What about your family?"

"We didn't exactly get off the *Mayflower* with the Peels, if that's what you mean. Cotton farmers, mainly, although acreage was sold over the years and there's less than a thousand acres left. As soon as the probate's resolved, the house and property are going on the market. I had my fill of boll weevils when I was growing up. I was sent to boarding schools back East, and cried every year when the spring semester ended and I had to go home for the summer."

She looked like she was on the verge of doing it right then, so Estelle changed the subject. "How did you and Todd meet? Did you have a class together?"

"Someone introduced us at a party. I wonder how much longer it's going to take to get to Graceland?"

"Five minutes," said Baggins.

Taylor glanced over her shoulder. "I hope Todd can hang on that long."

Somehow or other, he did. Baggins drove into a vast parking lot, cut off the engine, and put on his C'Mon Tours cap. "Follow that path to the visitors center, where you can buy your tickets for the guided tours and shop for souvenirs. Be back here at noon, 'cause I ain't waiting on you if you're late."

Todd was the last one to climb out of the van. Taylor reached for his arm, but he brushed past her and ducked around the back of the van. Unpleasant noises hinting of gastric distress suggested he had not yet recovered from what ailed him. Taylor grimaced, then followed his route.

Estelle nudged Ruby Bee. "Let's go on to the center. You know, in a funny way I feel like we're coming home for a cozy visit with kinfolk. Elvis wasn't like those conceited rock stars you read about today. He was one of us."

"I've always loved peanut-butter-and-banana sandwiches," said Cherri Lucinda.

"Fried?" said Rex, sneering at her.

"Yeah, fried," she said, then tugged at Stormy's arm. "We're wasting time we could be spending at Graceland. I can hardly wait to see the Jungle Room. Elvis himself picked out all the furnishing at a Memphis store in just thirty minutes. I'll bet not even Martha Stewart could have done it any faster."

Stormy looked at Baggins. "I asked you this once already, but you didn't bother to answer. Are you going to stay with the van?"

"I might get myself some coffee and a sandwich," he said. "I'll be sure to lock the van before I go, so you got no call to worry about your duffel bag. Remember to be back here at noon, everybody. I don't want to come looking for you all like you're kiddies on a school field trip."

"What about that sick boy?" Ruby Bee asked Estelle as they started for the footpath.

Estelle increased her pace. "The only thing that might

kill him is his fiancée. Do you want to have something to eat before we go to Graceland?"

They were trying to decide as they went inside the visitors center and stopped to take stock of the possibilities. Estelle had been worried about long lines to buy tickets, but the room was less crowded than the second night of a tent revival.

Ruby Bee grumbled as they shelled out eighteen dollars for the complete package, but quieted down once they went outside to wait for a shuttle bus to whisk them across Elvis Presley Boulevard. Elvis's voice could be heard courtesy of speakers somewhere above them; he sounded as sad and gray as the water trickling alongside the curb.

"Can you believe we're going to Graceland?" whispered Estelle. "My heart is pounding, and my mouth is so dry I can't hardly swallow."

"It's too bad Arly wouldn't come with us," Ruby Bee said, looking down at the pavement. "When I suggested it, she liked to have laughed so hard she fell off the barstool. I don't know what gets into her, Estelle. Sometimes she's moodier than Seezer Buchanon—and everybody knows to stay out of *her* way when she comes charging down the aisle at the supermarket. I was there when she couldn't find the tomato paste, and I thought she was going to chew Kevin up and spit out the pieces." She looked up. "Seezer, not Arly. Arly would never spit."

An elderly couple came outside, both looking a little bewildered. Seconds later, three solemn-faced girls wearing massive backpacks joined the line. They were speaking some funny language, but Ruby Bee didn't seem to notice and Estelle couldn't make out what it was. Next to appear were Cherri Lucinda and Stormy.

Cherri Lucinda waved at Estelle. "Isn't this exciting?"

"I was just telling Ruby Bee how my heart's doing the jitterbug," said Estelle. "Where are Taylor and Todd?"

Stormy made a face. "He bolted into the men's room as soon as they got to the visitors center. She said they'd catch up with us later. The professor went to see if there was some special new biography in the souvenir shop. I mean, how's anybody gonna write something new about a person who's been dead this long? It's not like he's making headlines these days."

"*If* he's dead," Cherri Lucinda said, then flinched as she received sharp looks from the foreigners. "My niece's roommate's boss saw him in Minneapolis not that long ago. I think Elvis must have learned something terrible about the mob in Las Vegas so the FBI faked his death and put him in that witness protection thing where they give you a new name and identity. They probably wanted him to have plastic surgery, but he would have refused because he didn't want to dishonor his mama. Elvis was real attached to his mama. Now you got to admit that makes perfect sense, don't you?"

The foreigners took refuge behind a trash bin. The elderly couple gazed blankly at her. Stormy tugged at the wisps of black hair along the back of her neck. Estelle was trying to find a response when a shuttle bus pulled up to the curb and the doors whooshed open.

"Next stop, Graceland," said the driver.

Minutes later they were crowding into the foyer of the sacred site, all too dumbfounded to speak as they gaped at the rooms on either side of them. The tour guide, who was petulant and pudgy rather than perky and petite, rattled off rules about staying together, not wandering off, and most certainly not touching anything, then turned her attention to a room with the longest sofa Estelle had ever seen in her entire life. Swirly blue stained-glass peacocks guarded a room at the rear that contained a black piano and a whole wall of golden curtains.

Estelle nudged Ruby Bee. "Isn't this awesome?"

"I suppose so, but I'd hate to see the bill from the upholstery store. And imagine what it must have cost to keep that white carpet clean."

Her disposition did not improve as they were herded past the dining room, paneled kitchen, down a mirrored staircase to admire the two rooms in the basement, and back up to the fabled Jungle Room, complete with a stone waterfall and gnarly furniture reminiscent of a rain forest.

"Would you look at this!" Estelle said, so dumbstruck she could barely get out the words. When she received no response from Ruby Bee, she cut behind the elderly couple and joined Cherri Lucinda, who at least had the common courtesy to look impressed. "Doncha love it?"

"Yeah," she breathed. "See those telephones? Elvis actually held them in his very own hand. I can almost hear him talking to his mama or telling the cook to fry up a peanut-butter sandwich. I may just pass out."

"It reminds me of my sister's house," Stormy said. "Up till now, I thought she had the worst taste in the entire world, on account of one whole wall in her living room is dedicated to her fishing-tournament trophies. I guess I was wrong."

Cherri Lucinda gasped. "How can you say that? This just proves Elvis was high on imagination."

"High, anyway. Remember the old whale died of a drug overdose."

"I should slap your face!"

Estelle caught Cherri Lucinda's wrist before she could carry through with her threat. "Don't do something that'll get you thrown out of the tour," she said in a low voice. "We haven't even gotten to the Hall of Gold and the Meditation Garden." As soon as she felt Cherri Lucinda's arm go limp, she turned to Stormy. "Now listen and listen hard, missy. If you don't love Elvis, you have no business coming on this pilgrimage and making the rest of us listen to your nasty remarks. You behave yourself or I'll—I'll make you sorry you ever got on the van in the first place!"

"What are you gonna do—poke me in the eye with a bobby pin?" Stormy said with a snide smile.

The guide cleared her throat. "Now we're ready to see Vernon Presley's office, where he and his secretarial staff handled Elvis's business affairs, correspondence, fan mail, and daily household management."

Still simmering with anger, Estelle stalked back to Ruby Bee's side. The group obediently trooped out a back door and along a sidewalk to a separate building. As the guide began to point out various items of interest in what appeared to be an ordinary office, Estelle heard a child's giggles. Putting her hand on her heart in case she was having some sort of supernatural experience and was about to see little Lisa Marie come skipping across the yard, she timidly turned around.

The child on the sidewalk was wearing a faded sweatshirt, plaid pants, and cowboy boots; her mouth and chin were stained red from some sort of candy. The woman who came after her looked like she'd be more comfortable in a double-wide than on the white sofa inside Graceland. Seconds later a guide came out the door, followed by another group of visitors, all craning their necks to look up at the back of the house, maybe thinking they'd see Elvis or his grandma Minnie Mae waving from behind a grilled window.

Estelle made sure nobody was up there, then looked back at the group and found herself eyeballing the man she'd seen the night before in the black car in the Starbright Motel parking lot. He was even uglier in daylight, his nose all crumpled and his lips thick and wet.

She spun around, hoping he hadn't seen her even though he'd been staring straight at her. The guide was busily talking about what all was on the walls behind the desks, but Estelle couldn't make sense of the stream of words that seemed to have everybody mesmerized like bullfrogs caught in a spotlight.

"What's wrong with you?" whispered Ruby Bee. "Now you're the one who's paler than a sow's belly. Did you see Elvis's ghost perched on the chimney or something?"

"We got to get out of here," Estelle whispered back. "I'll explain later."

She snatched Ruby Bee's arm and dragged her out of the office, not daring to look at the man on the sidewalk. She figured they couldn't go back through the house without encountering more groups and uppity guides, so she hung on to Ruby Bee and headed across the lawn in the direction of the Meditation Garden. Since it was the final stop on the tour, it seemed likely the shuttle buses would be nearby.

"Let go of me!" Ruby Bee yelped. "That guide's yelling at us to keep off the grass. The last thing I need is to be arrested for trespassing at Graceland. We'd be the laughingstocks of Maggody if somebody caught wind of it, and God only knows what Arly'd say."

Paying her no mind, Estelle kept going until they arrived at the curved brick wall and fountain. More than a dozen folks were lingering in front of the graves, some looking thoughtful and others honking into handkerchiefs and wiping away tears.

She stopped behind a stone column and peeked back at the yard. The bald man was not in sight, although this didn't mean he couldn't be skulking by the shrubs at the corner of the house, or even creeping behind the garden in order to nab them before they reached the circular drive.

Ruby Bee yanked herself free and rubbed her arm. "What's gotten into you, Estelle Oppers? I was looking forward to seeing all of Elvis's glittery costumes and his gold and platinum records. If we go back, that guide'll bawl us out for cutting across the lawn."

"Stop whining and look at the graves," Estelle said, keeping an eye on the sidewalk. "Afterward, we can go back to the visitors center, have something to eat, and do some shopping. Elsie made me promise to get her one of those paintings on velvet if they don't cost an arm and a leg."

Ruby Bee hesitated, then sighed and said, "I reckon that's okay with me. Let me sit down and catch my breath, then we'll be on our way."

Estelle stopped peeking around the column. "Are you sure you're okay?"

"As sure as Elvis is buried yonder."

Considering Cherri Lucinda's theory about his present whereabouts, Estelle felt a flicker of doubt.

F I V E

Although Reverend Hitebred could divine the persistent presence of satanists from a pink barrette and a couple of rubber bands, it seemed he couldn't tell time worth a damn. I'd been parked in front of his church, watching turkey buzzards drift overhead and listening to a staticky country music station for a good half hour before a car pulled in next to me.

A solidly built woman climbed out of the driver's side and came around to my window. I estimated her age to be somewhere between mine and Ruby Bee's, although closer to the latter's. Her brown hair, coarse and streaked with gray, was pulled back in a ponytail, her face devoid of makeup, and her coat the veteran of many winters. She approached warily, as if she suspected I was a member of a coven.

Somewhat sorry to disappoint her, I rolled down my window and said, "I'm Chief of Police Hanks from Maggody. I was supposed to meet Reverend Hitebred at eleven."

"I'm Martha, his daughter," she said in a flat, almost inflectionless voice. "Old Miz Burnwhistle decided that

this is the morning she's going to die, so she called my
father to go read the Bible and pray with her. She's been
doing this about once a month for the last three years.
She usually has a miraculous recovery before her soaps
come on at noon, although last month she gurgled and
wheezed right up until time for the Oprah show."

"And your father trots to her bedside every time?"

"She's ninety-eight years old and liable to get it right
sooner or later. Besides, it gives my father something to
do besides flipping over rocks in search of satanists." She
gave me a faint smile. "The members of the congregation are all too terrified of him to do much in the way
of sinning, and we don't get too many hymnal salesmen
out this way."

I got out of the car and leaned against the fender.
"What do you think about these purported trespassers?"

"You sound just like one of those cops on television.
Do they teach you to talk like that?"

"Not until the second year." I gestured at the door of
the church. "Any new evidence turned up in there?
More paper clips and cigarette butts, for example?"

Martha shook her head. "No, and my father came
over at the crack of dawn this morning to snuffle around
on the floor like a bloodhound. I could tell when he sat
down at the breakfast table that he hadn't had any
luck."

In that she'd failed to answer the more significant
question, I tried again. "Do you believe that someone
has been entering the church at night?"

"There haven't been any broken windows or
scratches on the locks, and my father and I have the only
two keys. He keeps his on a ring clipped to his belt.
Mine's in a drawer at home except when I'm using it."

"Has either of you ever given your key to a member of the congregation? It only takes a few minutes to have a copy made."

She thought for a moment. "I've never had call to loan mine out, and I can't imagine why my father would. He won't admit it, but he likes the idea that nobody can get into the church without calling on him. He makes 'em wait, too, just so they won't forget it."

"How often is the building used?"

"Services on Sunday mornings and evenings, prayer meetings on Wednesday evenings. Weddings and funerals by reservation only." She looked at the front of the building, and then at the low gray clouds. "My father's hardly competing with Methuselah, but he's getting on in years. The most foolish things have become real important to him. Food has to be cooked just so, shoes have to be lined up on his closet floor, books have to go back on the shelf from the exact place they came from. Otherwise, if you'll excuse the expression, all hell breaks loose."

"Are you saying these satanists are just another of his obsessions?"

"Maybe," she said, shrugging. "Anyway, I don't see what you can do, unless you want to set up a cot in the office and sleep over every night. You can come to the house for breakfast. It wouldn't be any trouble to fix another serving of oatmeal. No coffee, though. We don't believe in artificial stimulants." Again, the faint smile. "I used to sneak into town and buy a bottle of Dr. Pepper from the machine at the gas station. When my father caught me, you'd have thought from the way he carried on that it was whiskey."

"We're not quite to that point in the investigation," I

said. I took a small notebook out of my pocket and wrote down the telephone numbers of the PD and my apartment. "If you see any suspicious activity inside the church, call me. I can be here in less than twenty minutes."

She took the piece of paper, glanced incuriously at it, and folded it into a tiny rectangle. "Why don't you come to one of our services, Chief Hanks? You might find it interesting."

"If I get a chance," I said, then got back into my car before she could press me for a commitment. Martha was still standing next to her car, her hands in her pockets and her face tilted toward the sky, as I drove down the driveway to the county road. I supposed I might have been as impassive as she if I'd spent my life under the dour scrutiny of the Reverend Edwin W. Hitebred.

But I doubted it.

Brother Verber sat on the couch in the rectory, which, in spite of the fancy nomenclature, consisted of a mobile home parked in the yard of the Voice of the Almighty Lord Assembly Hall. He was marveling at the depth of depravity right there on the TV screen. Why in heaven's name a woman would go in front of a camera and tell the whole country how she'd had a lesbian affair with her husband's sister was beyond comprehension, he thought as he refilled his glass with sacramental wine and leaned forward to catch every last disgusting detail. Nothing like this had been covered in his correspondence course with the seminary in Las Vegas, and he figured sooner or later he'd be called upon to confront this particularly mystifying perversity. Surely he owed it to the Lord to be forewarned before he went into battle with ol' Satan hisself.

What was downright disturbing, he reflected as he idly scratched the tip of his nose, was that this woman looked so normal. Why, if he'd seen her at the Super-Saver, thumping melons or flipping through a tabloid at the checkout counter, he never would have suspected she was one of "Them." He'd heard tell of a book where a woman had been obliged to wear a scarlet A, so everybody'd know right off the bat that she was an adulteress. Maybe that wasn't such a bad idea. There were three or four high school girls who might think twice about lying buck naked with a boy on a blanket next to Boone Creek if they knew they might end up with a scarlet W nestled between their ripe, sassy breasts.

The idea was so intriguing that he found a pencil and piece of paper and started a list. "W is for whore," he murmured. "L is for liar, P is for pervert, S is for sinner, M is for Methodist. . . ."

He was so engrossed in his work that he came close to spewing out a mouthful of wine when someone rapped on his front door. "Coming," he called, then slipped the paper under a cushion and made a quick pass through the kitchenette to stash the wine bottle and glass in a cabinet.

He was darn glad he had when he opened the door and saw Sister Barbara (aka Mrs. Jim Bob) on the stoop. "What a charming surprise," he said, hoping she wouldn't notice that he was still in his bathrobe and slippers nigh onto noon. He'd had to explain to her more than once how staying up half the night to pray for various members of the congregation left him tuckered out the next morning, but she never looked real convinced.

"I need you to go unlock the door to the basement of the Assembly Hall," she said. "I've been out since eight this morning collecting items for the rummage sale, and my trunk's full."

Clasping his hands together, he beamed down at her. "You're an inspiration to us all. 'The path of the just is as the shining light, that shineth more and more unto the perfect day.' That's from Proverbs, chapter four, verse eighteen."

"You wouldn't think the day's so all-fired perfect if you'd been out in it. I stepped in a puddle in front of Millicent McIlhaney's house, and my feet are soaked. When I got out of my car at Fergie Biden's house, a brutish dog came charging from under the porch like it was bent on tearing out my throat. I barely escaped with my life. Furthermore, I had to pump gas, even though I must have told Jim Bob a half dozen times to fill the tank before he left town. I have a run in my stocking and I've lost a glove. There is a most unpleasant tickle in the back of my throat, and I won't be surprised if I have pneumonia by this evening. How long do I have to stand here in the cold before you put on your coat and go unlock the door for me?"

Brother Verber's eyes stung with unshed tears. "Why don't you come into the rectory and dry your feet, Sister Barbara? I'll make you some nice hot tea and you can rest up from all this trouble you've been going to on behalf of the heathen orphans in Africa. I'm surprised you ain't sporting a halo after what you've been through."

"Oh, all right," Mrs. Jim Bob said, "but only for a minute. There's more to do, and we both know the Devil finds work for idle hands." She cocked her head like a cute little ol' chickadee and gave him a piercing look. "Are you in your pajamas because you're working on your sermon?"

"I was scribbling so fast I must have lost track of the time," he said as he grabbed the remote control and turned off the TV. "You sit here on the couch and I'll fetch a towel. I'd consider it a blessing if you'd allow me to kneel in front of you and dry your feet."

She sat down, pulled off her shoes, and carefully inspected her toes for a hint of frostbite. Once she was satisfied that none of them required amputation, she looked up at Brother Verber, who was hovering in much the same fashion as a blimp over a football stadium. "So what's the topic of this Sunday's sermon?"

"I'll go get that towel." He scurried down the hallway to the bathroom, opened the linen cabinet, and spent several minutes trying to decide which color of towel she'd prefer. He finally grabbed an armful and went back out into the living room. "Where's Jim Bob off to?"

"He said he was going to the Municipal League meeting down in Hot Springs, but I'm not so sure that's where he is. He's been acting queer these last few weeks."

Brother Verber gasped. "He has?"

"For one thing, he made it home for lunch and dinner regular as clockwork, and he spent most every evening in front of the television. He only went back to the supermarket after dinner one time, and when I called, he answered the phone himself. I don't know what to make of it, Brother Verber."

He tossed the towels on a chair and sat down next to her. "It means he's finally seen the wickedness of his ways and decided to put himself back on the glorious path to salvation. Hallelujah! Why don't we both get down on our knees and offer a prayer of thanksgiving that his soul has been saved?"

Mrs. Jim Bob stayed where she was. "When he's carrying on with some hussy, he comes home at all hours of the night reeking of perfume and whiskey. He tells the employees all kinds of ridiculous stories about how he has to go to Farberville or Starley City in the middle of the afternoon to see wholesalers. That's the kind of behavior I'm used to. The way he's been behaving lately is just plain peculiar, and I know in my heart that he's up to no good, Brother Verber."

"Probably not," he said, squeezing her knee to let her know that he, in his role as her spiritual adviser, shared her apprehension. "The Lord must be testing your faith by giving you such an affliction. All Job had to deal with were painful boils from the soles of his feet to the top of his head. You've got a womanizing, whiskey-drinking, deceitful husband. It don't seem fair, but as pious Christians, we know the Lord moves in mysterious ways."

She removed his hand, which had mysteriously found its way to her thigh. Standing up, she said, "I've changed my mind about unloading the trunk just now. I'll come by later this afternoon."

Brother Verber blinked moistly at her. "It breaks my heart to see you like this, Sister Barbara. You're trying to be brave, but I can hear the anguish in your voice. I hate to think of you sitting all by yourself in your living room, the shades drawn and the lights out, battling to hold back tears of shame and humiliation."

She muttered a word of farewell and went back to the pink Cadillac Jim Bob had bought her after she found out about the redheaded Jezebel in the Pot O'

Gold mobile home park. The car had more than twenty thousand miles on it, and there was an unsightly stain on the passenger's seat from the time she'd taken tomato aspic to the potluck. It just might be time to replace it with a newer model, she thought as she drove toward the SuperSaver to search through Jim Bob's desk drawers for clues.

Estelle kept an eye out for the bald man while she and Ruby Bee gawked at Elvis's private airplanes, cars, go-carts, and motorcycles in the museum, and then had lunch at the Rockabilly's Diner. The only shiny head she'd seen belonged to a paunchy coot using a walker and slobbering worse than Petrol Buchanon (who was renowned for his saliva excesses, as well as for pinching fannies at the county old folks' home).

They were contemplating the wares in the souvenir shop when Cherri Lucinda joined them. "What on earth happened earlier?" she asked.

"Nothing," Estelle said in a chilly voice.

"I nearly swallowed my gum when y'all took off running like Elvis's pa had crawled out from behind a desk. The tour guide was so pissified that I thought she was going to chase after you and tackle you right there on the lawn."

Estelle pulled a postcard out of the rack and pretended to give it serious consideration. "It's a good thing she didn't try it." She realized Ruby Bee was looking thoughtful, which was a bad sign. "I reckon it's time to head back for the van. Baggins is mean enough to drive off and leave us in the middle of the parking lot. Where's Stormy?"

"Off having a cigarette," said Cherri Lucinda, "and I

couldn't care less if she makes it back to the van in time. She shouldn't have come on this pilgrimage in the first place. About the only thing she's done since we left Farberville is gripe. I didn't think the motel was so awful, but you'd have thought from the way she carried on that we were staying in a dungeon with spiders and bats. First she got it into her head that she was gonna leave and catch a bus back to Farberville. One minute later, she came back and said she was afraid she'd get mugged on the way to the bus station. After that, she was up all night long, smoking and watching out the window. I don't know if I can stand three more nights of sharing a motel room with her. I get these horrible dark circles under my eyes if I don't get my beauty sleep."

Estelle replaced the postcard and picked up a box of coasters. "Why did she come on the tour?"

"I don't know. She wasn't the tiniest bit interested when I told her about it a couple of weeks ago. Then the night before we left, she showed up on my doorstep with a suitcase and said she'd changed her mind and was coming after all."

Ruby Bee glanced up from a plate with a picture of Graceland decorated with Christmas lights. "Did you ask her what caused her to change her mind?"

"She wouldn't say exactly, but I sort of think she'd had a fight with her boyfriend and figured he'd be worried about her if she disappeared for a few days."

Estelle dropped the box of coasters. "You wouldn't happen to know what he looks like, would you?"

"Never met him," Cherri Lucinda murmured, distracted by a set of porcelain figurines of Elvis in his distinctive costumes. "Isn't this from the 'Aloha' special in nineteen seventy-three?"

"I believe it is. Ruby Bee, decide what you want and go pay for it. We need to stop by the ladies room and then get on out to the van. Neither of us can afford to take a taxi back to Farberville. You'd better hurry up, too, Cherri Lucinda, unless your duffel bag's full of money."

"Yeah, right," she said with a snort.

She was still frowning at the figurine in her hand as Estelle and Ruby Bee paid for their souvenirs. Estelle made sure the bald man was nowhere to be seen as they went through the main reception room, made a detour to powder their noses, and headed along the path back to the parking lot.

"Are you gonna explain or not?" Ruby Bee said, stopping abruptly.

"Explain what?"

"I may be feeling a mite crumpy, but not so much that I wasn't mindful of being hauled out of Graceland like a sack of turnips. I did not appreciate that, Estelle Oppers."

Estelle looked uneasily at the trees and bushes along the path. "You never know who might be listening. I'll tell you later when we get to the motel in Tupelo."

"Don't go to the bother," Ruby Bee said in her snootiest voice, which never failed to irritate Estelle. "You and Cherri Lucinda can have yourselves a fine time discussing Elvis's present whereabouts. Last week I saw a motorcyclist in a black helmet turn up the road that goes by Raz Buchanon's shack. Maybe Elvis's twin brother didn't really die at birth. Maybe he changed his name and grew whiskers so nobody'd notice any family resemblance. Maybe Elvis came down from Minneapolis for a visit."

"I'll say you're a mite crumpy," said Estelle with matching snootiness, which never failed to irritate Ruby Bee just as much, if not more so. "In fact, you're being as big a pain in the butt as Stormy. Why don't the two of you catch a bus home so the rest of us can enjoy ourselves?"

"You're a fine one to talk! I wouldn't be standing here if you hadn't bullied me into coming. God knows I had better things to do with one hundred and seventy-nine dollars than ride in a bumpy van and sleep in a filthy motel room. Diesel's cave is probably cleaner than that place."

Estelle squared her shoulders and gave Ruby Bee a disdainful look. "I may have been the one that found out about the tour, but I don't recollect twisting your arm till you agreed. Besides that, you're getting as set in your ways as an old grannywoman. The most exciting thing you ever do is change channels in the middle of a show. You may want to wither away, Rubella Belinda Hanks, but I ain't ready to join the antiques in Roy Stiver's shop."

Ruby Bee's face turned bright red, and she was sputtering out a mostly incoherent response when Rex Malanac stepped out from behind a clump of bushes.

"Please don't think I've been eavesdropping," he said. "I stepped off the path to—ah, have a moment to myself before returning to the van for the drive to Tupelo. When I heard voices, I thought it prudent to wait. However, it's very close to departure time and I have no desire to spend another night at the Starbright Motel."

Estelle and Ruby Bee glared at each other, then mutely stalked off toward the van with Rex behind them. Several of the pilgrims were already there; Taylor could be seen through one of the windows, her paperback inches from her nose. Stormy sat behind her, filing her nails. Baggins had the hood raised and was examining the dipstick.

Estelle was still fuming, so she took the seat next to Taylor. Ruby Bee plunked herself down next to Stormy, and moments later, Cherri Lucinda climbed aboard, sighed loudly, and sat down beside Rex.

Estelle did a quick nose count, then frowned at Taylor. "Where's Todd?"

"Curled up on the floor in back and feeling sorry for himself—as if it wasn't all his own fault. It looks as though I'll spend my honeymoon holding his head over a commode."

"Could it be something more than a hangover?"

"Like the flu? Considering the amount he had to drink last night, I doubt it. One of these days he's going to have to grow out of this frat-boy mentality. His father's law firm is very conservative, which is one of the reasons it's so prestigious. I have no intention of living on a legal-aid-clinic salary."

"I suppose not," Estelle said. "Did you and Todd take the tour of Graceland?"

"*He* took a tour of the men's room at the visitors center, and then we came back here. I've already done the tour, and Todd's eyeballs are so befogged that he can't see anything beyond his eyelashes. Perhaps this is one of those things that will seem hilarious in ten years, but at the moment it's hard to see much humor in it."

Rex leaned forward, and in a conspiratorial whisper, said, "Could he be malingering in order to postpone the nuptials?"

"Don't be absurd!" said Taylor. "Todd may not seem

enthusiastic about eloping, but he's just as eager as I am to get married and prove to his parents that he's prepared to settle down."

Estelle smiled reassuringly at her. "Of course he is. I'd bet some of his upset is due to excitement about the wedding. What time will it be?"

"Will I have a chance to rent a tux?" added Rex.

Taylor's hands were fluttery, but her voice was stiff as she said, "At seven o'clock. The site closes at four this time of year, but after some wheedling and the promise of a donation, one of the staff agreed to come back and let us in the chapel for a private ceremony. I tried to find out which motel we're staying in so I could arrange for a cake and a bottle of champagne, but Miss Vetchling refused to say."

"That's because," said Baggins as he took his place behind the wheel, "our travel plans have changed. We ain't staying the night in Tupelo."

"What?" yelped Taylor.

"It's like this," Baggins went on, watching them in the rearview mirror in case he needed to make a hasty exit. "It turns out that every motel in Tupelo is booked up for tonight. Shriners, I think they said. You know—those guys that wear funny hats and ride around on little motorcycles. I reckon there are thousands of them streaming into Tupelo right this minute. Miss Vetchling did her best to find us some rooms, but the only place that had any vacancies makes the Starbright look like Buckingham Palace."

Taylor shot to her feet with such fury that she banged her head on the van's ceiling. Wobbling just a bit, she said, "Baggins, I could wring your neck! Why didn't you tell us this earlier? Don't pretend you haven't been listening to every word we've said! If I'd known this yesterday, I would have tried to change the arrangements."

"I just found out about it myself. Miss Vetchling was still working on it when we left yesterday morning. I called her while you all were at Graceland, and that's when she told me. We're supposed to check into The Luck of the Draw over near Tunica by six o'clock, which means we have to leave Tupelo no later than three. If we're not there on time, they'll release the rooms and we'll have to go back to the Starbright for the night."

"You'll have to kill me first," said Stormy, "'cause that's the only way to make me spend another minute in that place!" She looked wildly at the others. "You would not believe the size of the hairy spider I found in the sink this morning! I'm almost positive it was one of those poisonous tarantulas from South America! What's more, I saw drug dealers out by the pool most of the night." She took out a cigarette and jammed it between her lips. "And don't give me any shit about smoking. I am so damn tired of being told that I can't smoke I could scream. Anybody worried about the danger of secondhand screaming?"

"But what about my wedding?" wailed Taylor, tears dribbling down her cheeks. "The justice of the peace can't come until after he gets off work."

"Could this be the classic example of a pair of star-cross'd lovers?" Rex said. "Can we look forward to daggers and poison?"

He might have been planning to elaborate, but Cherri Lucinda punched him in the shoulder and said, "Baggins, you have no right to change the plans like this. Taylor went to a lot of trouble to set this up, so you'd better just figure out a way for these two kids to get married in the Elvis Presley chapel."

"Can't do nothing about Shriners," he said.

Taylor crumpled into the seat and buried her face in her hands. "It was going to be so romantic," she said between noisy gulps and hiccups. "I brought a cassette player and a tape so Elvis could be singing in the background during the ceremony. Todd's mother wanted flower girls, bridesmaids, elaborate flowers, candles, a professional photographer, and all of that, but I just—I just wanted something different—special—something to tell our children and our grandchildren about. I think I'm going to be sick!"

A crude sound from the back of the van indicated that Todd had beaten her to it.

S I X

The Luck of the Draw Casino & Hotel could have been a stepchild of the fabled Las Vegas Strip. Lights flashed and flickered on every surface, and above the main entrance was a giant poker hand (aces and eights, oddly enough) outlined in red neon stripes. People were streaming in and out the doors, and the parking lot was filling up at a good clip.

Baggins stopped in a loading zone and looked back at his charges. "I reckon we're here," he announced cheerfully. When nobody responded, he sighed and went on. "Look, I already explained how there was no way we could spend the night in Tupelo, so it ain't gonna do y'all any good to be dragging your tails all the way home. You got to see the house where Elvis was born, didn't you?"

"For all of twenty minutes," said Cherri Lucinda with a grimace. "I felt like a calf at a slaughterhouse. I'm surprised you didn't chase after us with a cattle prod."

Estelle wasn't any happier. "I barely had time to stick my head in the chapel before you started hollering." She smiled at Taylor, who hadn't said a word since Memphis and had refused to set foot out of the van in Tupelo. "It was real pretty inside, with stained-glass windows and wood pews. It's a dadgum shame you couldn't have your wedding there, and I'll be the first to give Miss Vetchling a piece of my mind when we get home. The nerve of her switching the itinerary like that!"

"Perhaps," Rex said, "there's a wedding chapel on the premises here. If not, we can inquire about a bowling alley or a pancake house. Those are the fundamental hubs of social interaction in Mississippi. I'm sure weddings are not unusual in such establishments."

Stormy stubbed out a cigarette in a cup she'd been utilizing as an ashtray and aimed a finger at him. "That's enough out of you, asshole! You've been picking on her since the moment we left Farberville. I may not have a college degree, but my mama taught me to be polite to other people, no matter what they've done in the past. If you say one more rude thing to her, I'm gonna yank off your sunglasses and put 'em in a place where the sun don't shine. You follow me?"

"Go for it," said a hoarse voice from the rearmost seat.

Baggins decided he'd better regain control before an uncivil war broke out. "Here's what we're gonna do. I'll get out your duffel bags and you can take them into the lobby while I park. Soon as I get back, I'll see to registration. Don't be wandering off until you have your room key, 'cause I don't aim to spend the rest of the evening hunting you down in the casino. You're free to do whatever you want until tomorrow evening at nine, when we'll meet in the lobby for the show. There's a rumor that El Vez, the famous Latino impersonator, and the Lovely Elvettes may perform, but don't get your hopes up too high. We may have to settle for Elvision."

As the others got out of the van, Estelle noticed that Taylor was back to crying. She handed her a tissue and patted her arm. "It ain't all that farfetched for there to be a wedding chapel in this hotel. I'll bet lots of people come down from Memphis to get married and spend the weekend in the honeymoon suite."

Taylor wiped her nose. "I'm not sure Todd's still in the mood. He's blaming me for his hangover."

"Well, the worst that can happen is that you'll end up having the big wedding in Little Rock after all. I can just picture you in a satin gown trimmed with lace and your hair all soft and curly to frame your face. You'll look like a storybook princess, honey."

"What I'll look like is a princess who swallowed a watermelon. By August there's no way I'll be able to fit into the wedding dress Todd's grandmother wore forty years ago."

"You mean you"—Estelle licked her lips—"might be in the family way? Are you sure?"

"Yes, and six months from now, there'll be no doubt in anyone's mind. Girls from the 'right' families in Little Rock aren't supposed to do that. The ones that do it anyway either have an abortion or develop a rabid desire to spend a year abroad, perfecting their French culinary talents. Oddly enough, you don't find many recipes for soufflés and gâteaux in the Junior League cookbooks."

Estelle was struggling to find a reply when Baggins thumped on the window.

"Let's go!" he called. "Everybody else is already inside the hotel. I can't park until you get your butts off the van."

Only one duffel bag remained on the curb. Estelle collected it, then followed Taylor through the revolving door. The lobby was three times as big as the sanctuary of the Voice of the Almighty Lord Assembly Hall, and crowded with couches, chairs, potted plants, bellmen in crisp uniforms, piles of luggage, and folks wearing everything from diamonds and furs to plaid pants, cardigan sweaters, and caps with logos from tractor companies. A line beginning at the registration desk zigzagged between velveteen ropes on shiny posts. The babble of hundreds of voices, combined with canned music and crackly announcements over a PA system, reminded Estelle of a carnival on a humid summer night.

"Where's Ruby Bee?" she said.

"I don't see her, but there's Todd on a sofa over by the fountain. I suppose I'd better join him before he decides the only cure is a drink in the bar." A calculating expression flashed across Taylor's face, then disappeared. "Maybe a hot shower and room service will improve his mood," she added. "The poor boy hasn't had anything to eat all day."

"That might do the trick." Estelle stood on tiptoes to look for Ruby Bee. Blond heads bobbled here and there, but as far as she could see, none of them belonged to Ruby Bee. Leaving Taylor to tend to her fiancé, she forced her way through the wall of bodies. A woman in a bright yellow sweatsuit muttered a word of reproach as Estelle nudged her aside. A college-aged boy stepped on her foot, apologized, and then did it again in his haste to escape from her glare. Over the PA system, a man with a heavy accent advised the driver of a Toyota that he was in peril of having his car towed. Several of the men in the line bolted for the door.

Estelle spotted Rex and struggled to his side. "Have you seen Ruby Bee?" she asked, panting as if she'd just climbed to the top of Cotter's Ridge.

"No, but I heard our little spitfire offer to help her

find a ladies room," he said. He gestured at a corridor next to the registration desk. "The nearest one is down that way on the other side of the restaurant."

Estelle lowered her head and charged through the crowd until she reached the less populated hallway. After making sure her beehive was still well-secured, she stopped at a drinking fountain for a gulp of water, and was preparing to resume her mission when Ruby Bee herself appeared.

"If you're looking for the potty, it's right here," she said coolly.

"Why'd you go disappearing like that?"

Ruby Bee turned icy. "You are not my baby-sitter, so stop acting like it. I am free to come and go as I choose, and I don't need your permission to tinkle."

"If that's the way you feel, then you can just tinkle till the cows come home!" Estelle spun around and started back to the lobby.

She hadn't taken more than three steps when she found herself nose to nose with Jim Bob Buchanon, so close she could see the stubble on his chin and smell the whiskey on his breath. Neither was appealing.

"What are you doing here?" she demanded.

"What are you doing here?" he said, sounding equally surprised.

"I asked you first!"

"It ain't any of your fuckin' business what *I'm* doing here. I wanna know what *you're* doing here!"

"Don't you use that sort of language with me, Jim Bob. Didn't I hear that you were going to some kind of meeting in Hot Springs, and paying your expenses out of the town treasury?" She was going to elaborate when she heard a shriek from behind her.

She looked back. Cherri Lucinda and Stormy were on their knees next to a body sprawled on the diamond-patterned carpet. There was no mistaking the rubber soles of Ruby Bee's orthopedic shoes.

Dahlia was rattling pots and pans in the kitchen when Kevin got home from work. The babies were in a playpen in the middle of the living room; Kevvie Junior was staring at the light fixture on the ceiling, and Rose Marie was sucking on her fist with fierce determination and kicking her tiny legs.

Kevin stopped for a moment to watch them, wondering if Kevvie Junior'd grow up to be an electrician and Rose Marie a ballet dancer, then went on into the kitchen. He was thinking he might sneak up behind his beloved and nuzzle her neck, but she hunched her shoulders and said, "Cain't you see I'm busy? Why doncha do something useful for a change?"

"Like what?"

"I swear, when the Lord was passing out the brains, you were under the porch licking your balls with the dawgs. Bring in a couple of loads of firewood—and make sure you don't track up the floor while you're at it."

"Whatever you say," he mumbled, hanging his head.

Dahlia wiped her hands on her apron as she came over to him. "Aw, I dint mean anything, Kevin. You're a real fine husband and father. Your ma was telling me how your pa never once changed a diaper. You work long hours and still do what you can to help me with the babies." She leaned toward him and stroked his cheek with a damp, prunish fingertip. "I'm sorry I snapped at you like that."

Kevin was painfully aware of the closeness of the pendulous bosoms that had provided him with so many hours of bliss. They'd been declared off-limits for the time being, but his palms tingled as he recalled the overflowing handfuls of softness, downy hair, and nipples as big and pink and sweet as rosebuds.

"That's okay," he managed to say, sticking his hands in his pockets before he lost control and lunged at her. "I know you're tired all the time. The doctor sez the babies'll be sleeping through the night afore too long. That means you and me can go back to doing the things a married couple is supposed to do. Remember how we used to sneak into the storage room at the Kwik-Stoppe Shoppe?"

"And end up with more babies? We can't afford the two we have right now, and before you know it, we'll have to be buying shoes and bicycles and band instruments and party clothes and—" She sank onto a chair, her chins quivering and her face crumpled with misery. "We can't hardly afford vitamins and medicine, Kevin. What'll we do down the road when Rose Marie needs braces on her teeth?"

"Why, I'll be the manager at the supermarket by then," Kevin said heroically. "Jim Bob came near leaving me in charge while he's in Hot Springs, but then that dadburned Idalupino had to go and tell him that I took a nap in the lounge when I was supposed to be mopping the floor. From the way he carried on, you'd have thought I knocked over the display of canned pineapple again."

"Jim Bob ain't never gonna pay you more than minimum wage," she said, shaking her head. "All we can do is sell this house my granny gave us and move into a cramped trailer at the Pot O' Gold. Kevvie Junior and Rose Marie will grow up with a ditch for a yard. They'll start cussin' and lyin' and stealin' candy bars at the supermarket, and then drop out of school and take to selling drugs behind the pool hall. They'll be arrested and sent to prison, and when they get out, they'll have earrings all over their bodies. It's gonna kill your ma, Kevin. Then your pa'll have to move into the trailer with us, even though we won't have but one bedroom, and spend his days in a dirty undershirt, peeking through widows' bathroom windows and stealing their brassieres off the clothesline."

Kevin struck a manly, home-from-the-hunt pose. "We're not that bad off, my dimpled dumpling. According to the budget we made up, we can make ends meet as long as we don't waste money on extras like going to the picture show in Farberville or eating supper at the Dairee Dee-Lishus. It may get a little tight from time to time, but there's plenty of money in our bank account to pay all the bills."

If he'd been watching his wife instead of puzzling over what his pa was gonna do with stolen brassieres, he might have noticed the flush on her cheeks. He finally gave up (his pa having never shown much interest in underwear, including his own) and added, "So don't you fret about money. When we got married, I promised to see after you, and I'm gonna do it. What's for supper?"

"Beans and cornbread, just like every Friday night. Why doncha play with the babies till it's ready?"

He went back into the living room and began to prattle in a goofy, high-pitched voice. Dahlia poured the cornbread batter into a pan, stuck it in the oven, and sat down to rest for a few minutes. There wasn't any reason to ruin his good mood, she decided. There'd be plenty of time later to tell him that she needed the car the following afternoon. With any luck, she'd end up with cash to cover the payment to the hospital, and even leave enough for groceries till his next paycheck.

With any luck at all.

LaBelle was back at her desk when I came into the sheriff's department, but she was banging on a typewriter with enough fervor to bend the keys. Although she must have felt a gust of cold air as I opened the door, she kept her face down.

"I need to see Harve," I said.

"Well, he doesn't need to see you. Call next week and make an appointment like everybody else. This is not a convenience store where you can drop in and microwave a burrito whenever you please."

I took a deep breath and exhaled slowly. "Harve asked me to come by this afternoon and brief him on a case. Is he in his office?"

"Where do you think he is—Paris?" she said, at last giving me a hostile stare. "Of course he's in his office, but he told me that he doesn't want to be disturbed. I know for a fact that he locked the door as soon as I left. If a fire starts and he passes out from the smoke, he's gonna be in real trouble because there's no way anybody can get in to rescue him. My cousin Magenta always locked the bathroom door when she took a bath. When she slipped getting out of the tub, her husband called the ambulance and the paramedics had to break down the door. There she was, naked as the day she was born, with these two strange men ogling her every wart, scar, and stretch mark. To this day she claims she doesn't remember any of it, but that ain't what her husband says."

She resumed her assault on the typewriter. I went down the hall to Harve's office and knocked on the door.

"I tol' you to leave me alone, LaBelle!" he boomed. "I don't want to hear any more complaints about the dirty coffee cups in the break room. And stop calling it a 'war room,' fer chrissake!"

I identified myself and assured him I was alone in the hall. He unlocked the door, dragged me inside, and re-locked it.

"LaBelle's getting on my nerves," he said, running his fingers through what hair he had as he sat down behind his desk. "She's so crazy these days that she thinks I put a bathtub in here. Now you tell me—why in blazes would I have gone and done a fool thing like that?"

"Shall I assume the task force is still in operation?" I asked.

"Does a bear shit in the woods? Yeah, there are about a dozen of 'em on loan from various agencies in the county. They report to the prosecutor, so half the time I don't even know what they're doing—besides eating doughnuts and pizza." He took a cigar butt out of his pocket and stuck it in the corner of his mouth. "One of the fellows that was on the critical list died last night. The other one is on a respirator in the intensive care unit. A DEA agent's staying by his bedside, but I don't think we're going to be hearing a confession anytime soon."

"Why's this such a big deal, Harve? It's not exactly a secret that illegal drugs are cheap and plentiful in Stump County. Marijuana's more common than cocaine, but everything's available in the bars on Thurber Street."

"It seems we're smack in the middle of a new route from Mexico to Chicago. The DEA's been onto it for several months, but they've been waiting for a good-sized shipment so they can get publicity. They sure would like to know what happened at the Dew Drop Inn. The owner and bartender are in custody, but they seem to have been struck deaf and dumb. We're trying to find out who else might have been hanging around after the club closed." He took the cigar out of his mouth, studied it for a moment, and jammed it back in. He used a couple of matches to get it lit to his satisfaction, then leaned back and entwined his fingers on his belly. "Ain't your headache, though. You get anywhere in Scurgeton?"

"The only problem out there is a preacher with an overcharged imagination and too much free time," I said, trying not to squint as acrid smoke drifted across the desk. "There's nothing going on in Maggody, so I can keep driving over there to gaze wonderingly at whatever doohickey Reverend Hitebred finds under a chair. I may get bored with it sooner or later, however."

"Just keep him happy," Harve said with a chuckle that disintegrated into a spasm of coughing. When he regained control, he brushed ashes off his chest and said, "Or out of my hair, anyway."

"Sure," I said, waited a few seconds in case he had any more questions (or was going into respiratory failure), and then unlocked the door and went out to the hallway. Before I'd reached the reception area, I heard the lock click behind me, and from somewhere in the back of the building, brays of laughter and a phrase that sounded suspiciously like "straight flush." LaBelle ignored me as I went by her desk.

I stopped at the edge of Farberville and picked up a hamburger and fries for dinner. When I arrived in Maggody, I parked behind the antiques store and climbed the steps to my apartment. No interior decorating elves had been there in my absence; the linoleum was still buckled and the walls looked, if anything, dingier than when I'd left that morning. If I didn't do laundry before too long, my sheets would be able to crawl over to the Suds O' Fun on their own.

While I ate, I watched the local news, curious to see if the county prosecutor had held a press conference. The news anchor, a woman whose hair must have been highly flammable, briefly mentioned the second death and then moved on to a freight-train derailment in the next county. Drug traffickers could not compete with toxic spills, especially steamy green ones.

I was reduced to watching sitcoms, when the phone rang. Hoping I wasn't about to be recruited to go undercover at a topless/bottomless club, I picked up the receiver.

"Arly? Thank God, I found you!" shrieked Estelle. "The most awful thing has happened!"

"You found proof that Elvis was abducted by aliens?"

"This is serious. Ruby Bee is in the hospital. I kept after the doctor and the nurses, but none of 'em would say what's wrong with her. They've got her stuck with needles and wearing this tube in her nose!"

I put down my coffee cup and rubbed my forehead. "What are you talking about, Estelle?"

"I just told you, for pity's sake! Ruby Bee's in the hospital. Since I ain't kin, they won't let me in to see her. I don't know what to do! Here I am, not—"

"Calm down," I said, "and tell me what happened."

She gulped several times, then said in a voice slightly less likely to shatter crystal, "Not more than ten minutes after we got to the hotel with the casino—"

"I thought you were supposed to be in Tupelo tonight."

"Will you hush up and listen? We're here on account of a change in the plans. While I was talking to Taylor about her wedding in the van—"

"Someone got married in the van?" I said, increasingly bewildered.

"Are you gonna hear me out?"

"Go on," I said meekly.

"Like I said, while I was talking to Taylor, Ruby Bee went on inside the hotel with these two women in our group and went to the ladies room. I was on my way to find her when she came out, made a remark I won't bother to repeat, and then collapsed like a rag doll. Somebody called for an ambulance and they took her to the hospital."

"Are you there now?"

"I'm back at the hotel. The nurse made it clear that I couldn't even set foot inside the room where poor Ruby Bee's all trussed up. I'm supposed to call over there in the morning, but I'm afraid they won't tell me anything."

I was really glad I was sitting down. "And you have no idea what's wrong with her? Could it have been a heart attack?"

"I don't know what to tell you, Arly. She wasn't up to snuff these last two days, but she made it clear she didn't want to talk about it."

"She didn't mention any pain in her chest or shoulder?"

"I already told you what I know. Maybe I should have waited until the morning to call. It could be nothing more than a bad case of gas. She gets that when she's been eating cabbage, you know."

"*Had* she been eating cabbage?" I asked.

"No, but something else could have caused it. Chocolate, for instance, or that sandwich she ate last night at the motel. The bread looked a mite moldy."

"Give me the name of the hospital," I said. "I'll call and see what I can find out. If I don't get a decent answer, I can be there when Ruby Bee wakes up in the morning. Are you at the hotel on the brochure?"

I wrote down the information, told Estelle to try to get some rest, and hung up the receiver. This sort of thing wasn't supposed to happen. Ruby Bee was strong, if not invincible. When my father had walked out on her, she'd knuckled down to earn a living and never once referred to him. She'd steered me through school, starched my underwear and sent me off to the police academy in Camden, and, for the most part, held her peace when I moved to New York City with the hairball formerly known as my husband.

It took me several tries to dial the number of the hospital, and my throat was decidedly tight as I asked for the intensive care unit. By the time someone there answered, I sounded like a laryngitic rooster.

"Ruby Bee Hanks?" the nurse said. "Yes, she's in the cubicle right across from me."

I told her who I was and demanded details.

I may have been a bit brusque, because her voice turned chilly. "Hold your horses while I look at her chart. She was brought to the emergency room two hours ago, and transferred here almost immediately."

She paused, humming to herself. "It says she was complaining of sharp pains in the abdomen region. She vomited in the ambulance. Skin clammy, blood pressure elevated, feverish, and hostile when asked for a history. We have to take a history, you know. It's standard procedure, even though we're not a big, bustling hospital like the ones on TV. Our care is every bit as good as you'd get there. What's more, we have—"

"Could it be appendicitis?"

"The doctor ordered blood work first thing. Her white count is elevated, but not significantly. Red count was normal. EKG was within the acceptable range. She's scheduled for more tests, including an ultrasound in the morning. At the moment, she's resting as comfortably as can be expected."

"I'd like to speak to her doctor," I said.

"That's not possible. Dr. Deweese was at a stag party at the VFW when he was called, and he's gone back there. I can't page him unless there's an emergency."

Before I could argue, she hung up. I called Estelle and repeated what I'd learned, then watched a cockroach mosey across the floor while she faulted herself for everything that had gone wrong since the dawn of civilization, including Hiram's barn, Ruby Bee's abscessed tooth four years ago, and my failure to provide grandchildren.

When she ran down, I said, "I should be there in six hours or so, but I'll go by the hospital before I find your hotel. Call the desk and authorize them to give me a key to your room so I won't have to wake you."

"You think I'm going to get a wink of sleep tonight?" she said indignantly. "What do you take me for? I'll have you know that I'd have spent the night in the waiting room if they'd let me."

She was still expounding on her role as thwarted martyr when I replaced the receiver. I threw some clothes in an overnight bag, switched off the lights, and went down the stairs to my car. Only when I reached the county line did I allow myself to imagine Ruby Bee stretched out on a hospital bed, her face ashen with pain, needles in her arms and a tube in her nose.

Luckily, there was no other traffic. If there had been, I wouldn't have seen it through my tears.

S E V E N

I don't remember much about the drive from Farberville to Mississippi. I suppose I must have stopped for gas and coffee along the way, and crossed the bridge at Helena, but I was too benumbed to do much more than keep my eyes on the road and periodically search for new radio stations as I left old ones behind me.

The hospital was on the edge of town. It looked more like an elementary school than a towering medical complex, but I was damn glad to see it. There were only a few lights on inside, which was not surprising at that unholy hour. The main door was locked, the lobby dim and unoccupied. I tapped on the glass with my car key until a custodian shuffled into view and let me in.

Fifteen minutes later I was back in my car. Ruby Bee was asleep, her condition unchanged, her appearance no better or worse than I'd imagined. Dr. Deweese would be available in five hours. Hanging around the waiting room would accomplish nothing, and I needed sleep.

I headed north. The casinos were alongside the Mississippi River in a string of almost nonexistent towns. I spotted the sign for The Luck of the Draw and drove down a winding road that took me into a vast parking lot. I appropriated a space near the hotel entrance, grabbed my bag, and went into the lobby. Although it was better lit than the one at the hospital, it was not a good deal livelier. I fended off a bellman who believed with misguided optimism that he might earn a tip for carrying my bag fifteen feet, explained the situation to the very dim teenager posturing as a desk clerk, and eventually ended up with a plastic card that would allow me into Estelle's room.

I'd found the elevator and gone so far as to punch a button, when I realized I was too wound up to sleep. I was also reluctant to face Estelle and be treated to another round of self-incrimination. After six hours of time to brood, she might have regressed to the point of accepting blame for the unfortunate incident in the Garden of Eden, if not the annihilation of the dinosaurs or the Big Bang in all its cosmic splendor. Estelle is not one to take herself lightly.

It occurred to me that a nightcap might do the trick. I went to the end of the hallway and into the casino proper. It looked very much like the casinos I'd haunted a couple of times in Atlantic City. Acres of slot machines with bells and whistles promised instant wealth to players who'd long since gone to bed. Beyond them, the more sedate blackjack tables, a few sparsely populated. A group surrounded a craps table; volume indicated they were having a great time frittering away their hard-earned cash. Waitresses with skirts short enough to expose the bottoms of their buttocks glided between the tables, deftly balancing trays of drinks and empty glasses. Men in suits kept a prudent eye to make sure a good time was being had by all.

I stopped for a moment to watch an elderly woman on a stool in front of a slot machine. This was no one-armed bandit; the only thing required of her was to put a coin in the slot and push a button. She did so as if she were a robot on an assembly line, never pausing as the tumblers whirled or even glancing down when coins cascaded into a metal tray. Her face showed neither pleasure nor disappointment; she could have been feeding coins into a furnace vent. It seemed likely, if she kept up her rhythm, that her heirs would be disappointed when the will was read.

I continued in the direction of the blackjack tables. If the policy was like that of the Atlantic City casinos, drinks would be free to those who were gambling. A bit of cunning was in order. I found a table where two men were gazing intently at cards being flipped at them by a bored middle-aged woman in a tuxedo.

I sat on the stool at one end of the table and smiled brightly at them. "Is this what they call twenty-one?" I asked. "I used to play it when I was a kid, but I don't remember all the rules. Is anything wild?"

"Go play the slots," said a man with oily black hair and a cigarette dangling from his lip à la Humphrey Bogart. He scratched his fingernail on the green felt for an additional card, and then threw up his hands when the card, not to his liking, was tossed at him. "What is it with you dealers? Do you get a cut of my losings?"

I hoped he wasn't armed.

The second man, who had less hair but a kindlier disposition, nodded at me. "It's basically the same game, but it's called blackjack. In French, *vingt-et-un*." He nodded at the dealer. "Hit me, honey."

"Maybe I should watch for a minute," I said. "Could I possibly have a drink?"

"Drink!" yelled the dealer. She snapped down a card and waited without interest for further instructions.

A few minutes later, a waitress appeared at my side and agreed to bring me the classic Southern drink—a bourbon and Coke. When she returned, I tipped her a dollar, wished the two men luck, and slipped off the stool to walk off the soreness in my own decorously covered buttocks.

I headed in the direction of the noisy camaraderie of the craps table. People stood two deep around it, pressing against each other, cheering or groaning with each roll of the dice. At least, I thought, they were getting something for their money. When they found themselves back at work Monday morning, they could relate melodramatic tales of fortunes that had slipped through their fingers like fistfuls of smoke.

The drink was watery, but it seemed to be easing the taut muscles in my neck and back. I was beginning to feel as though I might be able to fall asleep when I saw what I dearly hoped was a figment of my exhausted mind. Surely not, I told myself as I stared at Jim Bob Buchanon as he flung dice onto the table and shouted something unintelligible.

His next remark was crystal clear, if contextually obscure. "Aw, shit! I knew I should have stayed on the hard eight."

"May I help you, miss?" asked a satiny male voice from behind me. "Would you like to sit down?"

The voice belonged to a black man in a stylish gray suit. His tie was red, his teeth were white, and his eyes (brown, not blue) were as impenetrable as the surface of the interstate. When I merely looked at him, he added, "You must not be feeling well. I'll be happy to escort you to a table at the bar or outside for a breath of fresh air." He glanced down at the drink in my hand and frowned ever so slightly. "Or have a waitress bring you a cup of coffee."

"No, thank you," I said. "I just stopped to have a drink on my way upstairs. What time does this place close?"

"Close?" His smile grew wider. "Like the Pinkertons, we never sleep. You, on the other hand, probably should. I hope you'll visit again tomorrow. We have raffles and contests every day at The Luck of the Draw. This weekend's grand prize is a trip to Jamaica. Be sure and enter."

He took my elbow and led me toward the door back to the hotel. I was too annoyed to resist, although I did crane my neck for a parting look at the craps table. If I'd actually seen Jim Bob—and I wasn't at all sure I hadn't been hallucinating—he'd vanished like a stack of five-dollar chips.

Estelle was snoring vigorously as I let myself into the hotel room. I undressed in the bathroom and crawled into the other bed. Sleep eluded me for a long while, and when it finally came, it was riddled with visions of Ruby Bee stretched out in a casket and Jim Bob doing belly flops across a craps table.

Neither was a pretty picture.

The hotel room was noticeably lighter when I was awakened by the sound of a siren. Groaning, I burrowed under the pillow and willed myself to go back to sleep, but the siren grew louder. Car doors slammed. People began jabbering in the hall outside the room. A second siren shrieked the approach of yet another official vehicle.

"What's going on out there?" said Estelle, sounding as if her mouth was filled with gravel. "Maybe you ought

should look out the window and see if the hotel's on
fire. I am not gonna scurry down some fire escape without putting on lipstick."

I did as she'd suggested. Eight stories below in the
parking lot, a police car was parked at an erratic angle,
its blue light spinning. An ambulance was speeding toward it. Guests and employees had gathered in the driveway. A woman dressed in jogging clothes and
high-topped athletic shoes sat on a curb, her head
between her knees. A police officer squatted beside her.

"There's been some sort of accident," I said, "but I
can't make out what happened." I pulled back the heavy
drapes, opened the sliding glass door, and went onto a
balcony large enough to accommodate two chairs, a
small table, and no more than three pigeons. My toes
curled as they met cold concrete, but I grabbed the rail
and looked down.

"Well?" demanded Estelle from the warmth of her
bed.

I retreated inside and closed the door. "It looks as if
someone fell from a significant height. A jogger must
have discovered the body."

"What a thing to wake up to," she said as she struggled out from under the blankets. "Why didn't you
shake me when you got here, Arly? I meant to wait up
for you, but I guess I must have dozed off. Did you go by
the hospital?"

I described my brief encounter with the ICU nurse at
the hospital, then went into the bathroom to take a
shower and brush my fuzzy teeth. When I emerged, she
was on the balcony.

"Can you tell what's going on?" I asked as I got
dressed.

"The body's been taken away in the ambulance, but from the way the police are measuring and looking up this way, the poor thing must have gone off a balcony right close to ours."

I prowled around the room while she took her time in the bathroom. It was too early to catch Dr. Deweese at the hospital; he wasn't slated to make rounds until eight. I ordered coffee and toast from room service and mindlessly watched some wake-up network show in which people seemed to be congratulating each other for breathing. Eventually I went back out onto the balcony, but the activity in the parking lot had melted away with the early-morning frost.

Estelle came out of the bathroom with her hair firmly pinned in place and several layers of scarlet lipstick defining her mouth. "I can't believe I went to sleep before you got here," she said as she poured herself a cup of coffee. "Night before last was rough, though, what with the gunfire well into the wee hours. I didn't think Ruby Bee'd ever fall asleep. When she finally did, I spent the rest of the night frettin' like a long-tailed cat in a room full of rocking chairs. I just want you to know that I did my level best to make her say what was wrong, but I might as well have been butting heads with Mrs. Jim Bob."

I squeezed her hand. "I'm sure you did whatever you could, Estelle. She'll be fine."

"What'll we do if she isn't?"

I couldn't bring myself to offer much in the way of blithe assurances, so I refilled my coffee cup and sat back. "What did you mean when you mentioned gunfire?"

"You would not believe the awful place we stayed! I

fully expected to be murdered in my bed. Stormy said she saw drug deals going on all night right outside our rooms. And of course there was the bald man that had the audacity to follow us on the Graceland tour, and then Baggins ups and sez we're not staying the night in Tupelo, which sent Taylor into a hissy-fit, even though Todd was—"

"Slow down," I said. "I have no idea who these people are."

"Folks on the tour, except for Baggins, who's the driver, and the bald man. I don't know who he is, unless he's Stormy's boyfriend. I was hoping Cherri Lucinda might know what he looks like, but she said she's never met him."

I held up my hands. "Forget I asked, Estelle. I drove half the night and I'm operating on three hours of sleep. You can tell me all the gossip and intrigue later."

She glowered at me, but fell silent and turned her attention to the TV set. I counted off minutes. It had taken me less than half an hour to drive from the hospital to the casino, and I wanted to be back there when Dr. Deweese arrived.

I was about to suggest we leave when there was a knock on the door. Wondering if room service had returned to repossess the coffee pot, I opened the door.

The woman in the hallway had noticeably bloodshot eyes and an ashen complexion. She put her hand to her mouth. "I am just so sorry for bothering you. I guess I have the wrong room."

"Is that you, Cherri Lucinda?" called Estelle.

The woman hurried past me, bent down to hug Estelle, and then sat down on the bed I'd recently vacated. "This trip is a nightmare! Everything's gone wrong. I wouldn't be surprised if that Miss Vetchling is some kind of nasty witch like the one that was going to eat Hansel and Gretel. If she was to walk into this room, I'd snatch the clipboard out of her hand and whack her over the head with it! I wouldn't be one bit sorry, either."

"I don't think she's responsible for Ruby Bee's ailment," said Estelle. "What's more, even though we didn't see any Shriners riding around Tupelo on their funny little motorcycles doesn't mean they weren't there. They could have been having their convention in another part of town."

Cherri Lucinda fell back across the bed. "That's not what I'm talking about. Don't you know what happened?"

Fearing that we were about to be treated to a lengthy discourse on the foolhardiness of high-stakes gambling or the effrontery of the male species, I said, "Estelle, we need to leave for the hospital."

"Didn't all the commotion wake you up?" persisted Cherri Lucinda. "I mean, I wouldn't be here if the cops weren't searching my room. I stood out in the hall for a while, but these ladies by the elevator started whispering and staring at me like I was some kind of freak just because the cops wouldn't let me put on makeup. They acted like they weren't gonna let me get dressed, either, but then the woman cop said I could if she stayed with me to make sure I didn't tamper with evidence. I don't see how I was supposed to do that when I don't know what evidence they were talking about."

"What are *you* talking about?" I asked.

"Stormy," she whispered.

Estelle's eyebrows shot up like missiles. "You don't

mean she . . . that was her down there . . . ? Oh, Cherri Lucinda, I just don't know what to say. I am sick about this. Was it because of the spat she had with her boyfriend?"

"How should I know? It's not like we were best friends or anything. When she moved to Farberville, she called me on account of a mutual acquaintance giving her my number. I helped her get a job. We had a beer every once in a while, but we never pretended we were sisters. Well, once we did at a bar when these two geeks tried to pick us up. She told 'em our brother had laid claim to both our bodies and would chew the dick off any man who thought different. They skedaddled like a pair of possums. It was real funny."

"Wait a minute," I said as I stared at her. "Are you saying that a member of your tour group committed suicide?"

Cherri Lucinda sat up and shrugged. "All I know is that some lady found Stormy's body on the ground long about dawn, and the cops seem to think she jumped off the balcony in the room we were sharing. They're going through her things now, maybe thinking they'll find antidepressants or a suicide note."

"She didn't seem depressed to me," said Estelle, "but I didn't know her very well. She was nervous about something, though. Remember how she attacked Rex when we got here?"

There were too many names without faces, and it was nearly eight. "I'm sure the police will sort this out," I said as I stood up. "I'm going to the hospital. What about you, Estelle? Do you feel as though you need to stay here?"

"Oh dear," said Cherri Lucinda. "I forgot to ask how

your friend is doing. Did they find out what's wrong with her?"

"Not yet," I said grimly.

Estelle told Cherri Lucinda to remain in the room as long as she liked, then followed me out into the hallway. No one whispered or stared at us as we waited for the elevator, descended to the lobby, and headed for my car.

"What a terrible thing," Estelle said, looking up at the facade of the hotel. "She wasn't more than thirty years old. She wasn't sweet like Taylor, or kindhearted like Cherri Lucinda, but she had spunk. You got to admire spunk."

Despite myself, I looked up at the balconies and then down at the unrelenting pavement. She'd had a moment when she must have realized what was about to happen. There'd been no opportunity to change her mind, no wings to spread, no bungee cord to save her.

"She'd had a fight with her boyfriend?" I asked as we got into the car and I backed out of the parking slot.

Estelle took a tissue out of her purse and dabbed her eyes. "She didn't exactly spill out her heart to me. When I was cutting her hair, she just sat like a chunk of cheese, not so much as watching in the mirror. Afterward, she mumbled something, took her bag, and sailed out of the motel room without bothering to thank me for my expertise. I did a right fine job, mind you, but she acted like I'd gone after her with pruning shears. You'd think I'd deserved a word of thanks, considering I did it for free. Back home, I would have charged her ten dollars."

"I don't think you'll collect it," I said as I turned onto the highway.

The hospital looked smaller and shabbier in daylight. Estelle trailed after me as we made our way to the ICU,

where a blond nurse with a sour expression had seized
control for the day shift.

"I'm here for Ruby Bee Hanks," I said.

"Hanks?" she said, pulling out a chart. "Dr. Deweese saw
her a few minutes ago. He wants to talk to the next-of-kin
when he or she gets here. I guess that'd be one of you. She's
over in that cubicle if you want to visit for a minute."

I'm not sure if Estelle was included in the invitation,
but she was stepping on my heels as she followed me.
Ruby Bee's eyelids fluttered open as we entered the cur-
tained enclosure.

"What are you doing here?" she asked me in a whisper that was both hoarse and hostile. "I don't recollect
asking anybody to call you."

Estelle crossed her arms. "I don't recollect you asking
me not to. She's your own flesh and blood, Ruby Bee.
Don't you think she has the right to know when you
make a scene like that in the hotel and have to be
brought to a hospital in an ambulance? It ain't like you
do this every week, you know."

"She has a point," I said mildly. "How are you feeling?"

Ruby Bee turned her face away. "Not real good, to tell
the truth. The bad pain's eased up, but I'm bloated and
having cramps. I told that doctor the only thing I needed
was a dose of bicarbonate of soda. He just kind of shook
his head and walked out." She looked back with a tight
frown. "I ain't sure he's a real doctor. If he tried to buy a
beer at the bar and grill, I'd darn well make him show
me his driver's license—and I'd still have my doubts."

"Why don't you stay here until they run you out?" I
suggested to Estelle. "I'll hunt down this impostor and
find out what's going on."

I left them bickering about the extent of the so-called

scene in the hotel lobby and asked the nurse how to find Dr. Deweese.

"His office is at the end of the main hall," she said. "The ladies auxiliary fixed it up and added all sorts of homey touches, but he seems to be in the cafeteria most of the time. I don't know why they went to the bother, and I'll be amazed if he sees much in the way of fruit-cakes and cookies next Christmas."

I wandered down the hall and found the cafeteria, which was no more than a room with pea green walls, a long table, rickety wooden chairs, and an array of vend-ing machines. The man who looked up was far from be-ing a medical wunderkind; his eyes were blue and his smile guileless, but his wrinkles put him near my age. In that Ruby Bee doesn't believe I'm old enough to drive, I wasn't surprised by her assessment.

"I'm Ruby Bee Hanks's daughter," I said.

"Good." He put aside the journal he'd been reading and opened a manila folder. "Last night she was admit-ted with abdominal pains and fever. The white blood count indicated a low-grade infection. I started her on glucose and an antibiotic, and gave her some mild med-ication to ease the pain. Even though she claims to be better, I'd like to do an ultrasound and keep her under observation for a few days."

"Then it isn't anything life-threatening?"

"I don't think so. If the symptoms intensify, she can be transported to a hospital in Memphis in a matter of hours. I have to warn you that it'll be expensive, though, and Ms. Hanks told me that she has no health insurance. Medicare may cover some of it—if she qualifies."

"She'd never admit it," I said. "You don't have any theories?"

"Gallbladder failure, food poisoning, pancreatitis, duodenal ulcer, blockage in the bile duct," he said rather casually, considering. "We'll keep her on a liquid diet and see what evolves. If it's nothing more than gall stones, we'll start her on some medication and she can go home. Surgery will be an option."

"An option?" I said. "Shouldn't she be having tests?"

Dr. Deweese regarded me for a moment. "Yes, she should. I'd love to order an MRI and tox screens and electrolyte analyses, but we lack the equipment. It's just as well, since most of our patients can't even afford a simple blood test. We do it anyway, and absorb the cost, but decent health care is for the wealthy. The tax benefits of these casinos have yet to dribble down to us. Look at the public schools in this community. Do you think we have computer labs and manicured soccer fields?"

"Don't the hospitals in Memphis have to accept charity cases?"

"If the patient's spurting blood or in the act of delivering a baby, yes. Sophisticated tests, no. We can do a decent job here, Miss Hanks. I'll make sure your mother is comfortable until we know what's wrong. Odds are good that she'll get through this attack and be able to have a follow-up with her own physician."

"How good are these odds?"

"I'd put them at three to one."

"Dr. Deweese," I said, grinding out each syllable, "I may decide to put a quarter in a slot machine, but I'm not going to gamble with my mother's health. Perhaps we should have a second opinion."

"Go right ahead, but you may have to rely on a veterinarian. I'm the only physician in the county." He put the folder down. "Would you like a cup of coffee?"

I shook my head. "You're the only physician in the county?"

"The glorious state of Mississippi paid my way through med school in exchange for a few years of indentured servitude. Before I came, all patients had to be transported to Memphis. A lot of the heart-attack and stroke victims didn't survive the trip. The poor folks couldn't afford to go to Memphis, so they had no access to prenatal care or ongoing therapy. My staff and I do the best we can." He gave me a smile meant to be downright dazzling. "Let's make the odds two to one."

"Let's do," I said as left. I may have paused in the hall to remind myself of the purpose of my presence, but I resolutely returned to the ICU and found Estelle outside the door.

"That nurse has a mighty high opinion of herself," she muttered. "To listen to her, you'd think she hung the moon and most of the stars. She shooed me out like I was a hen and said no visiting until this afternoon. What'd you find out?"

"Not much," I said as we went outside. I gave her the high points of my conversation with Dr. Deweese, stressing his confidence without quoting actual odds. "Shall we go back to the hotel for a proper breakfast?"

"How can you eat at a time like this?"

"At a time like this, Estelle," I said, "I'd like to buy a gallon of chocolate ice cream, a two-pound package of Oreo cookies, and find a nice, quiet place where no one can disturb me. So which is it—the restaurant at the hotel or a grocery store?"

Her sulky silence was answer enough. I drove toward The Luck of the Draw, for the first time seeing the bleak landscape scattered with shacks, abandoned gas stations, sickly trees that would never become mighty oaks, and litter attesting to the previous night's festivities.

"Tell me about the woman who committed suicide," I said, to take my mind off Ruby Bee.

Estelle was unable to resist the chance to make it clear she knew more about some things than I did. "Her name was Stormy Zimmerman, and she said she was an entertainer. I don't know exactly what she meant by that, but from the way she behaved, I doubt she was referring to singing in a church choir."

"Is that all you know about her?"

"No, it ain't. She said she had a tattoo. Now it's none of my business if a girl wants to have something like that done, but I don't see any reason to announce it in mixed company. Then she had the gall to make all kinds of vulgar remarks about Elvis, even though she should have known the whole reason for the tour was to see the most important sites in his life and pay respect for everything he accomplished in his forty-two years with us. It was like she was trashing kin. Even Cherri Lucinda started getting peeved at that point."

I turned onto the road back to the hotel. "You know, Estelle, there's something about Cherri Lucinda that seems familiar. I feel as though I've met her, but I have no idea when or where. It's been bothering me since I first saw her in the hall this morning."

"Me, too," said Estelle, nodding, "but I can't quite put my finger on it. When we were driving to Memphis, I noticed Ruby Bee giving her a funny look, like she was thinking the same thing. I wish I'd gotten around to asking her, but with one thing and another, it plumb slipped my mind. I guess it's too late now."

"She's going to be fine." I parked between a Lincoln Continental and a Volkswagen Beetle, cut off the ignition, and grabbed my purse. "If you want to sit there and work on your eulogy, it's your business. I'm going inside to have some breakfast." Scowling like Genghis Khan on a bad hair day, I climbed out of the car, slammed the door, and hurried toward the entrance.

"Keep your tail in the water," Estelle said as she caught up with me. "Of course she's gonna be fine, Arly. She sounded like her old self this morning, complaining about how she'd wasted all the money for the tour and would miss seeing the Elvis impersonators tonight. I'll ask Baggins if you can use her ticket to the show."

"No, thanks," I said curtly.

"Well, if you feel that way about it, forget I ever mentioned it—even though you might be missing a once-in-a-lifetime opportunity to see El Vez hisself."

I slowed down as I noticed two police cars parked at the end of the building. "I guess they haven't finished the investigation," I said to Estelle. "We'd better go up to the room. It's possible they'll want to question you."

"Me?" she said. "How should I know anything? Once I got back from the hospital, I called you and then got some pretzels and a ginger ale from the vending machines at the end of the hall. I was too worried about Ruby Bee to so much as stick my nose out the door after that until we left this morning."

"So that's what you'll tell them," I said.

The lobby was a good deal busier than it had been at three in the morning. Lines had formed for the optimists who wanted to check in and the disillusioned who needed to check out. Bellmen wheeled luggage carts in the appropriate directions. A mountain of suitcases indicated the arrival of a group on a much larger scale than that of C'Mon Tours.

"It was right crazy when we got here yesterday," Estelle said as we went down the corridor to the elevators. "I kept trying to spot Ruby Bee, but there were so many folks and all these loud announcements and . . ."

"And what?" I prompted her.

She sucked on her lower lip. "Maybe I was seeing things," she said at last. "Remember when Tiphini Buchanon kept telling everybody about how she'd seen glowing purple aliens at the foot of her bed? She could describe them from the antennas on their heads right down to the peculiarities of their privates. She never quit believing it, even when her pa had her carted off to one of those sanitariums."

"I must have missed that," I said as I nudged her into the elevator and pushed the button for the eighth floor.

"Lottie Estes had a time with her in home ec, let me tell you. It got to be where every kitchen utensil reminded Tiphini of something else about her aliens. Now I could see how a turkey baster or an oven thermometer might lead to certain ideas, but a spatula? If you ask me, the girl just wanted attention."

Instead of engaging in a conversation fraught with Freudian overtones (and having a hard time making the leap to spatulas, myself), I said, "What are the visiting hours at the hospital this afternoon?"

"Two to four. Remind me to take Ruby Bee her bag so she'll have her toothbrush and nightie. Those hospital gowns might as well be made of wax paper."

"Is it in the room?" I asked. "I didn't see it."

"It's in the closet. When the ambulance fellows were loading her onto a gurney, Stormy offered to take Ruby

Bee's and mine to our room as soon as Baggins got us registered. It's a good thing she did. I was so upset I would have left both of them setting in the hall."

When the elevator doors slid open on the eighth floor, we found ourselves facing a pear-shaped police officer. "You staying on this floor?" he said.

Estelle snorted. "Do you think we just came up to admire the view?"

I elbowed her aside and told him our names and the room number, then said, "Miss Oppers and my mother were both part of the same tour as the woman who fell."

"Yeah, then go to your room and stay there. The chief'll get around to talking to you before too long."

"He'd better not be all day," Estelle said. "I'm real sorry about poor Stormy, but we're not going to spend the day inside the room just because she committed suicide."

"That ain't what the chief thinks," said the cop.

E I G H T

Cherri Lucinda was no longer in our hotel room, which was the good news. The bad news was about to materialize with all the subtlety of an eruption of swamp gas. Estelle mumbled something about her slapdash makeup job and went into the bathroom to transform herself into a redheaded version of the redneck queen of mascara, Tammy Faye Bakker. I continued onto the balcony and looked out at the bleached flatness that stretched as far as I could see. Ruby Bee had lived all her life in the mountains; she would be disconcerted when she was confined to a bed in a room without a view.

I wished I knew if I could rely on Dr. Deweese's judgment. I certainly wasn't going to call in someone whose practice consisted of patients named Spot and Fluff. Tests at a Memphis hospital would run into thousands of dollars. Ruby Bee's income was apt to be only marginally healthier than my own—and I'd qualify for food stamps if I bothered with the paperwork at some bureaucratic quagmire in Farberville.

I was trying to think of someone I turn to for advice when I noticed a man on the next balcony. He was sprawled in one of the chairs, puffing on an unfiltered cigarette, sipping coffee out of a Styrofoam cup—and watching me as if I were a jewel thief who had rappelled from the roof.

"Yes?" I said frigidly.

"That your room?"

"That any of your business?"

He flicked his cigarette over the rail. "Might be, considering I'm investigating a crime. It's a little early for me to leap over there like a comic-book superhero, so I'll take the more routine approach and come around to your door."

I arrived at the door just as he knocked. Rather than usher him in, however, I said, "May I see some identification?"

"I left my badge at home on account of not being used to phone calls at the crack of dawn. My wife damn near whacked me to death when I told her to start some coffee, and I wasn't about to go back in the bedroom and grab my wallet. My name's Floyd Sanderson, and I'm the chief of police. If you want, call down to the desk and ask for Loretta. She's my niece. She don't know the particulars about my freckles and warts, but she can give you a general description."

He was unappealing enough without delving into the specific whereabouts of his freckles and warts. His belly was nearly the size of a beer keg, and his gray hair was cut so short it resembled the stubble on his jowls. His smile may have been good-natured, but his eyes were small and so deeply imbedded in his fleshy face that it was hard to imagine how light found its way to them. His shirt was stained. Much of what he'd had to eat for the last several days was memorialized on his tie.

"I suppose you can come in," I said.

"I thank you kindly," he said, brushing past me. "I don't recollect you telling me your name, missy. Would it be Estelle Oppers or Ruby Bee Hanks?"

"Arly Hanks." I followed him out to the balcony, not pleased with the need to address his broad backside. "Ruby Bee's my mother. She's in the local hospital, so I'm staying here for the moment."

"In the hospital? You be sure and give her my wishes for a fast recovery, you hear? We all feel real bad when someone comes to visit our little ol' town and fails to have a chance to partake of our hospitality. If our budget wasn't so skimpy, I'd send her a real nice bouquet of flowers."

"You're a prince, Floyd," I said as I put my elbows on the railing. "What can I do to reciprocate this generous, if empty, gesture?"

"We got us a problem, Arly. This morning we had a call that a body'd been found down there and over to your left a tad. Now this body was in real sorry shape. I don't remember much from high school, but I seem to think the formula for a falling body is sixteen feet per second squared." He looked down at the parking lot. "Or per second per second. I was too busy trying to figure out how to get into Mary Joleen Wanson's panties to pay much attention. Anyway, it's same as if you'd thrown a concrete block off a balcony, or a golf ball, for that matter. In this particular case, it was a young woman name of Stormy Zimmerman."

"I was aware that something took place," I said. "Why are you convinced it wasn't a suicide?"

"Are you from this town called Maggody?" he asked, going back into the room. He picked up a bobby pin off the chair in which Estelle had been sitting, studied it for a moment, and carefully placed it on the table before sitting down.

Wondering if he and Reverend Hitebred read the same tabloids, I closed the sliding door and sat down across from him. "Why are you convinced it wasn't a suicide?" I repeated.

Chief Sanderson gave me a discouraged look. "Thing is, we got the list of everybody on this Elvis tour, and the two ladies registered for this room are from Maggody. A couple of other witnesses admit to a connection with Maggody, and I ain't gonna pop a suspender if you're from there, too. I'd be in my bed, nice and cozy, if it weren't for all you folks."

"I'll pass that on to the Chamber of Commerce," I said, "but I'd appreciate some candor from you."

"Well, it's like this," he said in a drawl that was almost a Hollywood parody (but then again, he might have ambled off the set of *The Dukes of Hazzard*). "The deceased was sharing a room with a woman named"—he took out a notebook and flipped it open—"Cherri Lucinda Crate. She just happens to know the fellow in the next room, who just happens to be the mayor of Maggody. First off, he said he didn't know her from Adam—or Eve, anyway, that he'd met her in the casino and they'd hit it off real fine. When I said that didn't exactly agree with what she'd told us, he conceded that maybe he'd visited with her a time or two at the club where she works in Farberville, but of course he never dreamed she'd be within a hundred miles of Mississippi. Then I mentioned that the desk clerk had admitted to taking a ten-dollar bill to put him in the room adjoining hers, and he remembered that possibly she might have let drop something real vague about the Elvis Presley Pilgrimage."

"Jim Bob Buchanon?" I said with a grimace.

"Guess you know him, then."

"I know him, and his relationship with Cherri Lucinda is somewhat more intimate than he suggested. I was pretty sure I'd seen her before. I should have recognized her, but she had a towel wrapped around her hair when I went to her apartment to question her about a business swindle. Ruby Bee and Estelle caught a glimpse of her about the same time." I could see no reason to add that Ruby Bee's vantage point had been from the inside of a Dumpster; some things don't invite elaboration.

Chief Sanderson scanned the tray from room service, found a half-eaten triangle of toast, and jammed it in his mouth. "This is where it gets complicated," he went on, spewing whole wheat crumbs with each word. "She swears she wasn't expecting him, which may or may not be true. They went down to the casino and shot craps till dawn, then came upstairs to his room. She told him to go into her room and fetch her bag, then got into the shower. He says her room was empty, but a group of ladies on their way to breakfast heard an argument from inside. They stopped, not sure if they ought to do something. After a few minutes, everything got quiet and they went on toward the elevator. All of a sudden, they heard a scream. One of the ladies was so startled that she fell and twisted her ankle. While one went back to her room to call for a doctor, the rest of 'em stayed out in the hallway, fussing over their friend. They all swear nobody went in or out of any of the rooms between that moment and when a hotel employee showed up. He helped them get the accident victim back to her room, but they were still hobbling along the hall when my deputy got there."

"So," I said in an amazingly reasonable voice, considering I was in the unpalatable position of defending Hizzoner the Moron, "Stormy'd already jumped when Jim Bob went into the room to get Cherri Lucinda's bag. There certainly could be a short lapse between the time she jumped and when the woman in the parking lot saw the body and screamed. That would explain why he said the room was empty."

"You'd think so, wouldn't you?" he said.

"Yeah," I countered.

"Lots of folks would go leaping to that conclusion, Arly. My deputy did, but she ain't been on the job more than a month. Japonica's a good girl, mind you, and doin' her level best to prove herself. She just didn't think to wait until the witness stopped throwing up in the hydrangeas and started remembering more of what she'd seen."

"Which was?" I said.

"Two people on the balcony. One was the black-haired woman in a negligee. The other was a man. She couldn't make out much about him—about all she saw was an arm—but the ladies from Tuscaloosa are real sure no one left any of the rooms on this wing of the eighth floor. We're a backwoods operation, but we would have found someone hiding in a closet or lying under a bed. The only man who could have been arguing on that balcony hustled his butt back into the adjoining room, flopped down on the bed, and lit a cigar."

"I guess it has gotten complicated," I admitted. I thought for a moment, then said, "What if she was arguing with someone on the telephone? I was told that she'd had a fight with her boyfriend. She called him, and he said something that devastated her so much that she decided to kill herself. The ladies mistakenly assumed there were two people in the room."

"That doesn't explain why the witness saw a man on the balcony."

"With coaching, the witness might be convinced she saw Elvis on the balcony. Why was she looking up at the eighth floor anyway? Wasn't she more concerned with stepping in a pothole?"

Chief Sanderson blinked at me. "I hope you're not suggesting I coached the witness, Arly. I've been on the force for twenty-seven years. I may have been accused of being a little too rough with the local boys, but I ain't never been accused of playing fast and loose with a witness to a homicide. All I did was hold her hand till she calmed down, then encourage her to think more carefully about what she'd seen. As soon as she got outside, she stopped to tie her shoe and heard voices from above her. She did what any of us would do, which is look up. She saw a man on the balcony, and the only man she could have seen was Jim Bob Buchanon."

"Arly?" said Estelle as she came out of the bathroom. "Who're you talking to?"

"Chief of Police Sanderson," I said to Estelle, then gestured at her to keep quiet. "I have no problem with Jim Bob coming here to surprise Cherri Lucinda, and I'm sure he wasn't planning to give her a lesson in black-jack strategy after she finished taking a shower. But what's his motive for pushing a stranger off a balcony?"

Estelle's eyes bulged with astonishment. "Jim Bob pushed Stormy off the balcony? Jim Bob Buchanon?

Why would he go and do something like that? He didn't even know her."

"Not necessarily," said Chief Sanderson. "If he was in the habit of going to the club where Cherri Lucinda worked, he might well have met Stormy and become real interested in her . . . assets. That negligee of hers wasn't much more than a lace hankie. He coaxed her out onto the balcony and tried to get fresh. She attempted to slap him, so he grabbed her arm and twisted it behind her back. She was kicking and spitting at him, and he got so angry that he went berserk. Before he knew what was happening, he'd pinned her against the railing and was ripping at her negligee. I ain't saying he deliberately shoved her over the railing. It could have been an accident, although if the prosecutor sees it as attempted rape, the charge might well be murder in the first or second."

"I can't believe Jim Bob was responsible," Estelle said mulishly.

"We're still looking into it. No charges have been filed, but we'll keep him in custody for the time being. He can enter a plea with the judge come Monday morning."

Estelle squeezed my shoulder so tightly I winced. "Arly, you tell this man that he's crazy as a june bug. You and I both know Jim Bob ain't gonna win any blue ribbons for husband of the year, but he's not the sort to push women off balconies. Why, even if he was drunk when I ran into him last night, he wouldn't—"

"Drunk?" said Chief Sanderson. "What time would that have been?"

"I just saw him for a second, and he wasn't staggering or swaying or doing anything except being more than a mite surprised to see me. His language was crude, but it most always is. You have no business accusing him of being drunk!"

"You brought it up, Miz Oppers," he said.

"I did not!" Estelle glanced at me, then stalked back into the bathroom and slammed the door.

I waited a moment, then said, "So Jim Bob's in custody. Are there any witnesses besides the jogger?"

"Cherri Lucinda's at the station, making a statement. Her story's pretty simple—she came back from the casino with Jim Bob, took a shower, and was drying her hair when he busted into the bathroom and told her about the crowd gathering around the body in the parking lot. Cherri Lucinda said it never crossed her mind that it was her friend down there."

"Where did she think Stormy was?" I asked.

Sanderson tugged on his nose. "With a man she'd picked up in the casino or in the bar. Japonica said they acted real stunned when she went to the room in hopes there'd be a way to make a preliminary identification of the body. The driver's license photo is good enough for the time being, and it may take a long while to track down a next-of-kin, assuming there is one. Cherri Lucinda will be asked to make a more formal identification before the body's packed off to the state lab for an autopsy. I don't reckon there's much question about the cause of death, but we play by the book when we can."

"The ladies from Tuscaloosa are positive no one came out of any of the rooms?" I said. "Could the man have jumped onto another balcony?"

"Anyone tip his hat as he came through your room?"

"No, but what about the balcony on the other side?"

"Jim Bob's room? Why would he risk breaking his neck when all he had to do was return the way he came?" He paused in case I had a brilliant comeback, then added, "We're checking all the possibilities and we'll even make sure nobody saw a hang glider sail across the parking lot. After twenty-seven years, I've learned that the most obvious answer is usually the right one. People do stupid things. Maybe your mayor got drunk and lost a lot of money at the craps table. He was too ornery to back off when Stormy wouldn't co-operate. A good lawyer can bargain him down to manslaughter, even get him off with a plea of dimin-ished responsibility. Back before the casinos opened, I could handle anything that came along. These days we've got gangs, drugs, carjackings, and armed robberies. Folks get mugged in the hotel elevators. Sometimes they get killed. Husbands blow their paychecks, then go home and butcher their families."

He stood up and gave me a grim smile. "The only prosperity gambling's brought to the Delta is measured in court fines."

"Do you need a statement from Estelle?" I asked. "I don't think there's anything useful she can tell you. She was asleep when I came in around three this morning. The sliding glass door was closed and the drapes drawn, so neither of us heard a scream. The sirens woke us up."

"She didn't have any suspicion that Jim Bob was stay-ing just down the hall?"

I shook my head. "Not unless Cherri Lucinda let something drop, and it sounds as though she had no idea of Jim Bob's little scheme for the weekend. I thought I caught a glimpse of him in the casino, but it seemed so

ludicrous that I blamed it on fatigue. I only found out
my mother was in the hospital last night, and . . ." I
swallowed several times, desperately struggling not to
get teary. "Estelle was as preoccupied as I was. She
doesn't know anything."

"Can't see as she would. I'm gonna have Japonica get
statements from everybody on the tour, but she can
come here so you all won't have to bother going down
to the police department. Will you make yourselves
available?"

I nodded, then let him out and closed the door. There
were way too many things happening all at once, I
thought, my mind spinning like the tumblers on a slot
machine. Instead of cherries and oranges, I was seeing
free-falling bodies, and hearing a cry of terror that ended
with a most emphatic thud.

Oh, to be in Maggody, where nothing ever happened.

Kevin had dialed the telephone number of the police
department so many times his fingertip was beginning
to throb. Every darn time he'd gotten the answering machine and left a message pleading for Arly to come to
the supermarket, but it was finally sinking in that she
wasn't there—or if she was, she was ignoring him.

There was hardly any time left before his ma would
go to his house to baby-sit, freeing Dahlia to disappear
once more on one of her mysterious outings. Rather
than going back into the main part of the store to stock
the shelves, Kevin plopped down on the sofa in the
lounge and stared blankly at his shoes. Where could she
be going? Not shopping, since she never came back with
anything more than a scowl. Her clinic appointments
weren't more often than once a month. The doctor had

suggested a support group for mothers of twins, but his beloved had turned up her nose at the idea of listening to snooty Farberville women discuss how to go about hiring a nanny. If all she was doing was going to a movie theater, why wouldn't she just 'fess up?

He picked at a scab on his arm as he tried to think where else she might go. It was like she drove into a long, dark tunnel and came out hours later. What happened inside the tunnel that left her meaner than a polecat in heat?

He dug out the last of the change in his pocket and found thirty-five cents. Even though it meant he couldn't buy a soda pop later in the afternoon, he put the coins into the pay phone and called his house. He'd expected to hear Dahlia's sweet voice, so he was dumbstruck for a moment when his ma answered the phone.

"This is me, Ma. Is Dahlia there?"

"She just this second drove off. I practically got down on my knees and begged her to tell me where she was going, but all she said was to put ointment on Kevvie Junior's bottom when I changed his diaper. I don't understand it, Kevin. She is the mother of two—"

Kevin hung up the receiver and rubbed his eyes so ferociously he could see red and yellow splotches. His groan of despair seemed to fill the room like a particularly pungent fart. He was too late. She was gone again. All he could do was pray that she'd return. One of these days she wouldn't, and he'd have no idea where to even search for her. He took his wallet out of his pocket and gazed sadly at the photograph of Kevvie Junior and Rose Marie. Without their ma, their hearts would shrivel up like raisins.

Unless he could follow her.

Idalupino's handbag was on the shelf in the bathroom. Keeping his ears peeled, he took it down and dug through wadded tissues and empty cigarette packs until he found a key ring. He'd seen her drive up earlier in the day and park next to the Dumpster in the spot reserved for Jim Bob. She was up front, working one of the registers and telling everybody how she was the acting manager. There weren't no reason for her to come looking for him unless somebody dropped a bottle of ammonia or sent the apples rolling out of the produce display. That didn't seem likely, since business always slowed down in the early afternoon.

There was a voice whispering in his ear that maybe he shouldn't do it, but the voice in his other ear was a sight louder and pointing out that he was gonna lose his soulmate if he didn't. What's more, he owed it to his children to find their mother and bring her home. If she was lost in the woods, he wouldn't hesitate to go after her even though there might be a bear behind every tree. Idalupino was hairy, but she was nowhere near as vicious as a bear.

He stuck his head out of the lounge to make sure she wasn't nearby, then hurried across the storage room to the loading dock. No one hollered when he got into the four-wheel drive, closed the door as quietly as he could, and put the key in the ignition. There were some things on the dashboard he couldn't make heads or tails of, but he'd been driving a stick shift since he was twelve. If the wimpy city boys in TV ads could drive these across rivers and up mountains, he could, too.

He wiggled the stick until he found reverse and pressed down on the accelerator. The vehicle shot backward in a spray of gravel and gray smoke. He jerked his foot off the pedal and sat until his heart quit thudding, eyeing the dashboard with a newly discovered respect.

Time was wasting. Dahlia was most likely headed toward Farberville, with only a few minutes head start. He would follow her at a distance, even though there was no way she'd recognize him in this. Just to be extra safe, he took a scarf off the seat and tied it around his head, then found a pair of sunglasses in the glove compartment and put them on. After he'd checked his reflection in the mirror, he reopened the glove compartment, took out a tube of lipstick, and applied a thick red band over his lips. Now not even his ma would recognize him, he thought as he crammed the stick into first gear and eased down timidly on the pedal.

The car bucked across the parking lot but finally seemed to accept a stranger at the reins. Fully intending to bring bear meat home for supper, Kevin stuck out his chin and took off at a full gallop for Farberville.

Estelle was in no mood for breakfast, which was dandy, since I was in no mood for her company. I left her pacing around the hotel room and went down to the restaurant, determined to eat breakfast and read a newspaper in relative solitude.

I'd just ordered when a man approached the table. "May I join you?" he said as he pulled out a chair.

Recognizing him as the boorish blackjack player who'd attempted to banish me to the slot machines, I frowned and said, "I prefer to eat alone."

He sat down and filled his coffee cup from the pot on the table. "I hope I didn't offend you last night, or more accurately, this morning. I'm afraid I take my gambling too seriously, especially when I'm losing. The evening started so well, as it usually does. I am keenly aware of the percentages and play accordingly, but Lady Luck turned on me like an ungrateful mistress. It didn't matter what I did." He took the water glass in front of me and drank deeply. "There are moments when I feel like Prometheus, doomed by the gods to have my entrails ripped out at the gaming tables. In the wee hours, dealers take on an uncanny resemblance to predatory birds with razor-sharp talons."

"Perhaps you should take up needlepoint," I said without sympathy.

"Rex Malanac," he said, extending his hand. "You are, I believe, the daughter of Ruby Bee Hanks? I hope she's recovering."

I briefly touched his hand. "They're doing some tests at the hospital. She should be able to go home in a few days. Are you on the Elvis Tour?"

"Yes, but I must say it's been a disappointment. In Memphis, the driver did his best to convince us that we were staying in a motel where Elvis once slept, but of course everyone knows that he and his parents lived in public housing in the north part of Memphis. There is no documentation or reason to believe he ever stayed in any motels. One would almost suspect this was an economizing tactic on the part of C'Mon Tours."

"Estelle mentioned gunfire," I said.

"All of us were in abject terror that we would be killed by stray bullets. Only our little lovebirds had the courage to go out into the night, but they arranged to have taxis pick them up and deliver them to their motel-room door. Had your mother and her friend asked, I gladly would have taken up a post in their room in order to protect them. They're quite the innocents abroad, are they not?"

"Oh, absolutely," I said, stirring several spoonfuls of sugar into my coffee. "You heard about Stormy?"

"A terrible thing." He picked up the menu and beckoned to a waitress. "Be a dear and bring me scrambled eggs, two very crisp strips of bacon, and dry whole-wheat toast."

My appetite diminished, I ordered a bagel, then said, "What exactly did you hear, Mr. Malanac?"

"Please call me Rex. Otherwise, I'm apt to forget you're not a student and start lecturing you on the emergence of militaristic symbolism in the literature of prewar Germany. I'm sure you wouldn't care for that."

"What about Stormy?"

"All I know is that she fell to her death several hours ago. A rather uncouth police officer ordered me to remain in the hotel until I've given a statement. It will be a very short one, I'm afraid. I stayed in the casino until four, then went to my room and fell asleep immediately. I might still be in that condition had the police officer not banged on my door. I find it difficult to think kindly of him."

"Did you see Cherri Lucinda playing craps?"

"I do not allow my attention to wander when I'm at the blackjack table," he said primly. "I did see her enter the casino clinging to the arm of an unfamiliar man, and while on the way to the men's room, I noticed Stormy playing the quarter slots as if determined to win a kidney transplant for a kid sister or brother. Neither of them was of consequence to me, to be brutally honest. I came on the pilgrimage to do further investigation into Elvisian folklore, and divert myself with an evening at a casino. Calculating odds at blackjack makes a pleasant change from grading ill-written essays on Albert Camus and Günter Grass."

"Miss Hanks," said the same silky voice I'd heard in the casino, "you look as though you've had the opportunity to catch a few hours of sleep."

I looked up at the ostentatiously gracious young man in the lustrous gray suit. In that it was wise to avoid insulting likely members of a crime family, I said, "Yes, thank you."

"I was worried about you. If you will honor us with your presence tonight, I'd be delighted to offer you a drink."

"Drinks are free," I said, glancing at Rex, who was attacking his bacon and eggs with the dedication of a famished refugee. If he'd bent over any further, his nose would have made contact with the grease puddling the hash-brown potatoes. "Why don't you offer me a nice big stack of chips? You know you'll have them back at the end of the evening, but you'll have kept me amused and eternally grateful to the benevolence of The Luck of the Draw."

"I understand you're associated with the tour group that lost a member in a tragic fashion," he said. "All of us on the staff would like to share our condolences."

"So are you giving me chips to ease the pain?" I asked. "Red ones will do, but I'd prefer green."

"We'll have to see. You have the look of someone who might get lucky and make a run on the bank."

"I'll bet you say that to all the girls," I replied with a saccharine smile.

He looked down at Rex, who was still wolfing down his scrambled eggs as if they would scamper away if he didn't contain them with a fork, then nodded at me and wound his way through the tables to the exit.

I waited until Rex emerged from his close encounter

with carbohydrates. "When you saw Stormy playing the slot machine, was she alone?"

"Was she with someone, you mean?"

"That would be the question," I said, bemused.

"I don't recall anyone in close proximity. However, I only caught a glimpse of her. If she had a companion, he might have stepped away for a moment. Watching someone play the slots is slightly more boring than actually playing them. I prefer games of a more cerebral nature, in which a knowledge of the percentages is a factor."

"You must play a lot," I said. "Do you usually win?"

"Naturally." He put his napkin on his plate, finished his coffee, and rose. "I've enjoyed meeting you, Arly. Please tell you mother I wish her a speedy recovery."

I chewed on a bagel as I watched him leave the restaurant, wondering why he'd insisted on joining me. His expressions of concern for Ruby Bee were no more heartfelt than his superficial distress at Stormy's death. He hadn't attempted to elicit information, nor had he offered anything beyond a loose description of his activities during the last six hours. He'd played blackjack until four, and then gone to bed. I'd caught no glint in his eyes that suggested he was flirting with me, which was understandable, considering the grayish circles under my eyes and strands of hair jammed behind my ears.

When the waitress arrived with the bill, I realized Rex had stiffed me for the grand sum of two dollars and forty-nine cents.

The day was certainly taking shape.

N I N E

I hesitated in the restaurant doorway as a group of gray-haired women came out of the casino, each clasping a paper cup to hold her slot-machine winnings (or future losings). I had an urge to ask them if they were from Tuscaloosa, but instead waited until they'd marched by like a platoon of ducks and then trailed after them to the lobby.

I found a pay phone, punched in my card number, and called Harve's office. When LaBelle answered, I asked to speak to him.

"He's busy," she said. "So am I, what with all this ridiculous paperwork. Call back at the beginning of the week."

"Is he there, LaBelle? This is important."

"To the best of my knowledge, he's not in the building. Even though he's obligated to keep me informed of his whereabouts, these last few days he's been sneaking in and out the back door. I have better things to do than go knock on his door every time the phone rings. I most certainly am not about to do it now."

Short of a six-hour drive and a fistfight in the front

office, there was no way to win this minor skirmish. "Let me leave a message for him, LaBelle," I said. "I'm in a little town north of Tunica, Mississippi, and I may be here for a few more days."

"Why would that be?"

"Ruby Bee's in the hospital, having some tests. If that weren't enough, Jim Bob Buchanon's implicated in a homicide and I need to sort it out. It took place at The Luck of the Draw hotel, which is where I'm staying. This is strictly for Harve's information. Please don't spread it around."

"I beg your pardon," LaBelle said huffily. "I am not a person to go jabbering whenever I hear something. I'm right sorry to hear about Ruby Bee. Give her my best."

She slammed down the receiver. I moved on to a white house phone and called Estelle. She sounded peculiar when she answered, as if she'd been plotting to rob the casino in order to pay a Memphis hospital bill.

"Are you okay?" I asked.

"Why shouldn't I be? Just because Ruby Bee's on her deathbed and Jim Bob's in jail and Stormy's flatter than a Salisbury steak and—"

"Ruby Bee's not on her deathbed," I cut in. "The rest of it may be true, but there's not a damn thing you can do about it. You're not helping the situation, Estelle."

"And you are?"

"What am I supposed to be doing?"

"For starters, you can make sure Jim Bob's not being thumped with rubber hoses to make him confess. Scoot yourself over there and see if you can do something for him. He's from Maggody, after all, and no matter what problems you've had with him, you owe it to the community to look after its citizens."

"What are you going to do while I'm gone?"

Estelle harrumphed loudly enough to make herself heard in the hallway. "What do you think I'm gonna do, missy—go out on the balcony and yodel like a person of the Swiss persuasion? I thought I'd order another pot of coffee from room service and stay by the phone in case Ruby Bee takes a turn for the worse. I can use a little privacy after all that's gone on. I might just give myself a manicure while I watch a movie on cable. Is that all right with you?"

At that moment, if she'd said she had the ski mask in place and was loading an automatic weapon, I would have acquiesced. I told her I'd be back in an hour or so, then asked a bellman how to find the local jail and went out to the parking lot. I did pause for a moment to listen for mournful yodeling before I got in my car and drove out to the main highway.

The PD was in what amounted to an alley behind an abandoned grain silo. I parked and went inside. A young black woman with braided hair and a neatly pressed uniform gave me a toothy smile.

"Help you?" she said in a voice that implied she'd really like to be able to do so, no matter how much of a personal sacrifice might be required on her part.

"I'm here to see Jim Bob Buchanon."

Her smile dried up. "You his lawyer?"

"Not exactly," I said. "I just want to make sure he's all right."

"A relative, then?"

I peered at her name tag, which identified her as J. Jones. "I'm a friend from his hometown, Deputy Jones. May I see him?"

"I'd rather see a cross burning in my yard, but it's

your decision," she said as she stood up. We went into a short corridor lined with three barred cells. "You got a visitor, honey," she called. "She's a lady, so don't let me hear any more of that nasty language. You understand?"

Jim Bob was stretched out on a bare metal cot, his hands entwined behind his neck. His shoes were on the floor of the cell; the hole in his sock brought to mind my (and everybody else's) mother's admonishment to always wear clean underwear in case of an accident.

Or, in this case, an incarceration.

"Why, Japonica," he said, "I can't believe you'd say such a thing. I've been a perfect gentleman ever since you dragged me out of the hotel room and gave me a free ride to your elegant downtown establishment. I was just lying here thinkin' how I might spend my vacation in this very cell come summertime."

"Come summertime you may still be here," I said.

He jerked upright. "Aw, Jesus, like I need this on top of everything else? What the fuck are you doin' here?"

"It's okay," I said to Japonica before she could offer further commentary on his obvious lack of social graces. "I'm sorry to say I'm used to him."

"Well, I'm not," she said as she stalked toward the front room. "Call if you want me to come back with a nightstick and teach him some manners."

When the door closed behind her, I said, "You've gotten yourself into a helluva mess, Mayor Buchanon. Chief Sanderson mentioned the possibility of first- or second-degree murder. I don't know if they have the death penalty in Mississippi, but I do know they have endless acres of cotton to be chopped under the noonday sun."

"Don't give me that shit. I didn't do anything wrong

beyond telling Mrs. Jim Bob that I'd be at the Municipal
League meeting in Hot Springs. Nobody goes to prison
for that. When I get out of here, I'm going sue their sorry
butts for false imprisonment."

"*If* you get out of here," I said, "you'd better stay on
the far side of the river. You want to tell me what
happened?"

"No, I don't want to tell you what happened," he
muttered. "Guess I ought to, though, so you can convince that swinish chief of police to let me out of this
hellhole." He flopped back on the cot and resumed staring at the ceiling. "A couple of weeks ago Cherri Lucinda
said that she was goin' on this Elvis Presley Pilgrimage.
I thought I'd come over and give her a thrill. She wasn't
supposed to show up until today, but I figured I could
amuse myself in the casino for an extra night. You never
know who all you might meet, particularly at the craps
table. Most women are so stupid they don't have the
foggiest idea how to play, but they like the excitement
and the excuse to press their tits up against your back so
hard you can feel their nipples."

"Let's not go into that," I said. "So you didn't expect
to see Cherri Lucinda yesterday afternoon?"

"It's a good thing your job don't require much in the
way of brains. I just told you that she wasn't supposed to
get here until later today. I got to the hotel around five,
checked in, and was taking my bag up to the room when
I damn near tripped over Estelle in front of the elevators. Then Ruby Bee collapsed on the carpet and Cherri
Lucinda came dashing out of the ladies room and
Estelle started bleatin' like a sheep and everybody from
the bellboys to a group of Japanese tourists went crazy.
I returned to the desk, slipped the kid a ten-dollar bill to

change my room, then stayed in the bar until the excitement died down. Cherri Lucinda damn near peed in her jeans when I knocked on the door between the two rooms an hour later."

I waited in case he was going to ask about Ruby Bee, then sighed and said, "What about Stormy? Did you know she and Cherri Lucinda would be sharing a room?"

He sat up and frowned at me. "Is that the woman I'm accused of pushing off the balcony? Hell, I didn't pay any attention when Cherri Lucinda said her name. I had more important things on my mind—and in my pocket, if you follow me. I invited Cherri Lucinda into my room so she could express her gratitude for my going to the bother of driving all this way to see her. After that, we had ourselves a fancy prime rib dinner in the restaurant, then went to the casino so she could watch me shoot craps."

"She was at your side all night?"

"Ever' now and then she'd start whining that she was bored, so I'd give her some money to go throw away on the slots. She ain't the brightest thing to come down the pike." He smirked in a most unbecoming way. "Her talents lie elsewhere. On account of being an exotic dancer, she can get herself into some mind-bogglin' positions."

I leaned against the wall and regarded him with contempt. Back in Maggody, I was obliged to show a modicum of deference, but in this situation he was in a grimy little cell. It was an image I'd cherish for a long time to come, and my only regret was that I didn't have a camera. "At dawn you and she went up to your room, right? Did she go into her own room?"

"No, she went straight to my bathroom and started the shower, then asked me if I'd mind getting her bag so she could slip on her nightie. I went next door, stuffed everything back in it, and set it inside the bathroom. After that, I turned on the TV, lit a cigar, and waited for her to come out in a sexy little something, all steamy and warm and smelling of perfume."

"You didn't hear a scream?"

"I might have heard something, but I was trying to get the NBA scores due to a small wager with a gentleman that lives in Starley City. The siren was a mite harder to ignore. I pulled back the curtain to see what was going on, then went out on the balcony for a better look. Cherri Lucinda came out of the bathroom about then and joined me. We hadn't made heads or tails of it when that uppity colored girl banged on the door." He got up and came over to the bars separating us. Despite his display of bravado, his forehead was beaded with sweat and saliva dribbled out of the corners of his mouth. "You got to make them believe me, Arly. There wasn't nobody in the next room. The bathroom was dark and the only light came from a gap in the curtains. I just collected the bag for Cherri Lucinda. That's all I did."

"Did you hear any voices that might have come from the adjoining room?"

"Jesus, you are a few cans shy of a six-pack. If I'd heard voices, I would have expected to find folks in there, wouldn't I? The room was empty. There was a tray from room service next to the TV set. I noticed 'cause my belly was rumbling, but then I remembered there was a treat in the other room that was tastier than anything out of a hotel kitchen. The bag was on the bed, like Cherri Lucinda told me. I already told you what happened after that."

"There are several witnesses who heard an argument from inside that room," I said, watching him closely. "It's odd that you and Cherri Lucinda didn't hear it when you came down the hall."

"She was pretty loose and trying to sing that old song about a lovesick farm boy what jumped off the Tallahachee Bridge. She was having a real tough time getting out the words, and every time she screwed up, she'd start laughin'. I kept trying to shush her before somebody called the desk to complain, but it didn't do a damn bit of good." He jabbed his finger at me. "That's another thing wrong with women—they can't hold their liquor."

"So what's your excuse, Jim Bob? After all, we're on opposite sides of the bars here."

Even Hizzoner the Moron could see the folly in pissing me off, since I was free to waltz out the door and he was, in a manner of speaking, between a rock and a hard place. "What do you aim to do about this?" he said, attempting to sound humble. "Will they let me go if I promise to stay at the hotel until the judge hears me out on Monday?"

"I don't think so," I said. "You'd better be a tad more polite to Deputy Jones. It's likely she's the one who decides whether you get a dry bologna sandwich or a blue-plate special."

"I ain't kissing up to no colored girls!"

"Suit yourself. I'll talk to Chief Sanderson and find out if there are any more witnesses. Stormy seems to have been the type to cozy up to men in bars. Maybe she found a tightrope walker with a lousy temper."

I could hear him cursing as I went down the hall and out into the main room. Deputy Jones gave me another view of her white teeth, but the previous warmth was long gone and I figured she'd never offer to loan me her car or braid my hair.

"He's something, isn't he?" I said, shaking my head. "I'd like to be able to tell you that he's a decent guy at heart, but a lightning bolt would strike me dead in the middle of the sentence. One of his pastimes back home is buying up widows' properties for back taxes and evicting them."

"Known some like that,", she said. "All white, of course, since that's who has the money around these parts. None of the businesses you drove by on your way here are owned by my people, except Morton's Mufflers. Morton's my great-uncle. The Chamber of Commerce ain't asked him to join as of yet, but he's only had the shop for thirty-four years. He's real confident they'll ask him in another year or two. His wife's a maid at the hotel where you're staying. She's seventy-six."

I could tell from the way she was looking at me that she wouldn't be receptive to a generic apology for the abuses my race had heaped on hers for the last two hundred years. "Do you know what time you'll be at the hotel to take statements?" I asked.

"I'm waiting on Chief Sanderson. He went home to take a shower and have breakfast. Soon as he gets here, he'll take over the baby-sitting chores and I can leave. We wouldn't want your friend in the cell out back to hang himself with his shoelaces, would we?"

"Probably not," I said. "I gather Cherri Lucinda's gone back to the hotel. From what Jim Bob told me, it sounds as though she was pretty much out of it by the time they got to his room. She wasn't looking too robust this morning. I assumed it was her lack of makeup, but it's more likely to have been from a hangover."

Japonica's eyes narrowed. "That's what she said. You weren't on the tour. Where do you know her from? Did you know the victim, too? Maybe you ought to explain just who you are and why you're taking such an interest in this investigation."

I described my relationship with Ruby Bee and Estelle, but omitted any reference to my occupation since I was well out of my minuscule jurisdiction. Although Harve and I get along, there's plenty of jealousy among the various county law-enforcement agencies. The last thing I needed was for Japonica and Sanderson to think I was peering over their collective shoulder.

"As for Cherri Lucinda," I continued, "I had seen her before this morning, but it took the connection with Jim Bob to make me remember. They've been . . . carrying on for quite some time. I never met Stormy."

"Did you ever go to the club where they worked?"

"I couldn't tell you where Cherri Lucinda worked if you waved a winning lottery ticket at me."

Japonica's stare relaxed. "Yeah, you look kinda old to be going to nightclubs."

I was trying to think of a suitable comeback, when the telephone rang. She picked up the receiver, listened for a moment, and then held it out to me. "Sounds like you got a heap of trouble," she said.

My stomach constricted as if it had been pierced with an icicle. "My mother?"

"Your friend at the hotel. I'm beginning to wish all of

you folks had gone to a different casino, like in the south of France."

I forced myself to exhale, then took the receiver. "Estelle?" I said. "What's wrong?"

"Miss Hanks," said a male voice, "this is Mackenzie Cutting, chief of security at The Luck of the Draw. Miss Oppers is here in my office, doing her best to convince me not to press charges for burglary and criminal mischief. I'm calling you at her request. Would you be so kind as to join us at your earliest convenience?"

Kevin drove as fast as he dared, squirming with frustration whenever he got stuck behind a chicken truck or a car with out-of-state plates. Dahlia couldn't be more than five minutes ahead of him—unless she'd gone toward the Missouri line, which was possible, since he didn't have a clue where she was going. That didn't seem likely, however, since there wasn't nothing but fields and woods all the way to Branson. Just getting there and back would take close to four hours.

Of course she could have taken County 102 to Hasty, or turned at the Pot O' Gold trailer park and gone up the road that wound across Cotter's Ridge. Or gone bouncing down any of the dirt roads that led past rickety farmhouses and ponds covered with slime. Or parked in front of one of the units at the Flamingo Motel behind Ruby Bee's Bar & Grill, although he figured his ears would have been burnin' if that was where she'd been all these afternoons. Ruby Bee'd never been one to keep a secret any longer than it took her to whip up a batch of biscuits.

The four-wheel was a mite cumbersome to drive, but he was getting the hang of it. After some fumbling, he managed to turn on the heater, and after a good deal more fumbling, did the same with the radio. The music that blared out wasn't at all to his liking, what with the lack of a tune and the jumble of cusswords. He was trying to find a country station when he shot past the state police car lurking behind a billboard.

Brother Verber brought in his mail, tossed aside the bills and announcements of storewide sales, and took out the magazine that had arrived in a plain brown wrapper. In order to prepare himself for the shock and disgust he'd experience when he encountered the graphic depravity between the covers, he filled a glass with sacramental wine and set the bottle on the coffee table where it'd be handy if he started feeling woozy.

The afternoon stretched before him like a hot bubble bath. His sermon, "The Alphabet Sins," was written, rewritten, and fine-tuned for the following morning's service. Some of the letters had been downright challenging. He'd been on a roll for the first hour, racing from "atheism" all the way to "wickedness" without having to even gnaw on his pencil (except for a small problem with K, which he'd resolved in a somewhat fanciful manner).

But then he'd arrived at X and, shortly thereafter, at Y. Even Z had presented a quandary, although he'd finally chanced on a word that worked. What's more, he'd made it into a little ditty so that the congregation could memorize it and sing it under their breath when they were confronted with the choice between the paths of evil and righteousness. He'd originally set it to the tune of "Amazing Grace," but then he'd realized that the theme song to *Gilligan's Island* worked just as well and was a sight more spirited.

He was testing it once more to make sure the words

tripped over his tongue when the telephone rang. He picked up the receiver.

"Thank the Lord I found you!" said Mrs. Jim Bob. "The most terrible thing has happened! I didn't know where to turn. Brother Verber, this is indeed my time of trial and tribulation. I can't think when I've been so upset!"

"Tell me what's wrong, Sister Barbara," he said in a deep voice meant to comfort her, one of the techniques he'd learned from his seminary study booklets. "I'm here for you. If you'd like to take a moment to get a grip on yourself, that might be helpful."

"It's Jim Bob. He's gone and got hisself arrested for murder."

Brother Verber's face froze in horror. "Who did he murder?"

"Nobody," she said waspishly, sounding more like her regular self. "All I said is that he was arrested. He's accused of killing some hussy in Mississippi."

"I thought you said he was in Hot Springs."

"That's where he told me he was going. Don't you remember how I said that something fishy was going on? At least I'm not paranoid, Brother Verber. He said he was going to Hot Springs and now he's in Mississippi in jail for murder. If that's not fishy, I don't know what is!"

"That's mighty fishy," agreed Brother Verber. "Have you spoken to him?"

"He hasn't bothered to call. How busy can he be if all he's doing is sitting in a jail cell?" Her question being rhetorical, she went on. "I heard about it from LaBelle at the sheriff's office. She called to say how sorry she was and ask if she should mail him a tin of cookies. I had no idea what she was talking about, naturally, but she finally admitted that Arly had called her and—"

"Arly knows about this?"

"I don't think she'd call the sheriff's office if all she did was have a bad dream, do you? As soon as Arly hung up, LaBelle got on the phone and called the state medical lab in Mississippi. They admitted to knowing about this homicide in some little town, and before too long LaBelle had the details. Jim Bob's in jail, Brother Verber. He could end up in prison for the rest of his life, leaving me to fend for myself. The last job I had was working part-time in the church office when I was seventeen. What am I gonna do?"

"There's only one thing you can do, Sister Barbara."

"What's that?"

"Ask the Lord for guidance. Let's both just get down on our knees and—"

"Pack your bag. I'll be there in ten minutes."

She hung up before he could protest, not that it had ever done any good in the past. Brother Verber put the magazine away for another day, drained the glass of wine, drank another for good measure, and went down the narrow hallway to pull a suitcase out of his closet.

Idalupino stared at the space next to the Dumpster. There was a splotch of oil on the gravel and a scattering of rotten produce (orange peels and what looked to be a brown grapefruit) in the weeds, but there was definitely a big, fat nothing there.

She squeezed her eyes closed, whispered a little prayer in which she vowed never again to skip church or so much as sip a beer if the Lord would intervene, and then slowly opened her eyes. The space reserved for the manager remained most distressingly empty.

Canon was gonna kill her—no ifs or buts about it. She'd been nagging him for months to fix the exhaust pipe on her car; he'd finally agreed and even allowed her to borrow his precious sport utility van for the day. Now some thievin' sumbitch had stolen it right from under her nose, or at least from behind her behind while she was working the cash register.

She went into the lounge and found the telephone directory to look up the body shop where Canon worked. Then, trying not to imagine what she'd look like with two black eyes and a split lip, she put coins in the pay phone and dialed the number.

"I got to speak to Canon Buchanon," she said in a squeaky voice. "Tell him it's his cousin Idalupino. I got some bad news for him."

While she was waiting for him, she spotted a wallet on the couch. She picked it up and opened it. Kevin's face beamed at her from his driver's license. "I swear," she said as she stuck it in her pocket for safekeeping, "that boy'd lose his prick if it wasn't attached."

As soon as I arrived back at the hotel, I asked for directions to Mackenzie Cutting's office and was directed through a door marked "Authorized Personnel Only." Beyond it was a labyrinth of narrow hallways, but after a few false turns I found a door with his name painted on the opaque glass.

I wasn't sure of the protocol, so I went on inside. The security man with whom I'd had a couple of brief encounters was seated behind a desk. Nearby stood a thick-waisted blond woman in a maroon smock. Estelle was seated on the edge of a chair, twisting a tissue and trying to look anything but frightened. I wasn't fooled.

"Miss Hanks," said Mackenzie, "we meet yet once again, but under less congenial circumstances. This is Linda Billington, the head of housekeeping. I believe you already know Miss Oppers."

"What's going on?" I said.

He glanced at Ms. Billington, who flushed and said, "I have a new girl on the staff. She doesn't speak any English or I'd have her here to tell you her story. She was working on the fourth floor this morning, cleaning rooms as they became vacant. She finished up in one and came back out in the hall. Her cleaning cart was gone. Thinking she might be accused of theft and deported, she hid in a storage closet. Eventually another maid heard her sobbing, dragged her out, and determined the problem. I was called immediately. I rounded up several of my more reliable girls and we conducted a systematic search of all the floors." She turned her head slightly in order to glower at Estelle. "We found *her* on the sixth floor, dressed in a housekeeping smock and pushing the stolen cart. Based on the complaints we received in my office, she annoyed a large number of guests by ignoring the DO NOT DISTURB signs on their doorknobs and using a passkey to go into the rooms. That is strictly against our rules. We regard those signs with reverence. Many of the guests stay up very late and prefer to sleep until noon. A goodly number of them are too inebriated to engage the deadbolt before retiring."

"I don't see where burglary and criminal mischief enter into this," I said to Mackenzie, not trusting myself to look at Estelle.

"We haven't called the police," he said levelly.

I turned to Ms. Billington. "Did anyone go so far as to accuse her of theft?"

"No, but she stole the cart and used the passkey to

enter guests' rooms. I think it's obvious she hoped to spot money or jewelry on the dresser. Why else would she pretend to be a member of our staff?"

A very good question, I thought as I resisted the impulse to grab Estelle's scrawny neck and demand an answer. "If you'll overlook this minor indiscretion, I will personally supervise Miss Oppers's movements until we check out. Except for the times we are at my mother's bedside at the hospital, she will remain in her hotel room. Miss Oppers has no desire to give an interview to the press in which she explains how easily she gained possession of a passkey. It might reflect badly on security at The Luck of the Draw."

"It was all the new girl's fault," Ms. Billington put in. "She failed to follow procedure. The key should have been in the pocket of her smock."

Mackenzie Cutting raised his hand to cut her off. "You may go, Ms. Billington. Find someone who can communicate with this girl and see that the procedures are explained more clearly to her. Bring me a list of all those who complained this morning. Complimentary baskets of fruit will do much to erase any unpleasant feelings."

"Yes, sir," she said.

"All right, Miss Hanks," he continued, "we'll refrain from pressing charges as long as nothing further takes place. Miss Oppers, I have no idea why you felt the need to impersonate a hotel employee. Do not do it again."

Estelle nodded, gave me a wary look, and scurried out the door as if she could hear bloodhounds baying in the distance.

"I'll make sure she doesn't," I said lamely, then turned around and left.

It was not one of my grander exits.

T E N

By the time I reached the room, Estelle had locked herself in the bathroom and was running water in the bathtub. Niagara Falls was more subtle than her ploy.

"You come out of there," I said, wondering if I could order a crowbar from room service. It didn't seem likely.

Estelle had enough sense to stay where she was. "I am gonna take a bath to ease my jitters. I was never so terrified in all my born days when I was set upon by those women flapping down the hall in purple smocks. As a child, I was attacked by a flock of starlings, and it left me scarred for life. I feared for my very life this morning."

"Oh yes, I often lie awake at night worrying that maniacal maids will burst into my bedroom and dust me to death. Turn off the tap and get yourself out here to explain."

"I'll come out when I've a mind to. Now you just go about your business and let me have some peace and quiet."

I gave up and went on into the main part of the room. A maid who may or may not have been fluent in

English had made the beds, vacuumed, removed the breakfast tray from room service, and left a fresh pink carnation in a vase by the telephone. An opulent arrangement of orchids and birds-of-paradise would not have cheered me up.

The message light on the telephone was not blinking. I contemplated calling the hospital, but finally convinced myself that I would have been notified if anything critical had taken place. Ruby Bee was older than she admitted, but she was basically robust. More often than not, she was a pain in the neck, but I wasn't sure if I could do without her nagging.

Some of it, anyway.

I was struggling with unpleasant thoughts when someone knocked on the door. Doubting that Estelle was going to rise from the bathwater like a phoenix from the flames and respond, I wiped my eyes and opened the door.

"Oh," said the woman in the hall, peering at me through wire-rimmed glasses. "My name is Taylor. Is Estelle here?"

"Estelle is taking a bath," I said as I waved her in. If the Shriners and the ladies from Tuscaloosa showed up in the immediate future, I was more than willing to arrange liaisons in the casino. Maybe I could lure Japonica over to meet Mackenzie Cutting, and set up an intimate dinner for Rex and Ms. Billington. Cherri Lucinda might take a fancy to Chief Sanderson. Or I could mix and match with giddy abandon. All things were possible.

Taylor eyed me uncertainly as she came a few feet into the room. "Do you know how long she'll be? I really need to speak to her."

I pounded on the bathroom door. "Hey, Estelle, you've got company. Someone named Taylor. Shall I order tea and cream cakes?"

After a significant moment of silence, Estelle said, "Tell her what happened. I'll be out in a few minutes."

"Something happened?" Taylor said, giving me a smile that was as lackluster as her beige skirt and sweater.

"Nothing much," I said. "Estelle was busted for burglary, but it happens all the time."

"It's my fault. Well, it's more Todd's fault. He's my fiancé. It's just that when he disappeared, I couldn't stop myself from thinking the worst." Tears erupted, fogging up the lenses of her glasses and making me feel like a bully with all the compassion of Attila the Hun.

"Why don't you tell me what you're talking about?" I suggested gently.

"Okay, after we got the key yesterday afternoon, Todd and I went to our room, which is down the hall. He took a shower and shaved, and said he was feeling better. We decided to hold off on dinner for a while and go to the casino to have a look. We were walking past the bar when a bunch of his buddies from high school yelled at him. I would have preferred to keep on going, but Todd insisted that we join them for a drink. I thought it was a dreadful idea."

I may have been expected to agree with her, but I hadn't yet zeroed in on the transgression. "Buddies, huh? I guess you were uncomfortable."

"I felt like the barmaid, although they paid more attention to her than they did to me. All of them were smoking cigars—even the girls—and it was obvious they'd been in the bar all afternoon. I seriously considered going back to the room."

"And then?"

"One drink, two drinks, another round, another round. Pretty soon Todd was telling everybody how I'd arranged for us to get married at the Elvis Chapel in Tupelo. He made it sound so tacky that I wanted to die right there. His friends were hooting and carrying on like junior high kids at a mall. I was totally humiliated. Can you imagine how I felt surrounded by all those— those overbred pedigreed puppies who've never had to do more than whimper to their parents to get next month's rent? The only time one of those girls has been cold and hungry is when she's gotten herself locked out of the sorority house!"

I still wasn't making the leap between Taylor's unhappy experience in the bar and Estelle's more profound problem on the sixth floor. "Did you finally go to dinner?"

"The booze was coming too fast for that. I tried to convince Todd that he ought to eat something, but he ignored me and kept cracking up over all these inside jokes that made no sense whatsoever. I was like an orphan who'd wandered into a family reunion, so I told Todd I was going upstairs to order from room service. He said he'd join me in a few minutes." She took a shuddery breath. "I was waiting for the elevator when he and this slutty girl named Leanne or Luellen staggered up, hanging all over each other. According to Todd, she wanted him to fix a zipper. I had to think the zipper she had in mind was on her jeans, not her designer luggage. They got off on the sixth floor."

"And that's the last you saw of him?"

"It's been over twelve hours," she said, clutching a

wadded tissue to her nose. "He's either floating in the river or shacked up with this old girlfriend. I hate to say it, but I'm having serious reservations about him. You'd think he'd want to be with me on what's meant to be our honeymoon. I mean, what he's doing is so unbelievably inconsiderate of my feelings."

I finally got it. "And this morning when you woke up and he was still gone, you came here to pour out your problems to Estelle, right? You knew that if Todd was in the hotel, he was likely to be on the sixth floor. Estelle"—I raised my voice, even though I knew she had her ear pressed to the door—"being the idiot that she is, offered to don a disguise and see if she could hunt him down."

Taylor shifted uncomfortably. "We thought maybe she could find out which room he was in. I don't know what I was going to do when she did. Drag him out of there, I guess, and insist we get married as soon as possible. Once that happens, he'll settle down and behave like a corporate lawyer instead of a frat boy."

"Maybe he passed out," I suggested. "The girl figured it would be easier to leave him until he woke up this morning. He may be on his way to your room."

"I could tell from the way he was looking at her that he wasn't *that* drunk."

Estelle came out of the bathroom. "You said he hadn't had anything to eat all day," she said to Taylor. "Arly's most likely right."

"You didn't see him?"

"I made it into more than half the rooms," Estelle said, "and there wasn't hide nor hair of him."

Taylor dried her glasses on the tissue and settled them back in place. "Is there a way to make the hotel give us the names of all the single women with rooms on the sixth floor?"

I winced at the image of Estelle trying to wheedle that tidbit of information out of a desk clerk. "Listen," I said, trying to be assertive, if not dictatorial, "it's quite possible Todd went back down to the casino after he zipped her zipper. He might be playing blackjack as we speak. Why don't you go have a look before you get Estelle into more trouble?"

"It could have happened that way," Taylor said without conviction. "But I watched them on the elevator, and there was something going on. Todd's not exactly a choirboy when it comes to sex. He bragged to me how he slept with every single cheerleader during his senior year in high school. Is that repulsive or what?"

"Are you sure he's the man of your dreams?" I asked.

"No, but he most definitely is the father of my baby. His mother seems to have found a way to repress his father's libidinous impulses, or at least insist on a modicum of discretion. I'll just have to hope I can do the same with Todd."

It was not a marriage made in heaven, I thought as I went over to the sliding glass door and tried in vain to see the roof of the hospital. "Did you hear what happened to Stormy?"

"Wasn't that ghastly? She wasn't a very nice person, but I did my best to make allowances due to her inferior socioeconomic background and limited intellect. I'd be surprised if she even graduated from high school."

Estelle stiffened. "I can't see that matters, Taylor. It's not like she was on welfare. We can't all be doctors and lawyers—or executives, for that matter. We need mechanics and clerks and waitresses just as much as we need folks with flashy degrees. If you ask me, they're a darn sight more useful. When's the last time an accountant stopped and offered to look under your hood?"

"It's just that Todd's gone," Taylor said, beginning to cry once again.

I stayed where I was, but Estelle relented and sat down beside her to hold her hand and murmur inanities. I was less than impressed with her display of grief.

"Then you were alone all night?" I said.

"I just told you," she whined so piteously that Estelle glared at me. "I was so upset that I literally cried myself to sleep. What am I supposed to do now?"

"Go back to your room and wait for him to drag in," I said. "Either accept his apology or kick him out. It's your future on the line."

Taylor pushed her bangs out of her eyes so that she, too, could glare at me. "That's not a very nice thing to say. Here I am asking for a little compassion and all you can do is say mean things. You don't realize what it's like to be in my situation. It's not easy, you know. Todd's parents are like majorly important in Little Rock society. His mother is the committee chairwoman for the entire debutante thing, and she—"

"You're right," I interrupted. "All I can do is say mean things, and I'm thinking of a whole lot more of them. Why don't you go to your room and call someone who cares?"

"Arly!" Estelle gasped.

I crossed my arms. "My mother's in the hospital in critical condition. Jim Bob's in a jail cell down the road, likely to be charged with murder. You aren't allowed to leave this room unless you're on a leash. I simply don't have time for errant fraternity boys on drunken binges and social climbers who've misplaced their ladders."

Taylor stood up. "Well then, maybe I should leave."

"I never accused you of stupidity," I said as I stepped aside to facilitate her path to the door.

After she flounced out the door (and flounce, she did, as if she were a raven-haired vixen in a Civil War movie), I turned my attention to Estelle.

"This is why you stole the housekeeping cart and passkey?" I said.

"I don't need any lectures from the likes of you. I was merely doing a small favor for Taylor. It's obvious you've taken a dislike to her, but you ain't being fair. Here she is, all alone, pregnant, and going up against this snooty family. She's gonna come into a substantial inheritance before too long, but in the meantime she's doing the best she can to keep her pride intact. You had no business speaking to her like that."

I flopped down on the bed. "I met her type in Manhattan. Did you notice that she never even pretended to be worried about this fiancé who's disappeared? The only reason she wants to find him is so that she can get the gold band on her finger. After that, she'll slap him on the buttocks and send him right back out to fool around with all of his ex-girlfriends."

On that note, I rolled over and gave her an unimpeded view of my backside. She prowled around the room for a long while, then went out onto the balcony, pointedly leaving the door open to allow the cold air to emphasize her disapproval.

I fell asleep just to spite her.

Kevin kept craning his neck every which way, trying to make sure Dahlia hadn't parked in front of any of the businesses along the highway. She sure wouldn't have stopped at a taxidermy shop or a salvage yard, or at a pawnshop with a big sign promising genuine diamond rings at rock-bottom prices. He slowed down as he went past a couple of fast-food places, but she hadn't parked out front.

He braked as he came up on a station wagon crammed full of kids in muddy uniforms. Kevvie Junior, and maybe even Rose Marie, might want to play sports when they got older, he thought mistily, picturing himself on the sideline in a uniform that proclaimed him as head coach.

"Winning's not the most important thing," he'd tell the team during a timeout. "Doin' your level best is what matters most. Course, that don't mean you shouldn't go out there and kick some ass. That's why we're here—right? We didn't come to have a picnic lunch in the middle of the field. Now who wants to kick some ass?"

Suddenly he realized he was approaching the turnoff to the bypass that avoided the sluggish traffic in Farberville. Which way had Dahlia gone? He slowed down even more as he thought it over. If she'd gone on into downtown Farberville, he'd most likely never find her. On the other hand, if she'd taken the bypass, he most likely would spot her and be able to follow her to wherever she was going.

Kevin glanced in the rearview mirror to see how his lipstick was holding up. To his surprise, a state police car was all but riding on the bumper. Comforted by the knowledge that he was obeying the law, he put on the blinker, tapped on the brake pedal, and turned onto the bypass like a law-abiding citizen that was gonna kick some ass soon as he found it.

* * *

"Shall I order us bread and water for lunch?" Estelle said, poking me in the back. "I reckon that's what prisoners eat when they're under house arrest."

"Sounds yummy," I said. "What time is it?"

"Visiting hours at the hospital begin before too long. What kind of bread do you want?"

"Rye, with pastrami and Swiss. Mustard on the side." I sat up and rubbed the back of my neck. In college, we'd thought nothing about driving seven hours to Dallas for a concert or fourteen hours to New Orleans for oysters and Bloody Marys. Staying up night and day for the best part of a week during final exams was unremarkable. Maybe Ruby Bee was right when she pointed out (quite often) that I wasn't getting any younger. Few of us are.

Estelle ordered sandwiches and coffee from room service, then said, "I suppose I ought to let Baggins know what's going on. Ruby Bee and I sure won't be in the van tomorrow. Cherri Lucinda may have to stay on account of this mess with Jim Bob. If Todd doesn't turn up, I don't know what Taylor's gonna do. Rex may have the back of the van to himself."

"I met him in the restaurant," I said. "He told me about the motel in Memphis. I hope you and Ruby Bee had enough sense to stay in your room."

"We were the only ones. Luckily for us, Cherri Lucinda and Stormy found a store where they bought us sandwiches for supper. One of them mentioned that Taylor and Todd had gone out. When I was peeking out the window at the bald man, I saw Baggins come into the parking lot from the direction of the street. Not long after that, Rex showed up at our door, wanting change to use the pay phone by the office. It's a marvel none of them got shot."

"What's all this about a bald man?" I said.

Estelle's cheeks turned several shades pinker than her blusher, which was no easy feat. "Most likely nothing. He was in a black car out by the pool. Yesterday morning I thought I saw him at Graceland in the group behind ours. Maybe I was mistaken. There's got to be more than one bald man in Memphis, just like there is on television. For instance, there's Telly Savalas, Yul Brynner, Mr. Clean—"

"He never spoke to you or attempted to approach you?"

"I never gave him the chance. He looked way too old to be Stormy's boyfriend. If he is, though, he could have been following her instead of me. Baggins might have told him and the other man about the changes in our schedule. He could have been lurking around the hotel when we arrived, then waited until Stormy was alone in the room. She let him in, thinking he wanted to apologize, but he ended up pushing her off the balcony."

"That doesn't explain how he left the room without being seen by the eagle-eyed ladies from Tuscaloosa."

"I guess it doesn't," Estelle conceded, "but I still say Jim Bob would never do a thing like that. What's gonna happen to him?"

"I don't know. There'll be a bond hearing on Monday. The judge has the right to deny bond and keep Jim Bob in jail until the date of the arraignment, which could be anywhere from a month to ninety days."

"Ninety days? You can't let him sit in a cell all that time, Arly. The supermarket will have to close, and that means a lot of folks'll be out of a job. You've got to do something. Why don't you question Baggins? He might know who this man is."

"Because," I said with commendable forbearance, "it doesn't matter if he was Stormy's long-lost father, thought to have perished during a solo trek across the Gobi Desert. He couldn't have been in her room unless he mastered the art of transforming himself into an insect or a bird in order to fly away."

"You still ought to ask," she said.

I turned on the television. When lunch arrived, I continued to give my full attention to CNN while I ate. Estelle managed to grumble her way through her version of bread and water—in this case, a hamburger—then announced she was ready to go to the hospital if I could pry my eyes off the screen. I did.

Deputy Jones was in the hall, writing in a notebook. "Oh, good," she said, "I was just getting to you. Can you give me a few minutes?"

"We're on our way to the hospital," said Estelle. "Why don't you come back later?"

"Now will be fine," I said, forcing Estelle back into the hotel room. I'd wasted enough of my own time chasing down elusive witnesses to know how it felt to keep knocking on doors for days on end.

"I just need a few minutes," Japonica said as she sat down and opened the notebook. "You're Estelle Oppers, right? You and the lady in the hospital were part of the C'Mon tour?"

"I reckon that's right," said Estelle. "Look, you're making a big mistake about Jim Bob. There's only one thing on his mind, and it ain't murder. You've got no call to lock him up like a common criminal. He owns a supermarket and he's been the mayor of Maggody so long

that most folks can barely recollect when ol' Dinkus
Buchanon ruled the town council. Dinkus is the one
that insisted on the stoplight, even though there wasn't
hardly any traffic."

Japonica nodded thoughtfully. "Chief Sanderson and
I will take that into consideration, ma'am. You and Ms.
Hanks had no idea he was going to be here?"

"Why would we?"

"Just asking," Japonica said as she wrote in her notebook. "You saw him in the lobby last night. How did he
seem?"

Estelle stopped to think. "He was flabbergasted to see
me, and not real pleased. That'd be because he knew I
might say something to his wife and get him in trouble.
It's kinda funny, isn't it? Here he drove all this way,
thinking he'd be safe—and who's the first person he
runs into? Someone from Maggody."

I broke in before she could lapse into song about
what a small world it was. "Did he say or do anything besides express shock at seeing you?"

She shook her head. "No, that was about it. I didn't
see him after that, what with going to the hospital with
Ruby Bee and then coming back here to call you. It was
all so frantic that I plumb forgot about him."

"I saw him in the casino," I said to Japonica. "It was
just for a second, and I didn't notice if he was with
someone."

"Okay, then," she said, closing her notebook. "I need
to track down a couple more folks, then we're done.
Give me your addresses and telephone numbers in case
we have any more questions. Can't see why we would,
though."

I poked Estelle. "Tell her about the bald man."

"There ain't nothing to tell."

Japonica's heavy-lidded eyelids opened a tad wider. "Who's this mysterious bald man?"

Estelle reluctantly repeated what she'd told me, minimalizing it to the point that it sounded thoroughly inane. "I was just imagining things," she concluded. "That's not to say I believe Jim Bob Buchanon is responsible for Stormy's death. She was nervous from the minute we left Farberville. It could be because she'd decided to kill herself when we got here. That's reason to be nervous, isn't it? The idea of throwing myself off a balcony makes me so trembly I could almost throw up. No wonder she smoked so much and was saying all those rude things about Elvis like he was nothing but a Las Vegas celebrity. He was known as the Hillbilly Cat before he got famous, you know. He was always faithful to his roots, which is more than I can say for some folks who move up North and think they're hoity-toity."

One of the folks got a hard stare.

"Anything else?" I asked Japonica, who was looking rather bored by this time.

"No," she said. "Chief Sanderson's convinced he got drunk and assaulted the victim. We'll get it sorted out one way or another. Thanks for your cooperation." She smiled at each of us, then left.

"A lot of help you were," Estelle began belligerently.

"You planning to gripe much longer?" I said as I picked up my purse and made sure I had a key to the room.

"I'm coming."

We arrived at the hospital without further debate concerning Jim Bob's heretofore unacknowledged virtues or Elvis's fidelity. A woman in a pink jacket was seated at a desk just inside the lobby, resolutely defending the inner sanctum from light-fingered trespassers and misguided tourists.

"Are you looking for someone?" she demanded, making it clear she could see that we fell into one of the above-mentioned categories.

"We're here to see Ruby Bee Hanks," I said.

She looked at her watch. "Visiting hours begin at two o'clock. You're fourteen minutes early."

This was not Southern hospitality at its finest. "Okay," I said, "then I'd like a word with Dr. Deweese, her attending physician."

"Dr. Deweese is out on a house call. One of those trashy Claypitt girls insisted on giving birth at home. The midwife called an hour ago to say the baby was upside down and refusing to come out. Dr. Deweese had to set aside his lunch and go racing over to help. Claypitts are too miserly to come to the hospital like proper folks." She consulted her watch. "You've still got twelve minutes. Sit over there and I'll tell you when it's time."

Estelle may have wanted to argue, but I persuaded her to sit down on a molded plastic chair. After eleven minutes, we were told we could proceed to the ward where we would find our patient.

"At least Ruby Bee's no longer in ICU," I said as we walked down the hallway.

"I'm beginning to think this is some kind of prison camp," Estelle said, glaring at everybody we passed as if each was involved in sinister medical experiments. "What happens if you decide to die when it's not visiting hours? Is your family obliged to wait until the clock chimes before they can boo-hoo at your bedside?"

"Nobody's dying," I said evenly. "If you can't get that through your head, why don't you sit in the lobby?"

"Oh, Arly," she said, spinning around to squash me in a hug, "I never meant to imply that Ruby Bee was gonna do anything like that. I know you're worried. So am I, but we both have to believe that she'll be just fine. I don't know what else we can do." She released me and turned around, doing her best to square her shoulders and sound resolute. "After all, she's got a business to run, doesn't she? Where would all those truckers have lunch if not at Ruby Bee's Bar & Grill?"

"Yeah," I said as we went into the room.

Our topic of discussion was asleep. She still had an IV needle in her hand and an oxygen tube across her nose, but her color was better. I closed the drapes, pulled the blanket over her shoulders, and gestured for Estelle to follow me back into the hallway.

"What do you want to do?" I said.

"What do *you* want to do? We can stay here, or go back to the waiting room and hope the doctor delivers that baby and shows up, or even go on to the hotel and wait there. I can't think straight anymore."

"Neither can I," I said as we walked through the lobby. "Let's both go watch that movie on cable and relax."

I doubted I was going to be able to concentrate on a movie, but I knew I would crack if I didn't try to turn off my mind for an hour or two. I drove back to the hotel, found a parking spot, and shook Estelle, who'd dozed off.

"We're here," I said as I opened the car door.

"And ain't we lucky?" She checked her reflection in the rearview mirror, smoothed her eyeshadow (purple despite her childhood trauma), and patted me on the shoulder. "It's gonna be okay, Arly. Ruby Bee will wake up feeling fine and demand to go home. The police will realize Stormy killed herself and release Jim Bob. Taylor and Todd will live happily ever after. As for the rest of them, I don't give a rat's ass. Do you think I could have room service send up a glass of sherry?"

"Sure," I said, wishing I shared her optimism.

We were walking toward the hotel entrance when Estelle grabbed my arm. "Would you look over there?" she said in a stunned voice.

Expecting to see Elvis in sequinned finery, I did as ordered. "At what?"

"That's the C'mon Tours van. The man in the cap is Baggins." She dropped my arm. "You stay and find out what Baggins knows. I'll meet you upstairs."

Before I could react, she darted between two cars, came damn close to sideswiping a bellman, and disappeared into the lobby.

E L E V E N

I walked over to the man Estelle had identified in her typically
theatrical fashion, as if Charlton Heston—as opposed
to Moses—had descended on the scene with a matching
pair of tablets.

"Mr. Baggins?" I said. "I'm Arly Hanks."

"I know who you are. Don't go thinking C'Mon Tours
is taking any responsibility for this. Everybody signed a
disclaimer that said whatever happens ain't our fault.
There's no way we can be held liable if people get sick."

"Nobody's blaming you," I said.

"Nobody better be," he muttered. "I ain't never seen
a group more cantankerous than this. The bickerin'
started before we ever left Farberville. The professor
wasn't making it any easier, I'll admit, but all of them
were fussing every mile of the way to Memphis."

"At which time they discovered they'd be staying in
a dump in the sleaziest part of town. My mother forgot
to pack her bulletproof vest and sidearm. What kind of
company puts clients in that kind of danger?"

Baggins looked away. "Elvis slept there. I told 'em
that."

"And the overnight stay in Tupelo? Did he forget to sleep there?"

"Things changed. Say, how's your mama doing? I sure am gonna be sorry if she can't go back with us in the morning. She's a fine lady."

"I doubt she'll be allowed to leave for a few days, and Estelle will want to stay here with her. You know about Stormy, of course?"

"The police told me. It's real sad, her being so young and all, and C'Mon Tours will be sending a condolence card soon as we get an address. Listen, miss, I need to find an auto-parts store before we drive home tomorrow. You tell your mama how sorry I am about her ailment."

"I most certainly will," I said, smiling so sweetly my teeth ached. "By the way, I need to ask you about the man in the black car at the motel in Memphis. What's his name?"

"How should I know something like that? I don't work for the Memphis Welcome Wagon." He edged away from me as if I, like beef past its prime, had a pungent odor. "There's close to a million people that live there. I ain't on speaking terms with all of them. Why would I know what cars they drive?"

He was so nervous that I began to think Estelle might be onto something. I bore down on him and said, "Did he want to know where the tour group would be staying last night?"

"Why would anybody care about that?" he said as he continued to back away from me. "All he wanted to know was how to get on the road to Nashville. If I don't find a place to buy a fan belt, this van's gonna be dead as an armadillo on the interstate come noon tomorrow."

I grasped his shoulder. "I need to know if he's stalking Estelle. Who is he?"

Baggins flinched as my fingers tightened. "It don't have anything to do with Estelle, your mama, or you. Leave it at that. He's not somebody you need to cross paths with. His problem was with Stormy. Now that she's dead, he'll give it up and go home."

"Give what up?"

He squirmed out of my grip and gave me a churlish look. "Don't go trying to trick me like I just got off the turnip truck. It's nothing to do with you. When I get back to Farberville, I'll try to talk Miss Vetchling into returning some of the money your mama paid for the tour. She's tighter'n bark on a tree, but you never know."

He climbed into the van and drove away. I was thinking about what he'd said as I walked toward the entrance. It sounded as though Stormy had been followed all the way from Farberville to The Luck of the Draw, where her luck had clearly and most sincerely run out.

I paused in the driveway to look up at the balconies on the eighth floor. The metal railings hindered the view but did not completely block it; voices, especially agitated ones, could have carried in the stillness of dawn. Japonica had no doubt recorded the exact words the witness heard seconds before the body came slamming down onto the pavement. Jim Bob's lawyer would be given access to her report when the trial date approached, but I decided to see if I could wheedle a copy of it in a more timely fashion. She wouldn't cooperate as long as she saw me as Jim Bob's staunch defender. I was trying to envision a way to inveigle my way back into her favor as I went through the revolving door.

"Arly!" shrieked Estelle. "You make him let me go or

I'm gonna—I don't know, maybe I'm gonna do something we'll all live to regret!"

Mackenzie Cutting had her by the wrist. "Miss Hanks, approximately five hours ago you assured me that you would keep Miss Oppers out of trouble for a few days. I trusted you to keep your word. I think it would be better for all concerned if you and she checked out immediately and graced another hotel with your presence."

I stared at Estelle. "Now what?"

"I ain't saying a word until he lets go of me. He's gonna be darn lucky if I don't sue the hotel for a million dollars. Every time I turn around somebody on the staff's grabbing me and carrying on like I planted a bomb in a wastebasket!"

"A bomb?" said a cadaverous man in a lime green leisure suit.

"A bomb?" said the woman behind him, collapsing into a chair. "Julian, I need my pills!"

"No bomb!" Mackenzie yelled as the word began to ricochet around the room.

"We're all going to die!" screamed a woman clutching a bug-eyed spaniel. She dropped to her knees and crawled under a table. "Oh, Bertie, Mumsy's so sorry she brought you here!"

"No bomb!" Mackenzie yelled once more, releasing Estelle in order to thrust his arms in the air. "No bomb! Nobody's in any danger!"

"Julian!" the woman sprawled across a chair screeched. "I am having palpitations! Call an ambulance!"

I caught Estelle and propelled her to the side of the lobby as the babble of voices grew louder. "Look at this,"

I said. "You were in here less than five minutes, for pity's sake! What did you do this time?"

"I'll tell you when we get to the room," she said haughtily, then removed my hand from her arm and strode toward the elevators as if she were Cleopatra boarding a barge. The queen of denial.

I looked back at Mackenzie, who appeared to be going down for the third time in a sea of panicky guests. His mouth was moving, but it was impossible to hear him in the increasingly frenzied din.

It seemed like the time for a prudent, if also cowardly, retreat.

The sheriff of Stump County, Arkansas, was counting the number of days until he could retire and devote all his time to fishing, when LaBelle clattered down the hall and commenced to rap on the door. He put aside the calendar, popped an antacid tablet in his mouth, and said, "What?"

"There's somebody to see you."

"I ain't here."

"I swear, Harvey Dorfer, if you keep this up much longer, I won't be, either. My sister-in-law makes better money at the poultry plant in Starley City, and all she has to do is pull out gizzards and livers. She never has to deal with task forces and bosses that hide in their offices while other people have to deal with the public. Are you gonna open the door or are you gonna sit on your fat butt and listen to me while I go down the hall and out the front door for the last time?"

Harve considered his options. "How much does she make?"

"That's it! As of this very minute, I am no longer an

employee of this office. I am going to empty my desk drawers, rip up my time card, and go home to write a letter to the quorum court explaining why this job is unbearable. Your name is going to get mentioned more than once, Harvey Dorfer. I don't care if you're my cousin and your wife is having a bad time with her rheumatism and your son-in-law has so many speeding tickets that he could wallpaper his bathroom with 'em. My mind is made up. You can kiss my typing skills good-bye!"

"Aw, LaBelle," Harve said as he hastily unlocked the door, "you don't got any call to resign. What's going on?"

"A fellow calling himself Reverend Hitebred is sitting on the couch in the front room. He sez he'll sit there as long as it takes until you agree to hear him out. He has these creepy pale eyes and he stares at me like he thinks I'm doing the Devil's own work when all I'm doing is totaling up the monthly expenditures at the jail. I can't take any more of him."

Harve led her into the office and pushed her onto a chair. "You know you're the only one who keeps things running smoothly here," he said, going so far as to scoot a tissue box within her reach in case she turned weepy. "Soon as the task force gets some decent leads, they won't be here so much. I know for a fact that they're narrowing in on a couple of employees that didn't show up for work the day after the incident. Both of their apartments are under surveillance, and the minute either one of them comes home, we'll start getting some idea of what went on."

"I don't care," LaBelle said darkly. "It'd save us a lot of bother if they'd all shoot each other. That way there won't be any cocaine or crack dealers and we can go back to worrying about moonshine and marijuana."

"The good ol' days," Harve said as he sat down behind his desk.

"That's right."

"Along with polio, lead poisoning, bomb shelters—"

"I am not in the mood for this. You decide here and now if you're ready to resume your responsibilities. Otherwise, I may not enjoy plucking chickens, but I can do it. The going rate's eight dollars an hour, with benefits and two weeks' paid vacation."

The telephone rang. Harve looked at it, as did LaBelle. They looked at each other. The telephone rang again. LaBelle settled back in the chair and studied her fingernails.

Wheezing, he picked up the receiver. "Sheriff's office, Harvey Dorfer speaking."

He listened for a few minutes, making notes and mumbling, and then replaced the receiver. "That was the state police. Let everybody know to watch for a stolen vehicle. The driver is acting real peculiar, so tell 'em not to be heroes and get theirselves shot. All they should do is follow it." He handed her the slip of paper on which he'd written the license-plate number.

"Are they supposed to call the psychic hotline to find out what kind of vehicle?" said LaBelle, taking the paper.

Harve told her, then rocked back in his chair and felt in his shirt pocket for a cigar. Maybe he'd take his son-in-law deep-sea fishing down in Florida. There wasn't any way to get a speeding ticket for that, or so he supposed.

Rex Malanac was waiting by the elevators when I arrived on the eighth floor. "Oh, good," he said with all the cheerful sincerity of a telemarketer, "I was hoping I might catch you. Would you like to have a drink in the bar? I've been told they make passable margaritas here."

"Thanks, but I'm busy," I said, attempting to sidle around him.

He cut me off. "It'll do you a world of good to relax for a few minutes and stop worrying about your mother. I can give you some tips for the blackjack table. Do come down to the bar with me, Miss Hanks. I can assure you that I'm harmless."

In that we were the same height, I looked him in the eyes. "I said I'm busy. Is there something about this particular concept that baffles you?"

The elevator doors opened and Mackenzie Cutting emerged. "We need to talk, Miss Hanks."

Rex stepped into the elevator. "I'll see you later, then."

I waited until the doors had closed. "Have you heard anything more about the alleged homicide this morning?"

"As far as the casino is concerned, it was a suicide. Miss Zimmerman had emotional problems when she came. The croupier at the roulette wheel noticed how high-strung she was, and went so far as to suggest the pit bosses keep her under observation. This is meant to be a carefree place, Miss Hanks, where adults drink, socialize, and play games of chance. When people begin to lose heavily, we discourage them from further gaming by cutting off their free drinks and their credit. Habitual losers who get in over their heads are barred from the casino and given information about Gamblers Anonymous."

"Stormy was losing a lot of money?"

"No, but she was in a foul temper. She complained loudly whenever she lost a bet and used language that some of her fellow players found offensive. After a streak of ill-fated spins, she called the croupier a 'limp-pricked penguin.' He was taken out on break and she was asked to find other amusements."

"Was she by herself?" I asked.

"Our policy is not to gossip about our guests. We have a clientele that includes politicians, celebrities, investment brokers, and so forth. We show them every courtesy, of course, but we never discuss their companions for the evening or their outcomes at the tables. They would hardly give us their business if they weren't convinced of our complete discretion."

"I understand," I said, "but this doesn't qualify as gossip. A man followed Stormy from Farberville to Memphis, and possibly here. The witness in the parking lot is convinced that she saw a man on the balcony. I'd just like to find out who he is and if he's involved."

"Then you'll have to ask Chief Sanderson," he said dismissively. "Shall we discuss Miss Oppers's latest escapade?"

"Do I have a choice?"

"From all accounts, she burst into the men's room around the corner from the reception desk. Several gentlemen were at the urinal. She grabbed one of them by the arm and spun him around. In that he was in the midst of . . . ah, relieving himself, it resulted in an awkward incident. I was on my way to my office when I heard shouting, and was about to enter the restroom when Miss Oppers ran out. I detained her until I could find out what was happening."

"A men's room?" I said weakly.

"A very crowded men's room."

"And one of them . . . ?"

"Oh yes," he said, "and with an extraordinary range. I offered to cover dry-cleaning expenses, but most of them were speechless with outrage or embarrassment. Does she do this kind of thing often?"

"Not that I recall," I said. "Did she explain?"

Mackenzie's lips twitched a bit. "No, Miss Hanks, she did not, nor did she offer to apologize to the man she'd harassed. He's a state senator, and not happy that he might have alienated a dozen constituents."

"A vote by any other name," I murmured as I leaned against a table and tried very hard not to picture the scene. A giggle erupted. I turned around and stared out the window at the parking lot. "Estelle," I began, then did what I could to convert another giggle into a snort, "would never—"

"Never?" said Mackenzie.

"I'm sure she's really sorry," I said, now clamping down on my lip and making noises that were more suitable to a winded horse, "if what she did resulted in him pissing off constituents."

At which point I lost it. I needed to. I'd driven most of the night, then been obliged to deal with all kinds of officious nonsense, weird behavior—okay, very weird behavior—and a steady stream of people knocking on the door. My nose exploded with suppressed amusement. I waved him off and staggered down the hall, clutching my stomach.

"Miss Hanks," Mackenzie said, "my job's on the line. I'm paid to maintain a surreal microcosm. There is no dawn or dusk, no grocery money gone in the roll of dice or the flip of a card, no drunk hauled up to his hotel room to sleep it off until he wakes up and realizes that he's blown his life's savings. We cannot permit disruptive behavior. Can you control Miss Oppers?"

"I'll try to convince her not to piss off anybody else," I said, then doubled over and came near cracking my head against a wall.

"Will you please be serious?" he said.

I gnawed on my knuckles for a moment and willed myself to get over it. "If this senator still wants an apology, I can speak to Estelle about it."

"The last thing the senator desires is to relive the experience. All I need is your promise that absolutely nothing else will happen until you and Miss Oppers leave."

"Absolutely," I said, drawing a cross on my chest. "This senator—what does he look like?"

"He looks like the epitome of indignation," Mackenzie said coldly. "Do not approach him under any circumstances. Do I make myself clear?"

"Is he bald?"

"I am not going to discuss this any further. Keep her under control. This is not a video-game arcade where a limited amount of adolescent mischief is tolerated." He turned his back on me and jabbed at the elevator button.

I went to the room and let myself in. Estelle was perched on the edge of the bed, her purse in her lap and her ankles crossed. Her jaw was thrust out so far that I doubted she could see the carpet.

"Waiting for a parade?" I asked as I sat down.

"I called the hospital. Ruby Bee's still asleep. They expect Dr. Deweese in another hour or so. I was thinking it might be nice to take some flowers to brighten up her room."

"I'm not sure there's a florist shop around here."

"Well, then," she said, "maybe I'll buy her a couple of magazines in the gift shop. She used to like those true-confession stories where the gal does something real stupid but ends up living happily ever after anyways. I never much cared for them myself."

"I guess you're more interested in politics—or at least in politicians. That would explain why you were so thrilled when you spotted the senator that you lost your mind."

"What are you getting at?"

"Why else would you pursue him into the men's room?" I said. "I hope everybody washed his hands afterward."

She had the decency to look abashed. "Are they gonna let us stay here for the time being? The room's already paid for through tonight and I've unpacked my things. It'd be a shame to have to move to a different hotel."

"We're okay unless you decide to break into the safe or run naked through the casino. At this point, I wouldn't be especially surprised."

"I do not appreciate your attitude, missy. If you can't mind your mouth, I'll just go sit in the car and do my best not to die of hypothermia. There's extra blankets in the closet. They may not help much when it gets real cold tonight. I hate to imagine what condition I'll be in when you find me in the morning."

"Very stiff, I should think," I said. "So you thought you saw the bald man going into the lobby, right?"

"As sure as I live and breathe. I would have caught up

with him by the desk if I hadn't tripped over a suitcase and darn near broke my neck. As I was scrambling to my feet, I saw him go through a doorway. I went charging after him. I guess you know the rest."

"Indeed I do," I said.

"It's kind of odd, though," she said as she chewed on her lip, "because I was real sure it was him. He might have been doing his business in one of the stalls. Why don't I go sit in the lobby and watch for him while you do the same in the casino? I'll describe him for you. If you spot someone who fits what I've said, you can come get me."

"Absolutely not. I don't want you to go so far as the balcony without me. In fact, it might be better if you went on home tomorrow in the van. I'll stay until Ruby Bee is released, then bring her back with me."

"I am not about to abandon her in her time of need! After all the things she's done for me, I have no intention of going back to Maggody so I can give Elsie McMay a perm and trim Darla Jean McIlhaney's bangs like nothing went on. Ruby Bee was by my side when I received that unfortunate inheritance from my uncle, just like I was there when she found that letter."

"What letter?" I asked, leaning forward.

Estelle took a minute to answer, and I could see she was searching for words. "From your daddy, Arly. It was a hard time for her. Let's you and me go to the hospital and find out how she's doing. She probably doesn't want flowers or a bunch of silly magazines."

I couldn't think of anything to say. We drove to the hospital, went inside, and nodded at the pink-clad woman still defending the castle keep.

Ruby Bee was awake. Her eyes were dull and her

flesh seemed swollen, as if the constant drip from the IV was overinflating her with liquids. "What are you doing here?" she asked me.

"Same thing I was doing this morning," I said. "Making sure they keep you happy."

"This morning?"

I licked my lips. "Yes, this morning. Estelle and I came by to make sure you're not giving the nurses a hard time."

"Can I leave now?" she said, sitting up and picking at the adhesive strip that held the IV needle in place. "I want to go home, Arly. You fetch my clothes and my handbag. They ain't nice here. I'll get dressed and we can leave."

I took her hand and pulled it away before she could dislodge the needle. "You can't leave just yet."

Estelle touched my back. "I'll find a nurse."

Ruby Bee's face wrinkled with confusion. "Didn't you come to take me home, Arly? That's all I want. They keep coming in to poke and prod me like I was nothing but a piece of meat. Is Estelle mad at me? Did I do something wrong?"

A nurse came into the room and shooed me out. I could hear her murmuring as I sank against a wall in the corridor and ground my palms into my face. It took me a moment to realize Estelle was rubbing my neck.

"I'm all right," I said. "Let's find out if Dr. Deweese is here."

We went to the cafeteria and found him eating a sandwich. "Miss Hanks," he said as we came into the room, "I'm afraid I can't tell you anything about your mother. The X rays were inconclusive. The ultrasound is down, which is not unusual, and we're waiting for a technician from Memphis. If he can get it fixed, we'll do a scan this evening. She needs to stay here for a few more days, in any case."

Estelle nudged me aside. "She's all bewildered and upset. What if she yanks out that needle and goes roaming down the hall and out the back door? I don't reckon this hospital is more than half a mile from the Mississippi River. She never could swim."

"I'll order a sedative," he said. "We won't know anything for at least three hours. Why don't you go get some rest and come back this evening?"

I was too frustrated to do anything more than shrug. Estelle and I went back to the parking lot and got into the car. Rather than heading for the hotel, I suggested we drive around the area and look at the other casinos. We did so in gloomy silence, not bothering to comment on the gaudy exteriors and billboards advertising cheap buffets and forthcoming country music shows. We caught occasional glimpses of the muddy river; if Huck and Jim were on their way to New Orleans, they'd already passed by.

It was beginning to get dark as we arrived back at The Luck of the Draw. I stayed close to Estelle as we went into the lobby, praying she didn't see a bald head in the crowd and launch into action.

"Would you take a look at that?" she said, halting in midstep.

I poised my hand within reach of her elbow. "Do you see him?"

"Not hardly. If I'm not imagining things, that's Mrs. Jim Bob at the desk, and Brother Verber right behind her. What in tarnation would they be doing here?"

"They must have heard about Jim Bob," I said.

"I'd almost forgotten about him being in jail. Do you think he called 'em to come bail him out?"

I shook my head. "And be forced to explain why he was here in the first place? I should think he'd prefer to chop cotton for the next twenty years. Let's go up to the room before they spot us."

We'd almost made it to the hallway when Mrs. Jim Bob said, "Arly? Is that Estelle with you? I thought she was on some Elvis Presley tour."

"Shit," I said under my breath, then pasted on a smile. "This is the final destination."

"It shore is good to see some familiar faces!" boomed Brother Verber, grinning so broadly that several people near him shrank back.

Mrs. Jim Bob beckoned at me. "I want you to come over here and talk some sense into this young fellow. I have never in all my born days encountered such impudence. I have explained the situation to him at least a dozen times, but I might as well have been trying to communicate with Marjorie." She stared at the desk clerk. "Marjorie's a sow, for your information."

"What's the problem?" I asked as I joined her.

"He says we can't stay here."

"There aren't any rooms," the desk clerk said, looking as if he were prepared to duck behind the desk if she threw a punch.

Brother Verber rocked forward and pointed his finger at the hapless clerk. "No room at the inn," he said, "is what they told Mary and Joseph. Do you think that innkeeper was welcomed into heaven when his day came? Do you think ol' Saint Peter slapped him on the back and told him to come on in and make hisself at home 'cause there was plenty of room?"

The clerk gulped. "It's Saturday night. All the hotels from here to Memphis are always full. If you want to come back on Tuesday, we can fix you up."

"Do something, Arly," growled Mrs. Jim Bob.

"You planning to give birth?" I asked her. "I can probably get you a bed in the maternity ward at the hospital."

"You listen here, young lady," she began, quivering with rage, "if you don't curb your tongue—"

Estelle butted in. "Jim Bob's room is liable to be empty for some time to come. You all could stay there."

"Have you forgotten I am a respectable married woman? Some folks"—she turned a beady-eyed glare on those waiting in line—"may choose to share a bed with a someone other than their spouse, but I will never stoop to that kind of immoral behavior. I am a devout Christian, and when I got married, I vowed to love, honor, and obey. I disrecollect the preacher saying that infidelity was acceptable."

"It was just a suggestion," said Estelle as she stalked away.

I didn't know what Mrs. Jim Bob had learned about Jim Bob's current woes, but it didn't seem wise to suggest that she share a room with Cherri Lucinda.

"Okay," I said without enthusiasm, "here's what we can do."

T W E L V E

Kevin had long since driven all the way around Farberville and was heading west in the direction of the Oklahoma border. He hadn't seen Dahlia's car anywhere along the way—not parked in front of a store or next to the side of the highway, which is where he figured it'd be if she had a flat tire. He'd done his best to teach her how to change a tire, but she'd always just given him a puckery look until he fixed it himself and they could be on their way.

He glanced in the rearview mirror. The state police car was still behind him, and now there was another following it. Since he was being real careful to stay well under the speed limit, he wasn't worried about them. It was getting on toward Saturday evening, after all, and they were most likely going home to have supper with their families and watch television. If only he could be doing the same, he thought wistfully. Instead, he had no choice but to go search for his wife so he could bring her back to her sweet little babies.

It was hard not to imagine the worst. What if she'd been run off the road by a motorcycle gang and was plastered against the steering wheel, unconscious and in danger of icing over like a white wedding cake? She'd been frettin' about money ever since she came home from the hospital. What if she'd been so desperate that she'd been hired by a drug dealer to take his filthy wares to Oklahoma? She could be in a jail in Muskogee or Sallisaw, hanging down her head in shame. Or what if she'd met some fellow with plenty of money and was lying in his arms in a motel room? What if the room had velvety red wallpaper, a mirror on the ceiling, and a king-size water bed? That would explain why she kept slapping away her lawfully wedded husband whenever he wiggled up next to her under the covers and let his fingers ramble over her wondrous ripples of flesh. Was she doing it 'cause she loved this fellow—or was he giving her money?

Kevin's eyes clouded with tears. It was his fault, not hers. If he was bringing home more money every week, she wouldn't have been obliged to sell her body to a stranger, even if he drove a fancy car and bought her boxes of chocolates and great big bottles of perfume that smelled like diamonds.

He blinked as he watched a car with the sheriff's logo cut across the grassy median and fall into line behind the other two. Maybe there was some sort of policemen's ball up the road a piece, and they were all gettin' ready to dance the night away. He slowed down to encourage them to get on to their party, but none of them pulled into the passing lane. In fact, they were acting like he was leading them right to the door of the Elks Lodge or wherever they were going.

Kevin had never before considered himself a natural-born leader. This was kind of nice, though. Here he was, gathering up all the law-enforcement agents in Stump County so he could guide them to where they wanted to go. He rolled down the window and waved at them so's to assure them that they were in good hands; in response, they turned on their blue lights, adding a downright festive air to the occasion.

It was only fitting that he was in a Bronco, and a white one at that, since he pictured himself in a big white cowboy hat with a little feather tucked in the band. Feeling like the trail master at the head of a long line of covered wagons, each filled with stouthearted settlers, rosy-cheeked children, and all their worldly possessions, he took them onward into Indian territory.

I was keenly aware I was playing Russian roulette. After some dickering and many homilies from Mrs. Jim Bob emphasizing her moral superiority, she agreed to take my bed in the room originally assigned to Estelle and Ruby Bee. I moved my things into the next room, planning to sleep in what had been Stormy's bed. Brother Verber took Jim Bob's room. Cherri Lucinda, conveniently absent, had not been consulted, but I was pretty sure she'd rather have me than her boyfriend's acid-tongued wife or Maggody's spiritual guru (to use the term loosely).

I'd put my toothbrush in the bathroom and was hoping to sneak away to the hospital, when Mrs. Jim Bob barged through the adjoining door with Brother Verber in tow.

"Explain what's going on," she said. "Jim Bob is in jail for killing some woman? Why isn't he in Hot Springs? Have you spoken to him? I want answers, Arly Hanks—and none of your smart talk."

I looked longingly at the door to the hallway, but forced myself to stay put. "I don't know for sure why Jim Bob is here. He must have changed his mind when he reached the interstate, and decided to come to Mississippi instead. Two of the women on the Elvis tour were staying in this room. He invited one of them to . . . go down to the casino. I was there myself last night. Lots of good, clean fun."

"There's nothing good or clean about wagering," she said, her lips pinched.

Brother Verber loomed over my shoulder. "Sister Barbara knows of what she speaks. 'The wages of sin is death, but the gift of God is eternal life.' That's from a letter the Apostle Paul wrote to the Romans."

"I said *wagering*," said Mrs. Jim Bob. "You don't get wages when you wager."

"You don't? It'd seem like you would."

"Well, you don't." She looked at me. "I don't believe I've heard the whole story as of yet."

"Perhaps Jim Bob should tell you himself. I'm planning to go to the hospital in a few minutes. I can drop you off at the jail and pick you up later."

"I can see from the way you're squirming that you're avoiding the truth," she said. "I have to know what he did."

Brother Verber grabbed her hand. "I'm here for you, Sister Barbara, no matter how painful this turns out to be. I'll be at your side, praying for you night and day until your ordeal is ended."

"I'm not sure it's started," she said as she disengaged his hand, then retreated across the room. To my regret, she did not continue out the door. "Did he come here on account of this woman that died?"

"No," I said, relieved to be able to answer truthfully. "As far as I know, he'd never met her until late yesterday afternoon. The problem is that he had the adjoining room. Witnesses say he was the only man who could have been on the balcony"—I pointed at the one in question—"when Stormy was pushed. He claims he wasn't."

"Was he?"

I stood up. "He says not. Let's go into town and you can talk to him yourself. I'll get Estelle and we—"

"She's not in the room," said Mrs. Jim Bob. "She said to tell you she was going to take a shuttle bus to another casino. I hope she's not gambling. A fool and her money are soon parted, and the good Lord knows she's a quart low on common sense, probably on account of sniffing all that perm solution over the years. I have often prayed for her, just as I have for your mother and you as well. It's hard to picture you with a proper husband and children, but the flame of hope must never flicker and die out."

"Amen," intoned Brother Verber, then winced as I glowered at him.

So Estelle had escaped once again, I thought as I hustled them down the elevator and through the lobby. The only flame of hope I had involved Estelle's whereabouts; if she had left The Luck of the Draw, all was well—but if she hadn't, I was liable to find myself sleeping under a bush.

Or in a cell.

Japonica smiled as we came into the PD, but her heart wasn't in it. "Everything all right?" she asked me, eyeing my companions with justifiable wariness.

I introduced them, then said, "They'd like to see Jim Bob, if that's allowed."

"Sure. I feed him on a regular basis and escort him to the toilet when he hollers, but he's carrying on something fierce. I've already reached my limit on aspirin for the day. Maybe some company will shut him up for a spell."

"I think you can count on it," I said as I gestured for Mrs. Jim Bob and Brother Verber to follow her through the door to the cells. Rather than trail along to watch the fun, I studied the wanted posters until Japonica emerged. "Did you interview all the witnesses?" I asked.

"Did you forget to mention you're the chief of police in this town of yours?"

"Run a tracer on me?"

"The town can't afford a computer, but I've got one at home. Chief Sanderson pays me a little extra out of petty cash to stay linked. You'll be glad to know you don't have any outstanding warrants."

She wasn't overtly hostile, but I could tell she was annoyed with me. I considered various responses, most of them glib or evasive, then shrugged and said, "It didn't seem relevant. This isn't my turf. I'm just nosing around because of the local connection." I paused as I heard strains of a hymn resounding from the back room. "I don't like Jim Bob. He's pulled so much shit in his time that he could be the poster boy for small-town bullies—but he's not a killer."

"The evidence says he is," Japonica said, unmoved by my Clarence Darrowesque summation. She sat down behind her desk and began to align the scattering of pens and pencils.

"The investigation is done?"

"We won't have the autopsy for a few days, but all it's going to tell us is that she died from the trauma of the impact. It doesn't matter if there was the alcohol in her blood, or even drugs. She was pushed. The man who pushed her is locked up. The prosecutor will decide how to go with it. Yeah, it's done except for the paperwork."

"Did you interview someone named Todd?" I asked.

"The fickle fiancé? No, he's still missing, or at least he was as of a couple of hours ago. From what the girl said, I don't see how he could offer anything useful—if there was anything useful to be offered, which there's not." She opened a folder and shuffled through several handwritten pages of notes. "He got off the elevator on the sixth floor around ten o'clock in the company of an old friend, name unknown. His fiancée continued on to their room and went to bed. Rex Malanac stayed in the casino most of the night, then went to bed. Hector Baggins took the C'Mon van and went to visit family. When he got back at midnight, he went to bed. Your friend stayed in her room. She went to bed, too. It seems all God's children went to bed."

"With the exception of Cherri Lucinda, none of them has an alibi."

"None of them needs one. The only person the ladies from Tuscaloosa saw in the hallway was the hotel employee. They may be elderly, but they've spent their lives observing other people's private business. Even though Tuscaloosa's a sight bigger than your town, I'll bet they know every last soul who's drying out at a so-called spa, taking money from the cash register, and slipping in and out the back doors of all the divorcées in town. On the lily-white side of the tracks, anyway. The only 'colored folks' they take an interest in are their cleaning women and yard men."

I was developing an irrational dislike of the ladies from Tuscaloosa—and of Japonica as well. "I guess I'd better go to the hospital to check on my mother. I'll come back in half an hour and gather up Jim Bob's visitors."

"Hold on," she said, picking up the telephone receiver. She dialed a number and asked to speak to someone named Carlette. "Hey, girlfriend," she said, "how's Ruby Bee Hanks doing? You got time to poke your head in her room?" After a few minutes of silence, she said, "I'd dearly appreciate it if you'll call me at the PD if she wakes up. Save me a seat at church in the morning and I'll tell you what that fool brother-in-law of yours said when his wife caught him and Magda Maronni in the backseat of his car. Talk about lame!"

She replaced the receiver and looked up. "Your mother's sedated and sound asleep. The ultrasound machine hasn't been repaired. Dr. Deweese went home for the night. Carlette'll keep a real close eye on your mother, and let me know if anything changes. If it does, I'll call you."

"Ruby Bee's bag is in the car. I'm going to run it over to the hospital, stick it in the closet in her room, and come back here. It shouldn't take me more than twenty minutes."

"Take your time," Japonica said. "I'd sooner listen to hymns than complaints. If we leave them back there long enough, I'm liable to get a full confession. I'll be hard pressed to actually believe he kidnapped the Lindbergh baby, assassinated Lee Harvey Oswald, and slept with the governor's wife, but I won't be surprised. It might just perk up my day."

Tension was mounting in the cell block, if the three dingy cubicles could be described as such. Up until then, Jim Bob's day had not been all that bad, considering. Japonica had brought him a hamburger and fries for lunch, and had mentioned the possibility of meat loaf, mashed potatoes, and apple pie for supper if he behaved himself. She'd made it clear that a bottle of bourbon was out of the question, but then good ol' Chief Sanderson had slipped him one between the bars, like they were butt-slappin' cousins at a family reunion, checking out the dating possibilities. They'd passed the bottle back and forth while debating the hardships of deer hunting versus duck hunting.

Nobody'd asked him much of anything or made him go through his story over and over. He'd been daydreaming about Cherri Lucinda's exceptional talents, feeling real warm and smug, when the door had slammed open and a double-barreled shotgun had blown away his peaceful little world.

And they were still there on the opposite side of the bars, huffing, puffing, peppering him with questions, and doing their damnedest to rescue his soul. Jim Bob, being fond of his soul in its blissfully flawed condition, was getting cranky.

" 'Come, humble sinner, in whose breast a thousand thoughts revolve,' " sang Brother Verber, his eyes closed and his hands clinched so tightly his fingers looked like penne pasta. " 'Come with your guilt and fear oppressed, and make this last resolve.' "

"What about Hot Springs?" repeated Mrs. Jim Bob. "You specifically said you were going to the Municipal League meeting. You were supposed to get a new stoplight."

Jim Bob did his best to look guileless, even though Brother Verber's entreaties to 'come' were stirring up some seriously inappropriate memories. "Like I said earlier, it got called off. There I was, all the way down to the interstate, and I heard on the radio that the whole darn thing was canceled because of . . ."

"Because of what?"

"Snow," he said, then mentally kicked himself for getting himself in deeper in something a whole lot less odorless than snow. "They were worried that we might have a blizzard and everybody'd be trapped for days on end. It turns out they were wrong, of course, since we haven't seen a single flake. However, they had to be cautious on account of Hot Springs being remote like it is. I was too scared to risk driving back over the mountains, so I decided to come over here and wait until the weather boys said it was safe to go home."

Brother Verber gave him a look of profound disappointment. "Brother Jim Bob, you're only foolin' yourself if you continue to deny you took a detour on the highway to heaven. The Lord will forgive you this one time if you'll get down on your knees and beg for mercy. I have to say, though, He's losing patience with you. Even the most goodhearted shepherd gets weary of going out into the night to hunt for a strayed lamb. One of these days you're gonna reach out for Sister Barbara and she won't be there."

"She won't?" Jim Bob asked curiously. "Where's she gonna be?"

"Making sure the electric chair's plugged in," Mrs. Jim Bob said without hesitation. "After they've fried you to a crisp, don't think you'll be issued a halo and a harp. Fornication is a sin that's a sight more serious than sipping whiskey on the Sabbath or diddling with the supermarket accounts."

"Fornication?" Jim Bob said, slapping his hand across his chest. "I'd never do something like that. You know what, Brother Verber? Even though I know I'm pure of such wickedness, I would like to get down on my knees and repent right this minute, just because I may have—for no more than a few seconds—harbored lust in my heart while gazing at a sweet young thing when she was buying a candy bar at the checkout counter. I got to admit that sometimes the flesh is weak. Satan starts hissing in my ear, and my thoughts stray into the garden of forbidden fruit."

"Praise the Lord!" Brother Verber said, wiping his eyes as if they were blinded with tears of joy (which they weren't, but most likely should have been if he'd been paying proper attention instead of musing about fried catfish, hush puppies, and green tomato relish for supper). "Did you hear that, Sister Barbara? This particular sinner is gonna bare his soul and come back into the flock. I think we have a miracle in the making!"

Jim Bob looked up with an embarrassed grin. "It's just that I need to allow my bowels to purge themselves of the vestiges of overindulgence. It won't take but a few minutes. Could you be kind enough to ask Japonica to let me go to the restroom?"

Mrs. Jim Bob glared but held her peace, since she wasn't quite sure what-all was going on in his head. Salvation wasn't likely to be on the top of his list; she'd been dragging him to church for years and hadn't seen any improvement to date. Then again, he'd never gotten himself locked in a cell for murder. It could be that he was finally beginning to see the light, or at least the folly of his sinful behavior.

Japonica came down the short hall and unlocked the

cell. "You two want to sit down in the front room while you wait?"

Jim Bob was rubbing his hands as he came out of the cell. "Ain't that a thoughtful suggestion on Japonica's part! Due to all the stress, I may need a few minutes. Take a breather and think of some more of those soul-stirring hymns, Brother Verber. It's all I can do to stop from breaking out in song right this minute. Japonica, my angel of compassion, I hope you'll join us in prayer before the evening is over."

"You bet," she said as they all trooped out to the office. Mrs. Jim Bob and Brother Verber stepped into a corner to discuss this unanticipated turn of events as Jim Bob went into the washroom. He locked the door, turned on the tap, and assessed the possibilities. The window was high, and not more than two feet square. There might be garbage cans filled with rats on the other side of the wall. The lavatory looked like it might be wobbly. It wouldn't be easy.

Estelle was seated on a stool in front of a slot machine, a cup of nickels in her lap. Even though she had a good view of the crowd streaming through the casino, the noise was enough to drive her crazy, what with the machines around her dinging and ringing every time they spewed out a few coins. Folks who should have known better were shrieking, barging between the rows of machines, slopping drinks on each other, and smoking so many cigarettes that the air was thick enough to choke the cud right out of a cow.

Taylor sat down on the next stool. "Having any luck?"

Estelle stuffed a nickel in the slot and pushed a button. When nothing much happened, she said, "Not hardly. Are you here by yourself?"

"Are you asking if Todd came back? No, he didn't. I spent most of the day in our room, staring at the door and trying to decide what to say when he appeared. I went down to the restaurant several times, and walked around in here. I even went to the sixth floor and stood outside every door to listen for his voice. Not only has Todd vanished, but so have all of his old friends who were in the bar last night. I'm really starting to worry about him. Maybe he really was coming down with the flu or pneumonia or something like that. Could he have been taken to a hospital?"

Estelle dug through her purse and found a clean tissue. "Here," she said, handing it to Taylor. "If he's sick, someone would have called you. After all, you're his fiancée."

"Or was, anyway," she said glumly. "Does Maggody have a home for unwed mothers?"

"Now, Taylor, it's gonna be just fine. When he shows up, you can remind him of his responsibility to you and the baby. If he's scared of upsetting his mama, you and him can go down to Little Rock and have a cozy family wedding."

She blotted her nose. "I guess I'll go upstairs and see if he's there. The way things are going, I won't be surprised if his duffel bag is gone. This is all so Victorian, if you know what I mean. Here I am, a penniless orphan, pregnant with the young master's child, abandoned at the altar—"

"Oh dear!" said Estelle, turning back to the slot machine. "Don't look, but the security man is heading this way." She thrust the cup at Taylor. "Grab some nickels and start playing like you believe you're about to win a million dollars."

Estelle fed nickels into the machine for several minutes, all the while waiting to feel a hand clamp down on her shoulder and a cold voice to order her to leave the premises. She finally risked a quick look over her shoulder. Mackenzie must have missed her and moved on, she concluded, allowing her hand to drop. However, she didn't know in what direction he'd gone. If he was wandering around the casino, sooner or later he'd notice her, especially if she was doing the same thing in hopes of spotting the bald man.

"Why do people do this?" asked Taylor as she put a coin in the slot. "It's about as exciting as picking beetles out of a sack of cornmeal."

"You can stop. Go on upstairs, then come back if Todd ain't there. We can go to the show and distract ourselves from our worries. El Vez is supposed to be something. We'll just let ourselves go and pretend we're seeing the real thing in person, except for Elvis being dead and this impersonator being from Mexico. Other than that, it ought to be entertaining."

Taylor slid off the stool. "I'm not in the mood. I think I'll take one more tour around the casino, then go upstairs and pray that Todd shows up with a reasonably acceptable excuse. If I get bored, I can throw up. I do that a lot these days."

"There's no reason to . . ." Estelle said, then stopped and tried her level best not to gawk. "Just go on to your room. Odds are Todd will be sound asleep in your bed, and by tomorrow, everything will be back the way it was."

Taylor grimaced and headed for the door that led

back into the lobby of the hotel. Estelle automatically put nickels into the slot, ignoring the occasional clatter of coins in the tray, and tried not to stare as she watched Cherri Lucinda and the bald man settle down in leather chairs in the bar like they were bosom buddies.

She was still watching them when the machine erupted with dings, rings, flashing lights, sirens, and everything short of wild applause. That was provided by fellow gamblers.

Ruby Bee was still asleep. I tiptoed across her room, set the duffel bag on a shelf in the closet, then retreated out into the corridor. There was no reason to hang around; Ruby Bee was oblivious and Dr. Deweese was gone for the day. I could program a VCR with reasonable success, but I couldn't repair an ultrasound machine.

I was walking toward the door when a twentyish black woman in a green smock came trotting up behind me.

"Are you Arly?" she asked.

I admitted as much. "Is there a problem?"

"I'm Carlette, honey. Japonica called and said for you not to bother to come by the police department. She's gonna drive the folks back to the hotel herself."

"Why?"

"That's pretty much all she said. She didn't sound real happy about it, but she can be that way. She hates her job on account of the chief. He was obliged to hire her because of the affirmative-action thing. I suppose he does his best, but he acts like this is the nineteen fifties and gals like Japonica should be cleaning houses and sitting in the back of the bus. I look forward to the day he falls sick and has to stay here. There'll be some squabbling as to who gets to stick a needle in him."

"You have no idea why she's taking them to the hotel? She didn't mention anything else?"

Carlette shook her head. "That's all. Don't go worrying too much about your mama. I'll take real good care of her and let you know if she needs anything. Dr. Deweese is young, but he's smart."

"What does his wife do?" I asked ever so casually. "Is she a doctor, too?"

"He's divorced, but you'll have to get in line. Every unattached woman in the county is after him. Even though he's on the pale side, I could bring myself to pick up his dirty underwear and drink fancy wine if that's what it'd take. I was always a sucker for big blue eyes. Now you run along and get some sleep."

I had no idea why Japonica had offered to take Mrs. Jim Bob and Brother Verber to the hotel, but it didn't seem worth the energy to think about it. I drove back, parked, and walked hurriedly across the lobby, my fingers crossed that Mackenzie was occupied with mundane chores such as skimming profits or blackmailing politicians.

No one shrieked at me. I rode the elevator to the eighth floor and went straight to my room, not bothering to check on Estelle, or anyone else, for that matter. The Elvis Presley Pilgrimage had resulted in nothing but misery for all concerned. Stormy was dead, Ruby Bee was in the hospital, Jim Bob was in jail, Estelle was on Mackenzie's list of anarchists, an elopement had been foiled, and Mrs. Jim Bob and Brother Verber were both sleeping in close proximity to yours truly.

I had a key to the room, having found one on the dresser. I let myself in and sank down on the bed. A glass with a lipstick smudge suggested Cherri Lucinda had come and gone in the last hour. In that she hadn't been sobbing outside Jim Bob's cell, I presumed she'd found a replacement in the casino—and, if the luck of the draw was with me, might remain with him for the remainder of the night.

I tossed my coat on a chair and was reaching for the remote control when someone knocked on the door. I dragged myself up and went to peer through the peephole. The man in the hallway stood far enough away for me to see the hotel logo embroidered on his shirt.

"Plumber," he said loudly.

Despite the fact he had thick brown hair, I put on the chain before I opened the door. "I didn't call."

"The trouble's on the ninth floor in the room directly above yours. A pipe broke and I need to make sure there's no water coming down the inside of the wall in your bathroom. I can wait if you want to call the desk."

"No," I said as I disengaged the chain and stepped back to open the door.

Wrong.

THIRTEEN

The door slammed into me. I staggered backward, fighting without success to keep my balance as pain ripped across my face and shoulder. I hit the floor with a thud. The man stepped over me as he came into the room and snapped the deadbolt. The sound was as loud as a gunshot. Bad sign.

"Where is it?" he said.

"It?"

"The bag." He dragged me onto the bed and looked around the room. "I ain't in the mood for a guessing game. Just give me the bag and live to tell your story in the morning."

"Help yourself," I said as I gingerly examined my nose. Blood was dripping freely, but the basic structure seemed to be intact. "Take the toothbrushes and plastic cups in the bathroom while you're at it. I only have twenty dollars in my purse, but you're welcome to every one of them. Need an extra pillow or blanket?"

"Shut up." He grabbed Cherri Lucinda's duffel bag and dumped its contents on the other bed. "Where's the other bag?"

In the tradition of Lady Macbeth, I pointed a bloody finger at my overnight bag. "It's yours for the asking. I'm sorry I didn't bring my red flannel pajamas or whatever it is you want so desperately."

"You got some nerve. Has it occurred to you that you might just be in a real bad situation? The last thing you need to be doing is making me mad, you know?" He emptied my bag on the floor, pawed through my underwear and shirts, then looked down at me. "I don't know why the fuck you think you can get away with this. You know who you're dealing with?"

"No, I don't," I said. "Any chance you're going to tell me?"

"I don't have time for this shit. Get up."

"Get up and what?" I countered, assessing my chances of overwhelming him and dashing out of the room. His age was difficult to pinpoint, but there was little doubt he was several inches taller than I was and more than fifty pounds heavier. I would have preferred to take on the ladies from Tuscaloosa *en masse*.

"Get out of your clothes."

"You're not my type," I said as I wondered how effective the remote control might be as a weapon. If I clicked a button, could I change him into the Disney channel or Nickelodeon? "I don't know who you are or what you want, but if you leave right now, I'll give you a ten-second head start before I call security."

"You're not my type, either. You either strip or I'll do it for you. I won't be all that gentle."

"So you can rape me? There's nothing gentle about that." I may have sounded like a leather-clad warrior princess, but all of my internal organs were quivering with panic. He was too big, too assured—and possibly too experienced. In all my years in Manhattan, I'd only once been threatened on the street, and then by an asthmatic veteran in a frayed pea jacket that reeked of urine. I'd ended up admiring faded photographs of his children.

"I ain't gonna rape you," he said disgustedly. "I'm a professional. Now strip and let's get this over with."

"A professional what? A masseuse building up a clientele? A gynecologist who attacks women in hotel rooms in order to conduct pelvic exams as a form of community service?" Adrenaline was now controlling my mouth as well as my mind. I abandoned the idea of the remote control as a potential weapon and looked wildly at the room service menu. Thick, but plastic. Not promising.

"All right, then," he said, "just go out on the balcony."

I forced myself to suck in a breath and keep my pitch low as I said, "I don't think so. If you take one step toward me, I'm going to scream so loudly that the mayor of Memphis will hear me. I will scratch, kick, punch, and make every effort to claw your eyes. I'm not a black belt, but I had training in self-defense at the police academy."

He sat down on the other bed. "You're a cop? What the fuck are you doing here?"

"This is my room," I said, "which pretty much explains my presence. Your turn."

"This whole thing's a goddamn nightmare. You know that lady with the bright red hair that sort of looks like a fire hydrant balanced on her head? Where is she?"

"I don't know where she is. Who are you?"

He rubbed his eyes. "Like I said, I'm a professional just doing my job—okay? What do you know about this broad called Stormy? A lot shorter than you, big blond hair, enormous boobs? She went skydiving this morning, except she forgot to take along a parachute. She went splat." He slapped his palms together to re-create the sound.

I was beginning to think I might get out of this alive. "Let's talk about the woman with the red hair. What's she got to do with anything?"

"I wish I knew," he said. "Is she a cop, too?"

"Would it matter?"

"Okay," he said, standing up. "I don't have time to hang around and yak. Let's go out on the balcony."

"I wish you'd stop saying that. I'm not going anyplace with you."

He grabbed my arm, yanked me up, and propelled me out to the balcony. "You scream and I'll wring your neck. Understand?"

I nodded. He stepped back into the room, locked the sliding doors, and closed the curtains. I fell into a chair and put my head between my knees until the balcony stopped swaying and the roar in my ears began to fade. It occurred to me that I was ill-prepared to be outside, since I was wearing only a cotton shirt and jeans. This was, of course, infinitely better than being buck naked.

I looked over my shoulder at the curtains. There was not so much as a crack through which I could see what my uncivilized guest was doing in the room—if he was still there. I rose unsteadily and gauged the distance to the balconies on either side. Ten feet at a minimum, I concluded, and well beyond my prowess, since I had been thrown out of gymnastics class at the age of seven for declining to hop and skip across a balance beam six feet above the floor. A movie heroine would have climbed onto the railing, teetered for a tension-building moment, and then leaped onto the next balcony.

Lacking a stunt double, I leaned over the railing and looked down. Cars were pulling in front of the entrance to the hotel. Bellmen were taking suitcases out of trunks and piling them on carts. A woman with a dog on a leash appeared in the driveway, paused to light a cigarette, and headed for the nearest strip of grass.

Which happened to be directly below, proving there was no major cosmic plot against me.

"Psst!" I hissed as loudly as I dared.

The woman turned her head to stare at the bushes alongside the building. Her dog glanced up, then resumed sniffing the grass for the perfect spot to defile. After a few seconds, the woman looked down at him and murmured what I assumed were words of encouragement.

I made sure the curtain hadn't twitched, then bent down and said, "Up here."

The woman was clearly nobody's fool. Rather than responding, she began to speak in an urgent voice to the dog, which was engaged in the performance of an imperative biological process.

"Please," I said, trying to sound as whimpery and pathetic as a puppy. "I need help."

The woman tilted her head and scanned the facade, eventually spotting my fluttering hands. "Are you addressing me?"

I leaned over as far as I dared. "Please send security up to my room. I've locked myself out."

"That's ridiculous. How could you have done that? Are you drunk?"

"No, ma'am," I said. "Just go to the desk and tell them there's an emergency in eight-eleven. They'll need a passkey."

"Is this some kind of practical joke? I have no intention of embarrassing myself in front of hotel staff. Hurry up, Bertie. Mumsy wants to go back inside." Ignoring Bertie's yelps, she dragged him toward the entrance.

I straightened up and put my ear against the door. I heard nothing, but the glass was apt to be double-paned to withstand the increasingly cold wind. If the man had left and Cherri Lucinda had returned, she hadn't turned on the TV or gotten into a telephone conversation.

All the balconies I could see were vacant. Even during daylight hours the view was far from entrancing; it was hard to imagine why anyone would venture out in the dark to admire a skyline more than thirty miles away.

The chairs were too flimsy to break the glass. However, they might make serviceable missiles to catch somebody's attention. I made sure no was standing below the balcony, then held my breath and dropped a chair over the railing. It hit the grass and bounced into the bushes. I was about to try the second one when I saw a bellman staring up at me from the curb. Before I could call to him, he scurried into the hotel.

I put the chair back in place and sat down, confident that the report of a deranged woman throwing furniture off a balcony would bring a battalion, or at least a platoon, of security men. The Luck of the Draw did not tolerate adolescent mischief, or so I'd been told.

Jim Bob limped along warily, shrinking into doorways whenever a car or truck went by. Damn few of them did. He didn't know how many folks lived in the pissant little town, but most all of them must have been holed up at home watching Saturday night wrestling. The lo-

cal town council was a sorry group, he thought as he
went past burned-out streetlights and piles of garbage
bags and boxes. Obviously, none of them had ever been
to a Municipal League meeting and spent endless hours
in seminars listening to bureaucrats make no more sense
than Kevin Buchanon when he whined about the work
schedule.

He reached a corner and leaned against a crumbling
wall as he thought about what to do. There was no getting around the fact he was a fugitive. Japonica was uppity, but she wasn't dumb. She probably hadn't waited
ten minutes before forcing the door and discovering the
open window. She'd have been real pissed. Mrs. Jim Bob
was likely to have thrown a fit unlike anyone had ever
seen since the volcanoes erupted in Italy or wherever.

He reminded himself of his predicament. The hotel
was a good ten miles away. His ankle throbbed from
landing on a splintery crate. His coat was in the cell, and
his wallet was in Japonica's desk. This wasn't the kind of
town where taxis cruised, especially the kind willing to
accept welfare cases.

There were a few coins in his pocket. If he could find a
pay phone, he could call Cherri Lucinda and have her pick
him up. He couldn't go back to The Luck of the Draw, but
there were plenty of cheap motels in the area and she'd
surely brought some money to buy souvenirs. Come
Monday morning he'd start looking for a lawyer to get him
out of this damn mess. Mrs. Jim Bob could be dealt with later.

He must have walked for most of a mile before he
spotted a brightly lit convenience store. There were no
cop cars in the parking lot or uniforms bustling around
inside. He tucked in his shirt and tried to look like a man
on an evening stroll.

Inside, it was blessedly warm. He pulled out his change, hoping he'd have enough for a burrito once Cherri Lucinda was on her way. It didn't look promising, but he went on over to the pay phone. If there'd ever been a directory, it was long gone, so he continued to the counter, where a bored woman was thumbing through a magazine.

"Got a directory?" he asked.

"Yeah, somewhere."

"Can I see it?"

"I s'pose," she said, setting aside the magazine, "but only if you're buying something. The directory's for the use of customers."

Jim Bob fought off the urge to roll up the magazine and jam it down her throat. "I'll buy something after I make my call. I can't make my call until I look up the number, and I can't look up the number till you pass over the directory. You follow all that?"

"Ain't no need to get nasty," she said as she bent down and came back up with a thin directory. "This stays right where I can see it."

Jim Bob found the number of The Luck of the Draw, shoved the directory back at her, and was heading for the phone when a woman came into the store. Her hair was spiky and a bizarre shade of red, and she had safety pins stuck through her eyebrows and her cheeks. She was wearing a bulky jacket, but her legs were bare below very short shorts. Bare and shapely.

Despite the importance of calling Cherri Lucinda, Jim Bob stopped in his tracks and stared.

"Hey," she said, smiling, then went over to the case and took out a six-pack of beer. On her way to the counter she added a bag of potato chips and a handful of beef jerkies. "How much you want?" she asked the clerk.

Jim Bob forced himself to dial the number of the hotel and ask for Cherri Lucinda's room. When no one answered, he tried his own room in case she was sitting in there, feeling bad about what all had happened to him just because he'd done her a favor.

She wasn't there, either. He hung up the receiver and took his change back out to see what he had left. He figured he couldn't buy a bus ticket for seventy-seven cents, or a pack of gum, for that matter. The clerk wasn't gonna let him hang around for long, even if he had enough money to keep calling Cherri Lucinda till she got to her room.

The peculiar-looking woman came over to him. "You in trouble?"

Jim Bob did his best not to gawk at her choice of jewelry. "Yeah, somebody was hiding in the backseat of my car. He took my money and dumped me out on the road down a piece. All I want to do is get back to my hotel. Any chance you can give me a lift?"

"Sure," she said, going out the door.

He trotted after her, wondering if there was any way to get not only a ride, but also a beer and a beef jerky or two. "This is real kind of you to do a favor like this for somebody you don't know. What's your name?"

"Joy. Get in the car."

He was feeling downright giddy with his good fortune as he got into a big old Buick. The woman now known as Joy got into the driver's side, but before he could make a passing reference to the beer, a very bulky figure climbed in next to him and slammed the door.

"Who's he?" the man demanded, jabbing Jim Bob's

shoulder. Unlike his companion, his hair was blond and pulled back in a frizzy ponytail. His eyes looked like pennies imbedded in a wad of dough. "Fer chrissake, Joy, I leave you for thirty seconds and you're already picking up some scrawny little asshole."

"Shut your mouth, Saddam," she said. "You're the only asshole in this car. I have just about had it with you. The only reason I came here was to play in the slots tournament. The minute I turned my back, you took all the money out of my purse and bought a goddamn chainsaw. Now all we can do is drink beer and watch television—if you haven't hocked your set. You're not only an asshole, you're the biggest fuckin' asshole in the world!"

"You'd better watch it," he rumbled.

Jim Bob was about to suggest he leave them alone to work out their disagreement when the car squealed out of the parking lot and went flying down the highway. "If you could drop me off at The Luck of the Draw—"

Joy stomped down on the accelerator. "Do you realize how long I saved up for the tournament? The foreman was so mad when I called in sick this morning that I may not have a job on Monday. That wouldn't have mattered if I'd won some money, but that ain't gonna happen. You know what you can do when we get to your place, Saddam? You can fuck yourself, that's what!"

"You owed me three hundred dollars from when I bailed you out. I was just takin' what was mine."

"It was mine to enter the tournament," she retorted, swerving around a car and narrowly averting a head-on collision with a semi.

Jim Bob licked his lips. "I think my hotel's back the other way."

"Shut up," said Saddam. "Okay, maybe I should have said something before I took the money. I got all of twelve dollars in my pocket, and that's not gonna pay your entry fee. What do you want me to do?"

"Replace it," she said, then slammed on the brakes and spun into a U-turn so abruptly that Jim Bob sprawled across Saddam's substantial thighs.

When he sat back up, he saw they were approaching the convenience store. It looked a helluva lot cozier than it had a few minutes earlier, like an oasis in a desert of darkness. Joy pulled in and leaned across Jim Bob to open the glove compartment.

"You should be able to get a couple of hundred," she said as she pulled out a knitted cap.

Saddam pulled the cap over his head and down to his chin. Lopsided holes exposed his mouth and eyes. "Yeah, it's Saturday night. I'll be back in a minute."

Jim Bob watched in shock as Saddam got out of the car, took a gun from his coat pocket, and pushed open the door of the store. "Maybe I should get out here," he said, barely audible. "It was real generous of you, but I can see you're busy. I'll catch another ride."

Joy clenched his arm. "Can you imagine the nerve of that Saddam stealing money from me? If we were married, it'd be one thing, but this is fuckin' different. I worked overtime every chance I got to save up so I could play in the tournament. Then he goes and buys another chainsaw. I mean, how many goddamn chainsaws does he need?"

Jim Bob figured he was gonna have to leave his arm in the Buick if he got out. He was trying to squirm out of her amazingly tight grip when Saddam ran out of the store and dived into the backseat.

"Haul ass," he commanded.

As the car shot forward, Jim Bob saw the clerk standing at the window. She was staring at his face as if memorizing every last detail, from his beetlish forehead all the way down to his slack jaw.

It was possible that a certain amount of adolescent mischief *was* tolerated at The Luck of the Draw Casino & Hotel. Throwing chairs off balconies might be a time-honored Mississippi tradition, a unique display of gratitude for hospitality. The lawn maintenance crew might expect to pull some number of chairs out of the bushes each morning. I hadn't seen any other chairs fly by, but I was preoccupied with my plummeting body temperature. There'd been a heavy frost the preceding night.

The telephone inside the room had rung, but if my guest was still there, he hadn't answered it. The telephone in the adjoining room had rung, too. The lights were off, though, so I'd assumed no one was there.

I reached my limit for freezing my butt off. I picked up the remaining chair and stood by the railing. This time I'd aim for the roof of a car. Damage might result, but I wouldn't be ignored.

The light went on in what had been Jim Bob's room. I pulled the chair back and leaned out, hoping to see someone inside the room. By this time I was almost convinced the man responsible for my present situation was long gone. Then again, I was reluctant to scream and find out my supposition was wrong. I wanted no starring role in a second splat.

I lifted the chair over my head and flung it at the neighboring balcony. It landed with a satisfactory clatter, knocking over the chairs and table and almost going over the far railing.

The sliding doors opened and a head popped out. I'd been anticipating Mrs. Jim Bob, so I was pleased to see Japonica's braids.

"Over here," I said softly.

"Arly?"

"On the next balcony."

"You must be mighty bored tonight. There's a casino downstairs, you know. If you're not in the mood to gamble or drink in the bar, you can go to the show. Carlette saw it last weekend, and she said she damn near believed Elvis was gonna step down from the stage and give her a shiny new Cadillac."

"I need help," I said, glancing back at the curtains.

"A gambler, huh? There's a twelve-step program for that. You ought to do something before you get yourself in bad trouble. I got a cousin that lost his house—"

"A man came into the room, made me come out here, and then locked the doors. I don't know if he's in there or not. If he is, you need to be careful. He's the size of a refrigerator box, and his attitude is bad."

"Who is he?"

"Japonica," I said hoarsely, "I am turning an unflattering shade of blue. Can we discuss this once I'm inside?"

"How long have you been out there?"

I picked up the table and staggered to the railing. "See this? See that Mercedes pulling up? Want to make a small bet as to whether I can hit it or not?"

She went back into the room, and within a matter of seconds, slid open the door and let me inside. I immediately crawled under the covers of the nearest bed. "I am so cold," I groaned. "I was most definitely not an arctic explorer in a previous life. You did look in the bathroom and the closet, didn't you?"

"And under both beds," she said. "You want to explain whatever you were carrying on about?"

I told her what had happened. "Don't bother to ask," I went on, "because I have no idea who he was or what he wanted. It has something to do with Stormy, though." I sat up and pulled the blankets around my shoulders. "She must have been followed from Farberville. Estelle saw some suspicious characters at the motel the first night. Stormy demanded a new hair style and color, most likely to alter her appearance so she could get away. It didn't work, since one of the men was at Graceland, and possibly in this hotel earlier in the day."

Japonica shook her head. "This isn't some best-selling suspense novel with Mafia thugs. You had the bad luck to encounter a burglar. You're damn lucky you didn't find yourself out there without your clothes. Then again, the bellman wouldn't have scratched his head and gone off to polish the elevator buttons."

"So you're still convinced you have the killer in custody?"

"I'm still convinced we had the killer in custody until about an hour ago. He climbed out the washroom window and went hightailin' into the back streets. We'll find him before too long."

I did not allow myself so much as a tiny smirk. "So that's why you gave Mrs. Jim Bob and Brother Verber a ride back here. Where are they now?"

"Down in the restaurant. I told 'em not to come up here until I made sure he wasn't in the next room. His car keys are still there, as well as a couple of hundred-dollar chips from the casino. I wanted to check, even though there's no way he could have walked all this way. He's probably hiding in some vacant building not a hundred feet from the police department. I wouldn't be surprised if he was already pounding on the door, begging to turn himself in for a hot meal and a bed with blankets."

"The man wanted something from Stormy's bag," I said mulishly. "He's got to be involved in some way."

She gestured at the scattered clothes on the floor. "Well, he didn't find it in either of the bags out in plain sight. The bag in the closet has been emptied, too. There's no way of knowing if he found something in it. If he did, it's likely to be the last of him." She crossed her arms. "That doesn't mean he wasn't an ordinary burglar thinking he'd find jewelry or a stash of spending money. This is the time when most folks are downstairs enjoying themselves."

I crossed my arms. "He said Stormy's name. He knew what happened to her."

"Most everybody who works here has been gossiping about it all day. That's all the more reason why he'd expect the room to be empty. He was dressed up like a plumber so nobody'd notice him wandering around the floors. I'm surprised you fell for it, being a cop and all."

I let my arms drop. "I had plenty of time to think about it while I was out on the balcony, feeling like a damn fool. Don't you think you ought to dust for fingerprints?"

"And compare 'em with what?" Japonica said. "There are hundreds of folks on the staff, and thousands of customers in the casino. I don't think the hotel management would look kindly on me if I suggested they all get in line to be fingerprinted. Guys like him work one area for a few weeks, then move on like a tent revivalist making the circuit."

A beeper concealed somewhere on her body chirped. She slapped her pockets until she found it clipped to her belt. After squinting at it, she said, "I got to make a call. You mind if I use your phone?"

"Help yourself," I said as I leaned against the headboard and tried to come up with theories that would persuade her to reconsider the investigation.

"This is me," she said into the receiver, then paused. "That little store near the bait shop? Anybody hurt?" She gave me a curious look before turning around. "I've been on duty for more than twelve hours, Chief, and there's not really anything we can do tonight. On my way home, I'll stop by and see if she has anything else to add. I'm not about to set up a roadblock on a Saturday night."

When she replaced the receiver, I gave her a sympathetic smile. "You have had a long day, haven't you? A murder, an escaped prisoner, and now this. While you were running all over the place, did Chief Sanderson spend the afternoon watching basketball on TV?"

"He's got a hot tub on his patio. Most of the time he sits out there and lets his wife bring him beers while he listens to classical music. God only knows what he'll do when he actually retires." She began to zip up her coat. "Stay away from plumbers, you hear?"

She left before I could offer further arguments. I stayed in bed for a few more minutes, racking my brain for inspiration, then got up and went into the adjoining room. As Japonica had said, a ring with keys and a short stack of black chips were on the dresser next to a bottle of bourbon that was half empty (or half full, depending on your perspective; in that Brother Verber had not poured the devil's poison down the drain, I had a pretty good idea of his). Jim Bob's wristwatch was on top of the television.

A suitcase was overturned on the bed, as was a second one that had been set in a corner. The jockey shorts and undershirts were of no more interest to me than they had been to my assailant. Nor, for that matter, had been the items of obvious value (the chips) or of dubious value (the watch).

My assailant was after something that had been in Stormy's bag. He might have found it in the closet, but then why had he come into Jim Bob's room to root through more bags while I shivered on the balcony? There'd been more bags on the C'Mon van, I realized. Todd and Taylor had brought theirs, as had Rex. Baggins might have been allowed to bring a steamer trunk, but I doubted it. Estelle and Ruby Bee were the only ones of the group I felt confident were not transporting contraband across state borders.

It seemed prudent to alert the others to the possibility of a rogue plumber showing up at the door. Taylor, in particular, was in the most danger—unless her fiancé had returned with a damned good explanation. Having heard quite a few of them in my day, I would have been skeptical, but hormones can blind the best of us.

I'd picked up the receiver to call the hotel operator and ask for Taylor's room when I realized I didn't know her last name. Odds were good that the operator didn't, either. Baggins, on the other hand, was a last name, if one that summoned vague, unfocused images of hairy-footed creatures battling trolls and gremlins.

The hotel operator dialed the room, then came back on after a dozen rings and gently suggested that he wasn't there. She had a point.

I decided to see if I could find him in the casino.

FOURTEEN

The casino was lively. I wiggled my way through the crowd, peering over heads in hopes I'd be able to spot Baggins—or Estelle. I believed her story of shuttling to another casino with the same degree of confidence that I believed the Energizer Bunny would lead us to our salvation as a species. The fuzz-head would just keep on thumping and thumping as we tumbled over the cliff and into the sea.

The crowd was predominantly white, which helped. After some prowling, I saw Baggins beside a roulette table. I worked my way across the room and edged next to him as the wheel spun. He watched it with the intensity of a very hungry hawk.

"I need to talk to you," I said into his ear.

"Red, come red!" he shouted. When the ball settled into a black slot, he glared at me. "Fat lot of luck you are. I already told you everything you need to hear. Your mother may or may not get herself a refund. It's out of my hands. I'm off duty and having myself some fun."

"Well, I'm not."

Baggins bent forward to place chips in what I supposed were strategic spots. "Get on out of here. I ain't got anything more to say."

"Where's Estelle?"

"How am I supposed to know that? The show starts at ten. Till then, they're finding their own amusement. Mine happens to be roulette." He sucked in a breath as the ball once again dropped into a black slot. "I was doin' real fine up until a minute ago. Go pester somebody else."

I gave him an irritated look, but he was already slamming down chips and muttering incantations meant to influence the ball. I moved back and looked around. An unholy clatter came from the banks of slot machines, accompanied by outbursts of glee. Glaringly bright wheels whirled on several sides of me, reflected by mirrors on the ceiling. More lights flowed across the walls, flashing numbers. On a platform behind the bar, three hairy gargoyles jerked about with guitars, lost in personal rapture, while a fourth pounded on drums and shrieked about whatever was (or wasn't) on his mind.

Most of the accents around me were thick enough to pour over waffles. A few had the nasal intonation of the territory above the Mason-Dixon Line. As I pushed my way through the surge of bodies, I felt increasingly anxious. I'd dealt with crowds in Manhattan, but they'd been decorously dressed and ever so polite as they'd elbowed me out of line to buy champagne during intermission. In Maggody, a crowd was defined by the number of people who showed up for happy hour at Ruby Bee's Bar & Grill on a Friday afternoon.

Which wasn't always happy and rarely lasted an hour. Even with free popcorn.

All of a sudden I wanted to fight my way to the door

and drive to the hospital. So what if Ruby Bee was asleep? I could sit with her, stroke her hand, be there if she opened her eyes and wanted a sip of water. That was the reason I'd come; Jim Bob's problems were nothing more than a diversion. Japonica's version of the struggle on the balcony made perfectly good sense: Jim Bob had been drunk, upset by losses at the craps table, enraged by Stormy's rejection.

Except, I thought as I found a haven at the end of a blackjack table, Jim Bob hadn't lost money, if the chips in his room were indicative. He and Cherri Lucinda had made their way quite merrily to his room. No doubt he'd poured himself a drink before he settled down and allowed himself to fantasize about the woman taking a hot shower in his bathroom. They'd had sex twelve hours earlier, and he was expecting a repeat performance within a matter of minutes. He had no motive to attack Stormy.

"Miss Hanks," Mackenzie cooed in my ear. "Would you like a cocktail?"

I may have flinched just a tad. "No, thank you. I just came down to see the casino in all its glory on a Saturday night. I can almost hear the money being sucked in by the corporate vacuum cleaners. Nickels here, quarters there. It does add up at the end of the night, doesn't it?"

"Do you object to gaming as a form of entertainment?"

"Not when that's all it is," I said, watching for Estelle or her infamous bald man. "It can be an addiction, though."

"I told you this morning that we try to screen out compulsive gamblers. They do nothing more than cause us headaches. They demand credit when it's beyond their means, and become belligerent when we decline. We were once offered a three-year-old child as collateral. We don't do that."

I finally gave him my full attention. "Here in your make-believe world, it's an endless party. Free drinks for everyone willing to lose money. As you said, you never close. Aren't you preying on people's obscure hope that there really is a way to transform a five-dollar chip into a fortune?"

"That would be the essence of gaming," Mackenzie said dryly. "Something for nothing. We merely provide a reasonably level playing field. Some people do win a lot of money."

"Right."

"Let's take your friend Estelle, for instance. She won a thousand dollars with a single nickel. A remarkable return on her investment, wouldn't you say?"

"Estelle? She was here earlier?"

"Oh yes. I think she might have preferred to be elsewhere when the attention focused on her, but there was nothing she could do but accept congratulations with a gracious nod. We don't mind, since it encourages other players to persevere. Hope springs eternal, as someone said."

"Alexander Pope," I said, "and I doubt he was referring to slot machines. Is Estelle still here?"

"I couldn't say. She collected her winnings at the cashier's window, then she did what she could to fade into the crowd. I watched her for a while, but shortly thereafter we had an unpleasant situation at a blackjack table and I went to intervene."

"Is the senator here tonight?" I asked.

"I have no idea," Mackenzie said, "and it's not relevant—as long as your friend does not attack him again. I doubt he'll ever be able to stand in front of a urinal without recalling the incident. I must say I look forward to the morning, when this particular tour group leaves. In the future, C'Mon Tours will not be welcome at The Luck of the Draw. From what I was told, this Miss Vetchling is shrill and bullheaded. She called yesterday morning and demanded five rooms, four of them doubles. We were booked. She made such graphic threats that the manager finally gave her the rooms he keeps in reserve for emergencies."

"Was it an emergency?"

"I handle security, not reservations. What about Estelle?"

"As soon as I find her, I'll drag her back to the room and chain her to the bed," I vowed solemnly, if mendaciously. Dragging Estelle anywhere would be much like attempting to stuff a large cat into a small bag. "I don't understand why you're upset about tonight, though. All she was doing was playing the slots. That *is* what customers are supposed to do. Someone has to win every now and then to sustain the feeding frenzy."

"You betrayed my trust, Miss Hanks. That's the only reason I'm upset."

"Here's a better reason," I said as I gestured at the bar, where Brother Verber was teetering on a tabletop in order to preach at a noticeably disgruntled congregation. I couldn't hear him, but I could surmise the gist of his remarks. "Blame Miss Vetchling for this, too."

"You know him?" asked Mackenzie.

"Not in the biblical sense," I said, then deftly merged into the flow of bodies moving down the aisle. This time I would choke the answers out of Baggins.

I returned to the roulette table, but his place had been appropriated by a young woman wearing so much jewelry that she seemed in danger of toppling onto the green felt. There was no point in asking the croupier if he'd noticed in which direction Baggins had gone.

I made my way past the remaining roulette tables, but Baggins was not in sight. He was playing neither craps nor blackjack. The band was striving for new levels of auditory abuse, as if to provoke more hysterical action from the players. The waitresses were tight-lipped as they made their way from table to table. The sour stench of sweat, smoke, and anxiety was impossible to ignore. Men dressed as impeccably as Mackenzie attempted to scrutinize the proceedings with unruffled stares, but their eyes were darting as though they anticipated an event of cataclysmic significance at any moment.

An exit sign beckoned me. I wiggled my way to the door, then went outside and sat down on a planter to regain my senses. Had my self-imposed exile in Maggody led to a bad case of agoraphobia? The sidewalks of Manhattan were always jammed with pedestrians who blundered along like professional boxers who'd had a few too many blows to the head. Department stores, especially during seasonal sales, were crammed with women lugging screaming babies and rebellious toddlers. Waiters and clerks had been recruited from classified ads in the back of paramilitary magazines. Taxis had careened down the streets as if determined to rack up points by shooting through a dozen green lights before squealing to a stop.

I'd never paid much attention.

Once I'd calmed down, I decided to walk across the

parking lot to the hotel entrance rather than fight my way back through the casino. Brother Verber had undoubtedly inflamed a minor riot in the bar with his sanctimonious harangue, and Mrs. Jim Bob was apt to be in the vicinity, snarling like a red-eyed harpy. I had no idea how to find Estelle, Baggins, Jim Bob, or Todd. I had no desire to encounter Cherri Lucinda, the abovementioned evangelists, Mackenzie, Rex, or even Miss Vetchling, should she be skulking in the shadows to keep watch over her pilgrims.

I hadn't planned to be outside, so I'd left my coat in the hotel room. Fog was rolling in from the river, veiling the lights in the parking lot in a smudgy haze. I stood up, brushed off my fanny, and was about to take a reasonably short hike when a man approached from the parking lot. He was wearing a white satin cape over a jumpsuit emblazoned with rhinestones and sequins, and his hair was combed back in an improbable pompadour, with only a single black curl out of alignment.

"Evening, ma'am," he said. "I'm sorry if I'm alarmin' you, but you look troubled. Anything I can do to help?"

I appraised the distance to the door. "I just came out for some fresh air."

"Did you lose your money gambling?"

"No," I said irritably. "I wasn't handling the crowd well. I'm fine now."

"Crowds used to bother me, too, growing up like I did in a small town and all. I was only ten years old the first time I sang in front of an audience, and my knees were so wobbly I could hardly stand up. You sure I can't do something for you? Here you are, a pretty little thing out here in the cold. Are you lonesome tonight? Can I buy you a cup of coffee and a piece of pecan pie?"

"Don't you have a show to perform?"

"I wish I did," he said, then turned around and walked back into the parking lot, gradually disappearing as he moved out of the diffused glow of the red and yellow casino lights.

It was most definitely time to get some sleep. A couple of catnaps could not compensate for an all-night marathon drive. My nerves weren't just shot; they were flat-out riddled with bullet holes.

I began to walk along the sidewalk to the hotel entrance, unable to convince myself that the arctic wind was medicinal rather than punitive. It was likely that Estelle was in her room, counting out her money and eating bread and honey (which she could most definitely afford), or flushing Mrs. Jim Bob's utilitarian underwear down the toilet. I didn't much care.

I'd almost made it when Cherri Lucinda came skittering up to me and came damn close to knocking me into the bushes (where I would have banged my head against at least one chair).

"You got to do something!" she shrieked.

Jim Bob knew he had to do something, but damned if he knew what. He'd been told to sit on the couch, and that's what he was doing, trying not to notice how Saddam had gulped down the last beer, as well as half a bottle of whiskey he'd found under the sink, and looked ready to slide out of the recliner. Joy was flat on the floor, having injected herself with something Jim Bob figured wasn't along the lines of insulin. She most likely wasn't dead, but she didn't look like she was in the right frame of mind to drive him to the hotel.

He pasted on a smile. "You know, Saddam, I was

thinking I might head on out so you and Joy can have some privacy. Why, if you could see to loan me twenty dollars, I'll bet I could call a cab and be out of your hair in no time flat."

"I should have shot that bitch," Saddam mumbled. "I went to high school with her, fer chrissake. She probably got on the phone the second I left and fingered me to the cops. Any second now they'll come squealing down the road." He pointed a finger in the general direction of Jim Bob. "When they do, I ain't gonna go out the door with my hands in the air. You ever see *Bonnie and Clyde*? They didn't wuss out. Gawd, I loved that movie."

Jim Bob nodded energetically. "My all-time favorite. You know what, we could rent it and watch it this very night. Why don't I take the car and go to the video store? I could be back in twenty minutes. I'll pick up a pizza and more beer. It could be a regular party."

"On my sixth birthday, my pa took me to see Clyde's grave in Dallas. Ever since then, I've wanted to be on the FBI's most-wanted list." Saddam let out a belch that rattled the windows. "Fuckin' awesome, huh? You get your picture in every post office in the country. My last mug shot was kind of cool. I got this little shit-eatin' grin, and—"

"You asshole," Joy said as she sat up. "Next you'll be saying you want your handprints on that sidewalk in Hollywood. Armed robbery's no big deal."

"Is too," he said. "What's more, when the cops show up, I'm gonna get my shotgun and make my stand in the doorway. Nobody's walking away."

Jim Bob felt a chill run down his spine. For one thing, he didn't doubt Saddam's sincerity for a second; if the

cops showed up, all hell would break loose in the form
of tear gas and assault weapons. Nobody in the shoddy
little house would be in any condition to crawl, much
less walk away. What's more, he was not only a fugitive
waiting to be charged with murder, he was also implicated in an armed robbery. There was no way the police
would believe he was an innocent party.

Saddam lurched to his feet. "I'm gonna get a chainsaw."

Kevin realized he had to do something, and pretty darn
quick. If he ran out of gas and had to hitch a ride to a gas
station, it could be hours before he got the four-wheel
back to Idalupino, who probably had noticed it was
gone by now. She'd be madder than a wet hen. The
minute Jim Bob got back from Hot Springs, she'd be
griping in his ear and he'd have to promise to fire Kevin
to shut her up.

He glanced in the mirror. The police cars were still
there, their lights flashing, but they were keeping their
distance. It was making him kind of nervous, though.
It'd seemed like at least one of them would get tired of
driving so slow and go ahead and pass. There were a lot
of other vehicles back there, too. Something special was
going on over in Oklahoma. It was too darn bad he
didn't know what it was.

Dahlia was most likely already back at home, seeing
to Kevvie Junior and Rose Marie. Thinking he could find
her had been a dumb idea. About all he could do was
stop and fill up the tank, then take the Bronco back to
the supermarket and pray Idalupino didn't suspect him
of being the culprit that borrowed it.

Up ahead he could see the white lights of a service-center plaza. It looked like a right fine place to buy gas and maybe treat himself to a can of pop and a candy bar before he drove back to Maggody. The last thing he wanted to do was spoil his supper. Dahlia kept a real close watch on what he ate.

He put on the blinker and pulled into the parking lot. He'd sort of expected the police cars to git on about their business, so he was surprised when they all turned in behind him. He stopped at a pump, cut off the engine, and felt in his pants pocket for his wallet. He'd just remembered where he'd left it when he heard a voice amplified by a bullhorn say, "Get out of the vehicle and keep your hands above your head."

Kevin closed his eyes.

The Reverend Edwin W. Hitebred had determined through intensive prayer that he and he alone had been chosen to do something. Martha had pleaded with him, but his mind was clear and his mission set forth in words as plain and straightforward as the Scriptures, which he had quoted to her as he packed his bag: "Moreover this they have done unto me: they have defiled my sanctuary to profane it; and lo, thus have they done it in the midst of my house."

She hadn't looked real convinced, and had gone so far as to have raised her voice before he'd reminded her of the fifth commandment. Perhaps he'd erred when he allowed her to take a position at the high school as a secretary. None of her fellow employees came to the church; as far as he knew, she could be mingling all day with drunkards and atheists. This wasn't to say that he didn't trust her. She was stout, loyal, and submissive. When her mother had died, she'd accepted the burden of caring for the two of them and seeing to the time-

consuming chores required to keep the church func-
tioning smoothly. He might have been able to call on another member of the congregation to wax the floors,
sweep, dust, brush cobwebs off the rafters, and take the
preschool Sunday school class every week, but he'd
lacked volunteers. Besides, Martha was as stalwart as her
biblical namesake. She was eager to do God's work. Her
eyes shone with dedication every Sunday morning, just
as her mother's had done.

Hitebred threw the bag in his car and drove past the
church to a logging trail. He parked, wiped his forehead
with a handkerchief, and murmured a prayer for the
continued health of Miz Burnwhistle, who was again
convinced she was teetering on the edge of her grave.
He wasn't real sure who among the members of the
congregation would dare to criticize him if he missed
the big event, most of them having already dropped off
so many covered dishes after false alarms that the actual
funeral gathering would be a sorry affair when and if it
ever happened. According to Miz Burnwhistle's daugh-
ter-in-law, the freezer held no less than a dozen green-
bean casseroles, six pot roasts, and four lemon bundt
cakes (with powdered-sugar drizzle). The daughter-in-
law, who lived in Farberville and worked as a lawyer, had
sounded a bit stressed.

The current generation of Burnwhistles had all
moved away, as had most of the young folks. Scurgeton
had nothing to offer them. Family farms had been
bought out by corporations that bulldozed barns and
filled in ponds in order to construct endless acres of
chicken houses. Fewer children were joining 4-F and as-
piring to win blue ribbons at the county fair for little
heifers with shy brown eyes.

Hitebred took his overnight bag and walked back to the church. If the satanists were still bent on their wicked ways, they would hold their ritual on Saturday night in order to defile the holiness of the Sunday morning service. Never would they suspect he would be waiting for them in his office, erect in his chair, his ears tuned to the slightest sound, his hand poised to call the sheriff's department and summon a heavily armed squadron of men to burst into the church and cart them off to jail.

Although he knew that pride was a sin, Hitebred saw himself on the witness stand, his eyes blazing with righteousness and his words inspired by no less than the Holy Ghost. The jury would be spellbound, the judge and bailiff leaning forward, their mouths agape with awe. The miscreants, a sorry collection of slovenly, long-haired boys and girls—why, they'd fall down on their knees and whimper for forgiveness when they heard themselves condemned to eternal suffering. Whether or not he saw fit to forgive them would depend on the sincerity of their apologies. There was no room for ambiguity.

The church was dark. Hitebred let himself inside, locked the door, and groped his way through the folding chairs to the office door. He found the chair behind the desk, sat down, and set his Bible and a thermos of coffee within reach. Thus armed, he leaned back and awaited the arrival of Satan's onslaught.

Brother Verber was surprised when it began to sink in that he had been given the opportunity to do something that would expand his ministry. When he'd first climbed onto the table and exhorted the sinners to quit their drinking and gambling and spend the morning in church, he'd sensed that the message was not well received. However, once he'd pulled out the piece of paper with his lyrics and suggested that everyone present learn how to go about avoiding sin, his audience had turned oddly attentive.

"The thing is," he said, praying that the wobbly table would hold him, "you can't linger on the syllables. You have to keep moving along like draftees in boot camp. Now the first line goes like this: 'Atheism, bestiality, cunnilingus, drive-in movies . . . evolution and excessive body hair.' You want to try it, just to make sure we've got the pace?"

Those in the bar seemed willing to do their best. After a couple of false starts, it came together and Brother Verber beamed down at them as they applauded their group effort.

"Very good," he said, accepting a libation from a waitress who looked just like a miniskirted angel. "This is real kind of you."

"It's from an admirer," she said with a wink.

He thought about this for a second, then got back to the serious business of saving souls. "This next part is even trickier, but I'm beginning to feel the spirit—and I know you are, too. Before the night is over, we're gonna wash away all our sins and go forth like Christian warriors. Pay attention, 'cause here we go: 'Fornication, gluttony, heathenism, immodesty . . . jealousy and killin' with a pear.' Think you can do it?"

"A pear?" echoed a woman with white hair.

Brother Verber frowned. "Are you quibbling with the voice of the Almighty God? In Second Colossians, we are told: 'The fruit of the Spirit is love, joy, peace, longsuffering, gentleness, goodness, faith, meekness, and temperance.' A pear's a fruit, isn't it?"

"Well, yes," she admitted. "But I don't quite see how you'd go about killing somebody with one."

"You know the story of David and Goliath?" said Brother Verber. "Now I'm not saying this is the true story, but you remember how David put a stone in his slingshot, doncha? Only last week I was thinking of buying myself a ripe, juicy pear at the supermarket as a special treat. I could almost smell the sweet nectar dribbling down my chin. My mouth was watering with anticipation." He paused to allow his audience to share his anticipation. "But I groaned with despair when I discovered that the speckled yellow pear was as hard as a chunk of granite. I was so disappointed that I could have slung it across the aisle in frustration, just like David did."

The woman narrowed her eyes. "Are you saying that David slew Goliath with a pear?"

"We can't know for sure. It's an issue that's plagued biblical scholars for centuries. I think we need to move on to the second verse. We're not even halfway done." He paused, a little bewildered by the enthusiastic response he was receiving. This was a song about sin, after all, and those present were engaging in it in various degrees. "Okay, this second verse requires you to take off like you stuck a fork in an outlet. Ready?"

They all seemed more than just interested.

FIFTEEN

"**W**hat's wrong?" I asked Cherri Lucinda.

"I ain't sure. Well, I have my suspicions, but I hate to say outright 'cause I'm most likely wrong. Did you hear about Estelle winning all that money playing the slots?"

"I was told she won a thousand dollars."

"They gave it to her in chips. She stuffed them in her purse, then sailed right out of the casino like one of those ships on TV on the Fourth of July. You know what I'm talking about?" I nodded, unable to keep myself from picturing Estelle as a figurehead on a Viking ship, her jaw thrust forward and her wooden eyes focused on a yet unconquered continent.

Cherri Lucinda shivered as a gust of wind whipped around us. "I went to catch up with her so I could offer my congratulations, but I saw this man standing real close to her in front of the elevators, holding onto her arm. They got in one and the doors closed before I could get there. The thing is, she looked real perturbed. I don't think she wanted to go with him."

"And?" I said.

"That's about it. It was more than half an hour ago. I was trying to think what to do when I noticed you poking around the casino. I followed you out here, but, well, I got slowed down. You didn't see anything odd, did you—like a person or something?"

"No," I said curtly, not willing to pursue the topic. "Describe this man who was with Estelle."

She tugged on her lip with fingernails long enough to do damage in a crowded room. "Hefty. Brown hair, ordinary features. He was smiling, but the way he was doing it wouldn't have made me invite him into my apartment for a beer. He reminded me of my mama's third husband—and he ain't coming up for parole till the year two thousand and eight."

I was fairly confident I knew the subject under discussion. "He wasn't threatening her in any way?"

Cherri Lucinda gave me a look that implied she put my IQ somewhat lower than that of a slice of cheese. "Not that I could tell."

"Have you seen Baggins?" I asked.

"Since when? I saw him yesterday afternoon, when he gave us our keys. I saw him last night at the roulette table. I saw him this morning, tearing into eggs and ham. I saw him a while back, lined up at the cashier's desk."

"Cashing in his winnings?"

"Not hardly. He was using his credit card to get money. The professor was doing the same, although he was squabbling with them. I guess knowing everything there is to know about Elvis doesn't always cut the mustard. There were several casino guys arguing with him."

"I'd better go make sure Estelle is okay. Thanks for tracking me down."

"You sure you didn't see anybody wandering around

out here? A fellow dressed kinda funny, acting like he wanted to have a nice talk?"

I shook my head and went into the lobby. Everybody who was going to check in or out had done so, leaving the bellmen to share a tabloid (EXTRATERRESTRIALS IN CONGRESS!) and the desk clerks to stare at me with far more curiosity than I warranted. I took the elevator to the eighth floor and was digging through my purse for the room key as I stepped into the foyer.

Japonica damn near pushed me back into the elevator. I caught myself and said, "What's going on?"

"Hostage situation. Soon as we get backup from the sheriff's department and the state police, we can seal off the floor. You go downstairs."

I realized she had a gun in her hand. Chief Sanderson stood in the corridor, his weapon drawn. An anemic young man who appeared to be within seconds of both physical and emotional disintegration was slumped against the wall.

"What's going on?" I repeated. "Have the ladies from Tuscaloosa kidnapped one of those cute little croupiers to be their sex toy?"

"Get out of here," Japonica said as she moved behind her boss. "We can't know for sure, but we figure he's armed."

"Who?" I asked as I followed her.

Chief Sanderson looked back at me. "Would you mind relocating your ass elsewhere? The pertinent phrase is 'armed and dangerous.' We don't need civilians cluttering up the scene. Japonica here tells me you're a cop, but you're out of your jurisdiction, and you'd damn well better not be carrying. If you don't want to spend the night in jail, go play the slots."

"Floyd," I began in a reasonable tone, "I don't—"

"Put her under arrest," he snapped at Japonica. "Don't bother to charge her with anything; just lock her up and let the judge deal with it on Monday. Could be Tuesday, come to think of it, or even Wednesday. We're at the mercy of the circuit judge. He likes to go duck huntin' this time of year."

I stepped over the extended legs of the young man and positioned myself in front of the door to the stairwell, should the situation deteriorate further. "What the hell is the problem?" I whispered to Japonica.

"Hard to say. Somebody saw a man with a gun in the hall. He had a woman in front of him, and she was looking grim. We're not sure what's going on."

"Estelle?"

"I think so, unless there are two women on this floor with twelve-inch-tall hair. You know what room she's in?"

"Yes, but I think I'd better scoot downstairs before I get arrested. Why don't you call the desk? Ask for a man named Mackenzie Cutting."

Japonica grabbed me before I could push open the door. "They're paging him. Can you help us?"

"If you want me to," I said, sounding as sulky as a wallflower with an empty dance card, as opposed to someone who wanted to trample down Chief Sanderson and burst into Estelle's hotel room à la Mighty Mouse. "This is likely to be the man I was trying to tell you about earlier, the one who locked me on the balcony. He wants something. We should give it to him."

"Sanderson has his own agenda, and reelection is at the top of his list. How's it going to look if he lets this guy walk out of here?"

"How's it going to look if he lets an innocent tourist get killed because he failed to negotiate? Anybody who's ever been to the movies knows that the cops are supposed to negotiate while the SWAT team creeps over the roof."

Japonica grimaced. "You're looking at the SWAT team. That boy on the floor is Sanderson's nephew, Lloyd. Lloyd attends evening classes at the community college, working on a degree in agroeconomics. He's got bad allergies, especially this time of year. He's our sniper."

I looked down at the purported sniper, who was blowing his nose into a grubby handkerchief. "Hey, Lloyd," I said, nudging him with the toe of my shoe, "you ready to cover me if I try to break into the room?"

Lloyd sneezed. "Yeah, sure, just give me a minute. Japonica, did Uncle Floyd remember to bring my gun this time?"

I took a deep breath, then went over to Sanderson and tapped his shoulder. "Why don't I go talk to this man?"

"And get yourself blown across the hall? How am I supposed to explain that to the voters next fall? One more term and I'm officially retired. We've never had an unsolved homicide."

"It won't be unsolved if he shoots me," I pointed out in a remarkably cool voice. "You, Japonica, and Lloyd will all be witnesses. Well, Lloyd will have to get off his rear and come into the hall if he wants to watch the fun, but that's not important. What is important is that this man is holding Estelle in her room. I'm the only person who can talk to him."

"Why's that?"

I didn't have a good answer, but rather than admit it, I rolled my eyes and said, "Haven't you read Japonica's reports? It's all laid out like a recipe for lemon icebox pie. Maybe you should go to the office and get caught up. We'll wait here, our fingers crossed that no one gets hurt until you get back."

"You're one major pain in the neck," Sanderson said, holstering his gun as he stepped back into the foyer. "Anybody else ever tell you that?"

I gave him a tight smile as I went down the hall and knocked on the door of eight-eleven. "Estelle?" I called. "Are you in there?"

The door opened an inch. I could see Estelle's face, whiter than a pillowcase and dazed with fear.

"Arly?" she said huskily.

"You want to go down to the restaurant and have supper?"

"I don't think I can do that just now."

"Has someone got a gun stuck in your back again? I swear, Estelle, I can't take you anywhere without this happening. Let me talk to him."

The man who'd assaulted me earlier took her place. "You must think you're pretty damn funny. Any other jokes before I put a bullet in your friend's head?"

"And then dive off the balcony? In how many languages can you say 'Splat'?" I clapped my hands in case he'd forgotten his previous sound effects.

He grunted. "So what else you got to say?"

"There's a highly trained SWAT team in the parking lot. If you so much as step onto the balcony, you'll be hyperventilating in ways you never thought about before. I guess that covers it."

"Just take the money and let me be," said Estelle from

behind him. "I hadn't even gotten around to considering how to spend it. Easy come, easy go."

"That's not what he's after," I said. "It's something that used to be in Stormy's bag. Of course, if it's in the hotel safe, he's going to have to do more than wave a gun under your nose."

"It's not something she'd have put in the safe," the man said, curling his lip. "She didn't hide it in her hotel room or the one right next door, either."

"Why would she have hid it in here?" I asked.

"'Cause she saw me in Memphis and knew I was after her. Someone saw her carrying three bags yesterday afternoon. She must have switched 'em around."

"You want to look in mine?" said Estelle. "Be my guest."

Out of the corner of my eye I saw Mackenzie edging along the wall toward us. This was not good. I extended my hands. "I'm unarmed. Why don't you let me inside and we'll all search together? Afterward, you can keep me as the hostage until you're out of the hotel and on the road to wherever your heart desires."

Mackenzie was so close that I could hear his shoes scuffling the carpet. Surely he'd been informed that Estelle was in there, I told myself. I glanced toward the elevators. Japonica and Chief Sanderson were watching from behind a potted plant; Lloyd must have chosen a more prudent position, perhaps in a rapidly descending elevator.

"I already looked in here," the man said. "Besides, I don't trust those trigger-happy cops at the end of the hallway. Goddamn amateurs, thinking they'll get their pictures on the front page of the local newspaper for being heroes."

"I'll make sure they agree to meet your demands. They may not be able to arrange for a helicopter to land out front, but they'll cooperate if you want a car and a picnic basket. That's the only way you're going to get out of this, you know. Estelle's prone to fainting when she's scared. I can't see you tossing her over your shoulder like so much dead weight and trotting down the stairs."

Estelle's face reappeared. "I am not prone to anything, thank you very much. If this man wants me to be a hostage, then I can walk out of here on my own two feet. You make me sound like a dirty dishrag. I can't recall when I've ever fainted, not even when the doctor lanced a boil on my buttocks without bothering to give me a local anesthesia. It was not pleasant, let me tell you."

He looked back at her. "You are about the wordiest woman I've ever met. I ought to—"

Mackenzie shoved me aside, shouldered open the door, and fired his gun. The man gave him a stunned look, then crumpled to the floor. Rather than faint, Estelle opted to scream bloody murder (which was partly true). Japonica and Chief Sanderson thundered down the hall. I learned later that Lloyd was the guilty party who panicked and set off the deafening clamor of the fire alarm. An elderly lady in a silk bathrobe charged out of her room, swinging an umbrella. A dog raced past me and disappeared around the corner. Doors flew open and voices demanded to know what was happening. A sprinkler head on the ceiling began to mist us as if we were ferns.

I sat down on the floor. Mackenzie had continued into the room; the door was ajar but I couldn't see what he was doing. Chief Sanderson followed suit, but Japonica stopped and knelt beside me.

"You okay?" she asked.

"Just peachy," I said. "I had the situation under control. The guy was willing to allow Estelle to leave. I really didn't think he would hurt me, as long as everybody stayed calm. That did not happen, as you may have noticed. Why couldn't Mackenzie have held off for a few more minutes?"

"Kind of gung-ho, wasn't he?"

"No kidding." I pushed myself up and wiped water out of my eyes. "I guess I'd better see if Estelle's okay. Why don't you see if you can convince someone at the desk to cut off the alarm and the sprinkler?"

Japonica headed toward the foyer. I went into the room, stepped over the supine body in the same fashion he'd stepped over mine hours earlier, and sat down on the bed next to Estelle. Mackenzie was on the telephone, requesting an ambulance—no lights, no sirens, no unnecessary disruptions. Chief Sanderson was examining what I assumed was the perp's wallet.

"Well, you've still got your winnings," I said to her. "When Ruby Bee has recovered, you two need to take a really boring cruise in which your most pressing problem is how to eat your way through all the buffets without spilling out of your bathing suits."

She looked up with a faint smile. "I'll keep that in mind. Who was he, Arly?"

"I'm pretty sure he was the second man in the car you saw at the Starbright Motel. He was looking for Stormy's duffel bag, which he seemed to think might have ended up in here. Problem is, he already searched it earlier this afternoon. It was in the closet in her room. He also

searched mine, Cherri Lucinda's, Jim Bob's, and Brother
Verber's. He seemed to believe Stormy switched the
three bags she brought upstairs in the elevator. Hers,
yours, and"—I hesitated—"Ruby Bee's. Japonica told me
he'd gone through Stormy's bag and left the contents on
the floor of the closet. You don't think . . . ?"

"Think what?"

"Just sit here. I'll be back." I wormed my way through
the horde of security people who had appeared as if
they'd been delivered on a chartered bus, and went
down a couple of doors to the room I was sharing with
Cherri Lucinda. I let myself in, engaged the chain, and
opened the closet door. The faded flannel nightgown
and support hose were hard to overlook, as was the tube
of denture adhesive. These were not the items a sexually
active young woman packed for the weekend. I was
looking at the contents of Ruby Bee's bag—not
Stormy's. Which meant, of course, that the pertinent
bag was stashed on a shelf several miles away.

I should have returned to Estelle's room to do something, although I had no idea if my presence would be
tolerated, much less allowed. Instead, I went out to the
balcony and stared at the uninspired landscape of the
parking lot as I tried to sort out all the stray bits of information I'd been given.

A few ideas surfaced, but none were such that I could
dash down the hall and impress Chief Sanderson with
my insights. I went inside and dialed the number of the
sheriff's department. I'd expected LaBelle to be gone
for the evening, but she answered with her customary
charm.

"Stump County Sheriff's Department. State your
business."

"This is Arly," I said. "Any chance Harve's still there?"

"How's your mother doing?"

"Not as well as I'd hoped. What about Harve?"

"He's gone for the day, and the deputy in charge is picking his nose and gaping at a gun magazine. I was just on the way out the door, so if you don't have any more—"

"Do you have a list of the employees at the club where the drug bust took place?" I asked.

"Do you realize how many lists this task force has made me write up in the last four days? Every time I turn around, I'm typing up some fool list for them. And by the way, Reverend Hitebred was in here earlier complaining about you. You didn't exactly charm the socks off him. Harve is wanting to discuss that with you."

"Find the list, LaBelle," I said levelly. "I want to know if Cherri Lucinda Crate and Stormy Zimmerman are on it."

"Yes, they are. There's an APB out on both of them. I'd like to think you haven't helped them escape. That'd be aiding and abetting, you know."

"What's the story on them?"

"Both of them were working on the night of the incident. By the time the task force got around to them, their apartments were vacant. Supposedly, they're on vacation, but I know for a fact the DEA boys are looking for them real hard on account of them being at the club when the you-know-what hit the fan."

I sucked on my lip for a moment. "Anybody else missing?"

"I am missing my supper, if that counts. Other than that, various people are wanted for questioning. A couple of thugs were seen hanging around before midnight. A girl, probably not more than sixteen, was shooting pool and asking for trouble. A biker broke a cue stick over someone's head. A bookie got into it with a client. A truck driver put his fist through the front of the jukebox. A flasher was hanging outside the ladies room, doing the raincoat routine. Just your typical night at the Dew Drop Inn."

I made a note not to make dinner reservations there. "Has the money turned up?"

"No, and the DEA boys seem to think there's a kilo of cocaine floating around as well. Their solution is to hang around the bars on Thurber Street, ogling the college girls and drinking beer. Undercover, or so they say. If you ask me—"

"What's a kilo worth?"

"They're saying fifty thousand."

"Oh," I said, as if a mule were dragging a plow across my brain in a painfully slow progression. Furrow by muddy furrow, it came to me. "I think you'd better find Harve and have him call me."

LaBelle cackled. "Long distance? You think our budget is funded by the Publishers Clearing House Sweepstakes?"

"Just do it—okay?"

"I'll call over at his house, but if he's not there, I am most definitely going to my sister's for supper. I promised her I'd come make dried-flower potpourri sachets for a rummage sale at the Voice of the Almighty Lord Assembly Hall. Why she let herself get talked into it is beyond me. Here she is, with two boys under the age of four and a husband that can't hold a job for more than—"

I hung up and stared at the wall. I knew where one of the so-called thugs was, which was on the carpet in Estelle's room. I knew where the kilo of cocaine was, and quite possibly a lot of money. Since the second thug, presumably the bald-headed one, didn't know its location, there was no reason to send the troops (Floyd, Lloyd, and Japonica) to the hospital. The problem was that I didn't know where he was.

I decided to go back to Estelle's room and see what was evolving. As I came into the hall, I found myself in the middle of a stream of blue-haired women of varying size and shape. "Tuscaloosa?" I said hesitantly.

They all stopped and stared at me. "Do we know you?" one of them demanded.

"Aren't you one of Joe Henry Blakeman's daughters?" asked another, staring at me.

A third shook her head. "She has the same jaw, but her build isn't right. The Blakeman girls all have broad hips. Good for childbearing, I suppose."

A dozen sets of eyes assessed my hips. Feeling as if I should give birth in the hall to prove my worth, I said, "Did you all happen to be out here this morning when the woman fell off the balcony?"

"Why's that any of your business?"

I expected at least one of them to smack me with a handbag. "Mama's in the hospital," I said, sucking in my cheeks and doing my best to snivel in an acceptably genteel fashion. "It's all so confusing. I drove all night so I could sit by her bedside, and then this morning I heard that dreadful scream and I guess someone told me you could help me understand what happened. Mama isn't doing so well. If she doesn't get better, I just don't know where to turn. My brother is over at the state hospital, and no one's seen Daddy or any of the dogs since the fire gutted the house."

It didn't make much sense, granted, but they bought

it. Amidst much clucking and patting, I was escorted back into the room and settled in a chair. Seconds later, a damp washcloth was pressed against my forehead. Had it been within their power, I'm sure a cup of tea laced with brandy would have materialized as well.

"You drove all night? It's good to hear young folks still have that kind of regard for their parents," said one of the women. "I'm real sorry your husband couldn't accompany you. Were you able to find someone to look after him and the children?"

There was one and only one right answer. "My sister agreed to see to them," I said, gulping ever so bravely. "LaBelle has three of her own, all as sweet as they can be, but she promised to pick up Kevin and little Rose Marie after school and take them to their piano lessons. Harve will read them a bedtime story as soon as he gets home from the bank." I gazed up at their concerned faces. "You heard that scream?"

All of them nodded. The one who seemed to be the spokeswoman said, "We were on the way to breakfast when we heard it. Hattie stopped so abruptly that poor May ran right into her and fell backward, sending Dorothy crashing into Jewell Ellen. I can't remember when I've seen so many feet and fannies in the air at one time. We were all trying to catch our breath and get everybody off the floor when we realized Jewell Ellen had twisted her ankle. I don't know what we would have done if that nice man from room service hadn't come along. He helped Jewell Ellen back to her room and even called the desk to send up a doctor."

"Someone ought to inform the hotel manager about this conscientious employee," I said. "Did you happen to get his name?"

"There was some Mexican name on his name tag," said one of the ladies. "I was a bit surprised, since he did not have a accent."

"No, he didn't," added another, "and his hair wasn't the least bit greasy."

"What sort of hair did he have?" I asked.

"Short, and fuzzy on top. He reminded me of that unpleasant man from the bakery just down the street from my house. Do you remember him, Hattie?"

"How could I ever forget him?"

I jumped in before we digressed into stale cinnamon buns. "How old was he?"

The general consensus was that he was young, but as I looked at each in turn, I decided that from their perspective youth was relative. Children believe anyone over twenty is ancient; septuagenarians believe anyone under fifty is adolescent.

"But he most definitely had hair?" I asked. "No one would say he was bald?"

They were intractable on this point. Knowing I would never convince them otherwise, I thanked them for their concern and promised to give "Mama" their best wishes for a speedy recovery.

When I returned to Estelle's room, paramedics had arrived and were preparing the body to be transported to the local morgue. Japonica was questioning Estelle, but I could see from both of their expressions that nothing substantive was being communicated. I didn't see how it could be—Estelle had no prior awareness of the man who'd taken her hostage. It was likely he'd been in the car at the Starbright Motel in Memphis, but she'd never seen his face.

Mackenzie Cutting was still on the telephone, speaking in a low, urgent voice. Wondering if he was ordering fruit baskets for everyone on the eighth floor, I sat down across from him and glared until he replaced the receiver.

"Why on earth did you pull that shit?" I said angrily. "Didn't it occur to you that Estelle might have been hurt—or me, for that matter? What if his gun had gone off as he fell? The situation could have been resolved peacefully if you hadn't blundered in like that!"

"It seemed like the quickest and quietest way to handle it."

"To shoot him?" I said, raising my eyebrows. "If you develop a hangnail, are you going to cut off your finger or your whole arm?"

Mackenzie glanced up as the paramedics wheeled the gurney out the door. "Be sure and take the service elevator," he said to them, then looked at me. "My primary concern is the well-being of our guests. I perceived one of them to be in danger. The man had a gun, Miss Hanks. Should I have invited him to join me in the bar for cocktails and counseling?"

"No," I said, "I suppose not."

"What did you mean when you mentioned all these bags? Do you have a reason to think someone from C'Mon Tours has brought an illegal substance into the hotel? If so, you need to tell me where it is right now. We don't want any hint of scandal at The Luck of the Draw. We rely on our reputation to renew our gaming license each year."

Estelle came out of the bathroom, her lipstick applied by a noticeably unsteady hand. "Arly," she said as she sat down next to me, "that was a brave thing you did—talking to that terrible man like he was nothing but a backwoods Buchanon. You risked your life, and I appreciate it." She glowered at Mackenzie. "You, on the other hand, made a real mess of it, didn't you? Arly here had everything under control, but you had to come charging through the door like a professional wrestler. You're darn lucky no one else got hurt."

"What is going on in here?" demanded Mrs. Jim Bob as she came into the room. "There are all sorts of wild stories being repeated out in the hall. I must say, Estelle, that these stories seem to imply that you're involved with the wrong sort of people. I have enough to worry about without being exposed to a procession of gangsters all night long. Perhaps it might be better if you moved your things to another room, preferably not on this floor."

Chief Sanderson cleared his throat. "Even though we all saw what happened, Japonica is going to have to get signed statements. It can wait till morning, long as nobody's planning to leave town anytime soon. Any problem with that?"

No one, including Japonica, seemed inclined to argue. Chief Sanderson jammed his hat on his head and left the room. Japonica and Mackenzie followed him.

"Well?" said Mrs. Jim Bob. "Is someone going to explain why my bag has been emptied on the floor? If you wanted to borrow toothpaste, you should have asked instead of just pawing through—through my things and making such a mess." Tears began to slide down her cheeks. "Would that have been too much to ask?"

SIXTEEN

Estelle opened her purse and handed Mrs. Jim Bob a tissue. "You're tuckered out from the long drive. You just sit down and I'll gather up your things."

"Thank you," Mrs. Jim Bob said as she dabbed her nose. "This has been a trying day. First, Jim Bob goes and gets himself arrested like a common criminal, and then has the audacity to—" She took a deep breath. "You do believe he's innocent, don't you?"

"Yes," I said, "I know he is. I just wish he'd sat tight until I could convince Chief Sanderson and Japonica. Anyway, you don't need to worry. Everything will be straightened out by morning."

She tried unsuccessfully to suppress the dribble of tears down her pale cheeks. "I just feel so confused. It's obvious Jim Bob came here for reasons I can't bring myself to consider. I don't know what to do."

Holding her hand did not appeal. "Is Brother Verber still in the bar? I can try to find him for you."

"Brother Verber is in his room. He assured me that he felt the need to read the Bible and pray in solitude for the redemption of Jim Bob's soul, which appears to be in need of all the assistance it can get." She took a final swipe at her eyes. "It is well past my bedtime. I'm sure the Good Lord will not begrudge me a few hours of rest." She took her bag and went into the bathroom.

"I need to go downstairs," I said to Estelle, "but first, I want you to tell me every last thing that happened from the moment you and Ruby Bee climbed on the van."

Estelle seemed to enjoy her few minutes in the limelight. We went through hairstyling, tuna-salad sandwiches, and so many petty squabbles that I myself would have preferred to take a swim in the muddy Mississippi than put up with the pilgrims.

Once she'd run out of steam, I said, "Can I trust you to stay here?"

"Never in all my days have I broken my word when it mattered. I think I'd rather wait in your room, though. Mrs. Jim Bob doesn't sound like she's in the mood to order sandwiches from room service and watch movies. Besides, I'd like to have a word with Cherri Lucinda."

I gave her my key. "Put the chain on the door, and don't open it for plumbers, hotel security, other people on the tour, cops, room service, anybody. Got that?"

Estelle nodded. I took the elevator down to the lobby, wondering if there was any way to find Baggins in the Saturday night chaos of the casino. As I pushed open the doors, I came close to recoiling. The music was louder, the voices more strident, and slot machines cacophonic in their desire to assure all players that fortunes awaited those who risked one last coin. The shouts from the direction of the craps tables brought to mind a pack of hyenas closing in on a wounded gazelle.

I wound my way toward the roulette tables. A dozen were active, ringed with optimists wearing everything from T-shirts to minks. As before, Baggins had one of the few dark faces. I grabbed his arm and literally dragged him to the relative calm of the bar.

"What's your problem?" he said sulkily.

I pushed him down into a chair and waved off a waitress. "Why did the itinerary change?"

"You need to ask Miss Vetchling. I'm nothing but the hired help. I do what I'm told."

"Not good enough."

"Sweet Jesus, why don't you go on over to the hospital and worry about your mama? Here she is, sick as a dog, and all you can do is—"

"Yesterday at noon you announced that the tour would not be staying the night in Tupelo as promised in the flyer. Why?"

Baggins sank back and rubbed his forehead. "Miss Vetchling got a call from this lady in Little Rock who'd caught wind that her son was eloping. It seems him and Taylor ran into someone on Beale Street who spilled the beans. The lady insisted that the tour not stay the night in Tupelo, but instead come on over here. Miss Vetchling agreed."

"For a sum, I suppose."

"She ain't the patron-saint of travel agents. I felt real bad about disappointing Taylor, but I didn't have any choice. The motel in Tupelo wasn't much fancier than the Starbright, anyway. At least you get clean sheets and cable here."

"When were you informed of the change in the plans?" I asked.

"While everybody was at Graceland. Soon as I got off the phone, Todd staggered out of the men's room and damn near barfed on me. Taylor and I hauled him back to the van. The rest of them showed up within a few minutes and we left. Do you mind if I get back to my game?"

"Go on," I said, taking his seat. Baggins would never admit he'd discussed the itinerary with the thugs in the motel parking lot in Memphis—but his information that night had been wrong. The tour had not stayed in Tupelo the previous night.

Interesting.

"Miss Hanks," said Rex Malanac as he sat down beside me, "are you ready for that margarita I promised you earlier? Frozen or on the rocks?"

I bit back an annoyed response and looked at him. His face was mottled. Sweat beaded on his earlobes like pearl earrings. His hair resembled a rigid cap of carbon.

Before I could reply, he grabbed my hand and said, "I was wondering if you could do a minor favor for me. There's been a most embarrassing mix-up with my credit card. If you loan me a few hundred dollars, I'll pay you back later tonight. My luck has to change; I can feel it in my bones. I've studied the fine art of blackjack and I know how to play the percentages. Anyone can have a momentary bad run. A couple of lucky hits and I'll be where I started, and then some. Why, I can even give you a small fee for the use of your funds for an hour. Ten percent, shall we say?"

"I don't have a few hundred dollars in my checking account," I said, "and my credit cards are maxed out."

"Then whatever you've got."

"Let me ask you something, Rex. If you're such a well-known authority on Elvis, why did you come on this tour? I'd think you've been to Graceland and Tupelo more times than you can count."

"Well, yes, I have been to those places in the past." He found a paper napkin on the next table and wiped his forehead. "I just thought it might be refreshing to stand beside someone viewing them for the first time. A neophyte might see something that we popular scholars have overlooked all these years, or at least offer an amusingly naive interpretation. I brought along a notebook to record such observations."

"But you didn't go on the Graceland tour."

"I intended to catch up with them as soon as I'd taken a look in the souvenir shops." He wadded up the napkin and dropped it on the table between us. "About that loan . . . ?"

"Did Cherri Lucinda recognize you?" I asked abruptly. "Do you frequent the Dew Drop Inn out by the airport?"

"Why would I do a ludicrous thing like that? I'm a tenured professor at Farber College, not some sleazy miscreant who finds bliss in drinking longneck bottles of beer and listening to atrocious music on a jukebox. I spend my evenings at concerts, poetry readings, and theater productions, or at home in the company of Brahms and Beethoven. I'd never seen Miss Crate until she climbed onto the C'Mon Tours van two days ago."

"You've never utilized the services of a bookie at the Dew Drop Inn? Your name won't be on the list of members?"

Rex stood up. "It most certainly will not. Feel free to confirm this in any way you see fit."

He stalked away. I leaned back and tried to think, despite the sensory overload that was as aggravating as the wind outside the casino. A waitress approached and looked inquiringly at me. I shook my head, further addling my thoughts. What were the odds I was totally and hopelessly wrong?

Three to two, or something like that.

Brother Verber was in the fanciest suite he'd ever seen in his entire life. Not only were there television sets in the sitting room and the bedroom, but there was also a little one in the bathroom, along with two commodes (one without a proper seat) and a telephone.

He dried his hands and went back out to beam at his new friends. "I'm just tickled pink about your enthusiasm," he said, having the tiniest bit of trouble with the syllables of the final word. "I can almost see us marching into the casino and bringing all that sinfulness to a halt."

"Oh, preacher," said a woman with tawny hair and big violet eyes, "so can I—as soon as you teach us the rest of your delightfully prudish song. How about a little something to wet your whistle?"

Brother Verber had always had a weakness for violet eyes. He allowed her to put a glass in his hand, then surveyed the dozen or so young people sprawled around the room. "All right," he said, "the second verse goes like this: 'Lustful thoughts and masturbation and naked breasts; obscenities, promiscuity, queers, and rape; sacrilege and titillatin' bathing suits; unseemly shorts that make a man to gape.' "

"That's divine," drawled a young man who was draped across a chair. "Todd, you must allow us to sing it at your wedding. I can't think when I last heard someone use the word 'queer.' It's so quaint. Your mother will love it."

"Inspired by the Almighty Lord," said Brother Verber. "It all came to me yesterday morning like a bolt of lightning from above. I was so overcome that I bowed my head and offered heartfelt thanks for the blessing."

The tawny-haired woman took the paper out of his hand. "Okay, everybody, listen once more to the lyrics and then we'll take our best shot. If Todd's mother won't let us sing it during the ceremony, we'll do it at the reception at the club."

Brother Verber wanted to give her a hug to express his gratitude, but instead drained the glass and gave her a broad grin. Who said young folks had lost their appreciation for that old-fashioned religion?

Saddam was snoring like a rock-crusher. Joy had staggered into the bedroom half an hour earlier and was currently stretched out across the bed, her feet twitching every now and then like she was a dog dreaming about a coon hunt.

Jim Bob eyed the crumpled bills on the floor next to Saddam's feet. A few of them might solve his problem with paying for a taxi back to the hotel, but might also lead to an unpleasant incident with a chainsaw if Saddam woke up and discovered his loss.

And how the hell did he think he was going to find a taxi, anyway? If there was one in this pissant town, the driver surely had been alerted to watch for the escaped prisoner last seen holding up a convenience store in the company of two of the most disturbing people Jim Bob had ever met.

It was hard to know exactly where he was. He'd seen flat fields on all sides when Joy had careened up the road and slammed on the brakes in front of the sorry excuse for a house. Headlights had flashed on a distant line of trees. He had an idea which direction the highway was, but if he headed that way, Saddam would know where to look for him.

Holding his breath, Jim Bob turned the knob and eased open the door. There was no sudden bellow from behind him. He stepped down on the cement block that served as a porch, pulled the door closed with only the faintest grate, then sprinted around the corner of the house and ducked behind a tool shed.

He made himself stay down until he'd counted to a hundred. What moonlight there was was filtered through clouds, but he could make out trees not more than a hundred yards away. Even if Saddam woke up, he might figure Jim Bob had stepped outside to piss. In a couple of minutes, though, he would realize what was happening.

Jim Bob wasted a second considering the wisdom of his actions, then began to zigzag across the field, grazing his knuckles on the jagged stalks and praying he didn't make a decent target. Chainsaws demanded proximity; guns didn't.

The field was a mess of mud and icy puddles, and it wasn't nearly as level as it had looked. Jim Bob lurched across endless rows, tripping and sprawling every third step or so, trying his best not to imagine a gun aimed at the middle of his back. If he'd ever wondered where his hackles were, he was damn sure he knew now.

When he reached the line of trees, he was gasping so raggedly that he could see blotches of light inside his head. He threw himself down and rolled under what proved to be a patch of briers. The stench of decay was nearly overwhelming, but he burrowed deeper until he was sure no flashlight could penetrate the branches.

He wasn't technically a fugitive from a chain gang, he

thought with a sigh, but there were some noticeable similarities.

Martha Hitebred studied her reflection in the mirror. Changing clothes in the church was not only difficult in the dark, but a bone-chilling ordeal as well. Now, with her father down there, most likely hunkered on his desk like a turkey vulture, she could take her sweet time adjusting her skirt and combing out her hair. She didn't quite have the nerve to smoke a cigarette in the house, but she put one between her lips and pretended she was a slinky torch singer in a nightclub thousands of miles away.

"Anton," she murmured to an invisible suitor, frowning ever so slightly, "how presumptuous to think I'll share a bottle of champagne with you this evening. I am leaving for Paris at midnight. Go away."

Anton obediently faded. Martha pinched her cheeks until they pinkened, turned out the lights (her father seemed to equate the electric bill with the national debt), and went out to her car. She couldn't trust the old fart to stay at the church all night, but she figured she was safe for several hours. Even if he came home, he'd assume she was at the homeless shelter, as she claimed to be several nights a week, spreading the gospel.

Close enough.

SEVENTEEN

I brooded long enough to hatch an illusionary egg or two, then went back into the hotel and down the hall to the private offices in the netherworld behind the registration area. Mackenzie was seated at his desk, scribbling what was apt to be a vaguely worded press release to explain away a teeny disturbance on the eighth floor.

"I have a question about security," I said as I sat down and propped my feet on the corner of his desk. The posture wasn't as comfortable as in my personal domain in Maggody, but it was not time to be picky.

"Shoot," he said, then winced. "Poor choice of words. What's your question?"

"Let's say I arrive at the hotel in search of my great-aunt, who's eloped with her hairdresser. I don't want her to know I'm on her trail. If I slip the desk clerk twenty bucks, will he tell me her room number?"

"Absolutely not. It's grounds for immediate dismissal. The only jobs in this region are in the hotels and casinos, and all of us crosscheck references very thoroughly. Nobody with enough wits to determine the room number would dare give it out."

"That's what I figured," I said, frowning. "I wonder how he knew which room Stormy was in."

Mackenzie sighed. "Is this an obscure reference to this enigmatic bald man? Give it up, Miss Hanks. The police have the killer in custody. Twelve witnesses have sworn that no one else could have been in the hotel room."

"I ran into the ladies earlier, and I have to agree that they seemed reasonably sharp."

"Well, then, if you don't mind, I need to continue working on my report of the incident." He picked up a pen and began to shuffle his notes.

Politely overlooking his hint that I make myself scarce, I said, "Actually, there were thirteen witnesses. The ladies from Tuscaloosa and the guy from room service. Did you talk to him about it?"

Mackenzie slapped down the pen. "No, I did not. I have no idea if Chief Sanderson or Deputy Jones bothered with him. I hope not. The food service employees are an edgy group; the presence of a uniformed officer in the kitchen area would have caused a major stir."

"I want to talk to him."

"Out of the question. This is a very busy time for them. Besides, his appearance at dawn suggests he's working the midnight shift. If you're going to be stubborn—and I can see you are—then perhaps I can arrange for you to meet with him early tomorrow morning."

"I really don't want to spend the night in this chair, Mackenzie. Can you get me a rollaway bed?"

Glowering, he snatched up the receiver and jabbed a button. I felt a twinge of sympathy for whoever had the ill fortune to answer at the other end. "Cutting here," he snarled. "I want to know who delivered a tray to the east wing on the eighth floor this morning around six. I don't know the room number. Once you have the name, find out if he's currently on duty. Call me back as soon as possible."

He hung up and gave me a chilly look. "Satisfied, Miss Hanks?"

"Want to play a couple of hands of gin while we wait?"

Estelle searched through Cherri Lucinda's bag, not sure what she thought she'd find that might explain who the bald man was. She found nothing more damning than some dingy bras and a lace nightie with some mighty peculiar holes. All the plastic bottles of shampoo, conditioner, and moisturizer in the bathroom seemed innocent, although she was afraid to dump out the contents to make sure there were no precious jewels at the bottom.

She was about to open the closet and rummage through coat pockets when she heard a key slide into the lock. Her heart pounding, she scurried over to a chair and was reaching for the clicker when Cherri Lucinda and Rex came into the room.

"Estelle?" said Cherri Lucinda. "What are you doing in here? I found a note saying Arly was going to sleep in the other bed. Has there been a change in plans?"

"I decided to sit in here in case the hospital calls. Why's he here?"

Rex smiled so broadly that Estelle couldn't help but think of crazy old Merle Hardcock in his Evel Knievel period. "Cherri Lucinda offered to loan me a bit of money for a few hours," he said.

"But you have to pay it back," Cherri Lucinda said primly. "Jim Bob won't like it one bit if he gets out of jail and finds out you took his winnings from last night."

"No problem," he said. "I have analyzed and identified the flaw in my method. Once corrected, the contents of the casino coffers will be mine, and you will have your cut. I'll even add a chip to Jim Bob's stash. We'll all have champagne for breakfast."

"I don't much care for champagne," said Estelle, feeling contrary for no good reason. "Rex, would you step out to the balcony for a minute? There's something I want to ask Cherri Lucinda here."

"Girl talk, I suppose," he said, chuckling as he opened the sliding door and went onto the balcony. "Don't be all night, please. I'd like to get back down to the casino and start raking in their money. Unlike the three of us, the night is young."

"What's his problem?" Estelle demanded as she pulled Cherri Lucinda into the bathroom. "Is he drunk?"

"I don't think so. He was kinda mopey when he found me downstairs, but once I said he could borrow Jim Bob's chips, he cheered up. Do you know anything about Jim Bob? Do they have strict visiting hours at the jail? Should I take him a toothbrush?"

"Now that Mrs. Jim Bob's here, you'd better pretend you never met him." Estelle peeked out the bathroom door to make sure Rex was still on the balcony, then said, "Who was that bald man you were talking to in the bar earlier?"

Cherri Lucinda studied her reflection in the mirror. "Him? He came into the club the other night and bought me a drink between shows. I don't recollect him telling me his name, but most of the customers don't. The ones that do are all named John or Joe. Strange, isn't it?"

"Real strange. Did he ask you about Stormy?"

"No. We mostly talked about how the weather was better than it was up north. I told him about the Elvis Pilgrimage, but I might as well have been talking about my favorite brand of shampoo. He couldn't have been less interested."

"And this evening?"

"He said he was real surprised to see me, that his company had sent him over to Memphis for the weekend and he'd just happened to come down to The Luck of the Draw to relax for a couple of hours. Considering how many casinos there are, it's pretty funny, isn't it?" She shoved a handful of curls across one eye. "Unless it's destiny, of course. My horoscope said I might encounter someone from my past. I guess the middle of last week counts as the past."

Estelle managed a nod. "Fate can't be ignored. What else did he have to say?"

"He was real curious about what we'd done in Tupelo and if we might have stopped somewhere other than the museum and birthplace. When I told him how Baggins had allowed us all of half an hour before heading the van toward this place, he told me that if I ever got back to Memphis, he'd take me over there so I could poke around to my heart's content. I thought that was a mighty kind gesture on his part. He ain't the handsomest man I've ever seen, but he has nice manners."

"That's all you know about him? He came to the place where you work, and then popped up here today?"

Cherri Lucinda leaned toward the mirror. "You got it.

Now maybe I don't have what you'd call prominent cheekbones, but my chin doesn't pooch and these little lines around my eyes are on account of exhaustion. I mean, I haven't had a decent night's sleep since before I can remember. I may be puffy, but I don't see how you can say my face is plump. I feel like I've been accused of looking like a piece of fruit."

Estelle tried not to let her eyeballs roll back. "Your face is not plump. All I said was—"

"I distinctly recall the word 'plump.' "

"Pleasingly plump," said Estelle, sitting down on the edge of the bathtub and trying to think.

"Okay," I said to Mackenzie, who was hardly the most scintillating company I'd kept lately, "look at it this way. The men whom we shall call Brown and Bald determined that Stormy ended up with a kilo of cocaine and a lot of money. She couldn't go back to her apartment or so much as set foot in the bus station or airport. She decided to join the tour and jump ship in Memphis. You with me thus far?"

Mackenzie continued to scratch on a piece of paper. He was making a very faint sound that might have involved the grinding of teeth, but I opted to ignore it, since he was clearly under duress.

As were we all.

I recrossed my legs, leaned back in the chair, and let my head fall back. "So Stormy got on the C'mon Tour van with every expectation of slipping away into the night in Memphis. However, Brown and Bald showed up at the Starbright Motel and made it clear they were watching her, and the neighborhood was so dangerous that she could hardly duck down alleys. She had Estelle restyle her hair, but B&B were at Graceland the next morning, still after her. Once the schedule changed, she must have thought she'd be safe here for the night—especially since she'd stashed her bag in a safe place."

Mackenzie glanced up at me. "Perhaps you could play solitaire until the head of food services calls?"

"Only the lonely play solitaire," I said. "So Stormy went down to the casino and shoveled coins into the slots for a few hours. Eventually, she got bored and went to bed."

"You are about to put me to sleep with this story," Mackenzie said. "If I give you a hundred dollars' worth of chips, will you promise to go fritter them away in the casino? How about a dinner voucher for the restaurant? A ticket for the floor show? We were unable to book El Vez this weekend, but we have a fantastic total-sensory presentation called 'Elvisaromatica.' "

"You jest," I said, crunching my heels down on his thickening pile of yellow papers. "What we need to think about is the fact that B&B were under the impression that the tour group would be in Tupelo last night. Baggins, who does not strike me as a morally upright individual, no doubt told them what he himself had been told about where the tour group would be staying."

To say his sigh was long-suffering would be an insult to his prodigious effort, which might have been an attempt to blow me out of his office. "So what, Miss Hanks? Based on your reasoning, neither of these insidious 'B' men was in the hotel when Stormy was pushed off the balcony. We know who pushed her. Is there anything short of calling armed guards to make you go away?"

"Try room service."

"They're busy, but as soon as someone has a moment to look at the records . . ." He picked up the receiver and hit a button as if it were a pustule. "Cutting. I want the name now. I don't care if Bill and Hillary are awaiting dinner in the Presidential Suite." After a moment, he shook his head and put down the receiver. "The problem is they can't find an order to the east wing at any time between midnight and eight. This doesn't mean there wasn't one. Computers screw up, as we both know. Why don't you go on to bed, and I'll call you in the morning when I have the waiter's name?"

"Jim Bob saw a tray when he went into the room to get Cherri Lucinda's bag. When was it ordered?"

"He was drunk. Doesn't it seem likely that Stormy decided to have dinner in the room before she went down to the casino? I cannot keep badgering the staff. At this hour, as many as a hundred orders are backed up."

I shuffled the cards. "How about blackjack? You'll have to run through the rules for me. Does a straight beat a flush?"

His composure seemed to be cracking around the edges. He took a neatly folded handkerchief from his pocket, blotted his forehead, and then reached for the telephone. "I solemnly swear this will be my final call, Raoul. Last night someone delivered a tray to room number eight-thirteen. I need to know the exact time, and I suppose the name of the waiter." He took another swipe with the handkerchief as he waited. "Are you quite sure? No orders from that room yesterday or today? No, no, there hasn't been a complaint. Thanks, Raoul. I will not call again."

I stood up. "I need your gun."

"What you need, Miss Hanks, is a therapist to help you work through your persistent paranoia." The telephone rang. "Raoul must have found it. If the employee is not on duty, I'll give you his home address. I'm sure he and his family will welcome an unexpected guest with a long list of questions." Smirking, he picked up the receiver. "I hope this hasn't disrupted—"

He listened for a long moment, his mouth tight with irritation. "I think, Miss Oppers, that you share Miss Hanks's affinity for fantasies. Jim Bob Buchanon must have left his coat on the balcony for some reason. The wind blew it into a corner. Or maybe someone with an immature sense of humor dropped a bag of garbage from a higher floor. However, if it will ease your mind, I'll get a key and have a look."

"What?" I said as he hung up.

"According to Miss Oppers and other members of this wretched tour, there is a body on the balcony of room eight-fifteen. She acknowledges that it's dark, but she's adamant that they can see the outline of a human form. The adjoining door is locked, so they're unable to investigate. This is too much, Miss Hanks. I will personally make sure that C'Mon Tours is not allowed to enter the state of Mississippi ever again."

"Let's go, Mackenzie," I said, "and for pity's sake, bring your gun."

Not even Muzak could have enlivened our elevator ride to the eighth floor. As we went down the hall, Mrs. Jim Bob came out of the room she was sharing with Estelle. She stared at Mackenzie, no doubt thinking I'd lapsed into the ultimate moral depravity and would end up with a two-toned infant, then said, "There you are,

Arly. The doctor at the hospital called and wants you to call him back. Also, Harvey Dorfer called, but didn't leave a message. It's been impossible for me to so much as close my eyes."

"Is Brother Verber still in his room?" I asked.

"How should I know? I am not his keeper any more than I'm your private secretary."

I took a breath. "Estelle says she can see a body on his balcony."

Mrs. Jim Bob's eyes widened, but before she could sputter a response, Mackenzie said, "This is not confirmed, ma'am. Miss Oppers has been seeing all sorts of things today. I will not be surprised when she claims to have encountered Elvis in the stairwell."

"Actually, he's out in the parking lot," I said, then went into the room that had originally been assigned to Stormy and Cherri Lucinda. Estelle was slumped on a bed. Cherri Lucinda was on the balcony, holding up a flickering cigarette lighter as if she were a human lighthouse. As I joined her, I noticed Rex leaning against the rail.

"What do you see?" I asked.

"I'm darn near positive that's a shoe," Cherri Lucinda said. "Where there's a shoe, there's apt to be a foot and a leg and . . . so forth."

I could make out a mound next to the sliding door. I went back into the room and said to Mackenzie, "I can't tell from here. It could be an overcoat, or it could be a very inert person."

"Oh, dear God," gurgled Mrs. Jim Bob. "It's Brother Verber, isn't it? He went out for a breath of air, then fainted and froze to death. I feel like I'm being visited by the plagues of Egypt. Are frogs gonna start raining down on my head?"

Mackenzie tried the door that adjoined the two rooms, but it was indeed locked from the opposite side. "I guess we'd better take a look," he said to me.

I told Estelle to restrain Mrs. Jim Bob, who was gulping noisily and carrying on about lice, locusts, and flies. I trailed Mackenzie out into the hall and waited while he unlocked the door.

"I didn't think anybody was staying here," he said as we went inside. "Who's Brother Verber?"

"I'll explain if necessary." The room did not appear to have been disturbed since I'd been in it earlier. It hadn't been tidied up, either. The whiskey bottle was still half full—a promising sign that Brother Verber had not come back for his purported solitary prayer vigil.

Resisting the urge to allow Mackenzie to do the dirty work, I opened the sliding door. "There's a body, all right," I said over my shoulder. "I feel as though I should consider him an old friend, but I don't know his name."

Mackenzie nudged me aside. "Well, Miss Hanks, you're not quite as paranoid as I'd assumed. He most definitely is bald."

"He *was* bald. Now he's dead," I added, gazing at the wire that had been twisted tightly around his neck.

"Is Dahlia home?" said Kevin as he and his pa drove away from the county jail.

"You plannin' to show her how purty you look in lipstick, boy?" growled Earl. "When this gets out, I'll be ashamed to show my face at the feed store. Everybody's gonna assume you're a faggot. Why'd you have to go and put on lipstick before you stole the four-wheel?"

Kevin cringed against the door. "It's kinda hard to explain. I dint want Dahlia to recognize me if she looked in the rearview mirror. If I caught up with her, I mean. Is she back home?"

"No, your ma was still over at your house when you called. You're damn lucky you're not spending the next five years in jail for grand theft auto—and if you'd taken anybody else's vehicle, you would. Despite being kin, Canon was ready to press charges. He finally backed off when I reminded him of the money his pa still owes me for that parcel of land down by Boone Creek. I ain't never gonna get it now."

"I'm real sorry, Pa," Kevin said, staring at the dashboard. "I was trying to keep my family together. I guess Dahlia's run off with another man. I should have seen how tired she was and figured out a way for her to rest up until she was her regular sweet-natured self again. The doctor called it something fancy, but I just thought of it as the baby blues times two."

"I can't see her running off," Earl said. "Buchanon women don't do that. Well, there was Maizie Grace, but she was always flighty. You recollect her?"

"Yeah, Pa." Kevin turned away to hide the tears forming in his eyes.

Earl cleared his throat. "Quit your sniveling and see if you can get a ball game on the radio. You're stupider than cow spit, but you ain't a faggot—okay?"

The Reverend Edwin W. Hitebred's eyes flew open. It took him several seconds to remember where he was and, more important, why he was there. The Mount Zion Church was under siege by satanists, and he alone was willing to risk his life to defend it. He'd armed himself with a Bible, a crucifix, and the vial of holy water he'd purchased at a tent revival back in 1967.

But he couldn't allow himself to nod off again. No matter how uncomfortable the chair, no matter if his back started aching and his knees began to throb, no matter if the satanists set fire to the church, he would be ready.

He started as he heard a creak. It seemed to come from overhead rather than out in the main room. Could that be how they were breaking into the church? Hitebred held his breath and strained to hear the sounds of footsteps on the roof.

After a good thirty seconds, he exhaled. He'd pretty much convinced himself that most likely it had been nothing but wind when he heard a hoot from outside. It could have been an owl—but it could have been a signal. He forced himself to go over to the window and peer out. If they were crawling on their bellies like the serpents they were, they were staying too low to be seen.

He'd just resettled in the chair when he heard a car drive by. Either folks down the road were on their way home—or the satanists were making sure the church was empty before coming inside.

It occurred to Hitebred that he might be in for a long, cold night.

Mackenzie was calling Chief Sanderson as I left the room and went next door. "There is a body," I announced, "but it's not anyone you know. Estelle, let me have your room key. I need to make a call."

"You're sure it's not Brother Verber?" whispered Mrs. Jim Bob, who was calmer but still trembling.

"I'm sure." I went to Estelle's room and called the hospital. "Dr. Deweese, please," I said.

"He left about an hour ago for Memphis. He'll be back on Monday. If there's an emergency, you're supposed to—"

"Is Carlette there?"

"She damn well better be. Hang on and I'll transfer you to the nurses' station."

I recognized Carlette's voice when she answered the phone. I identified myself, then said, "How's Ruby Bee?"

"Just doing real well, honey. She passed an enormous gallstone. It wasn't like a basketball or anything, but it was big enough to have caused all her misery. She's out of pain and sleeping like a baby. Dr. Deweese said she can go home in the morning."

I fell back on the bed as a knot of anxiety three times bigger than a basketball began to unravel. "She's okay? Her fever's down?"

"Coming down. Her head'll clear up now that she's off the pain medication. She told me to tell you to leave her be so she can get a decent night's sleep. She'll expect you at eight o'clock tomorrow morning, and she wants biscuits and gravy for breakfast."

I forced myself to sit up. "Thanks, Carlette. I'll tell Dr. Deweese how supportive you've been. I hope you get a raise or something."

Carlette laughed. "About all I can expect is to be named employee of the week. That means I get to decide what kind of pizza we'll order on Friday. Other than that, I'll be making minimum wage till I retire in forty years."

"I need another favor," I said. "I left Ruby Bee's bag in the closet in her room. Could you find a safe place to keep it until tomorrow, preferably a locked cabinet or storeroom?"

"Somebody hot to steal her nightgown?"

"Just do this, please, and don't mention it to anyone else. I'll explain in the morning."

"Whatever," she said.

When I went out to the hall, I found Estelle waiting for me. I told her the news about Ruby Bee, and both of us were damp when we finished hugging. "That means we can leave tomorrow," I added. "I can hardly wait to see this place in the rearview mirror."

"Mackenzie said that the body on the balcony is the bald man. What in tarnation was he doing in there? Was he looking for Jim Bob?"

"I don't know why he went in there. His colleague had already searched the room earlier today. Maybe the two of them had a falling out late this afternoon. The man with the brown hair thought the room would be a safe place to leave the body for the rest of the day."

Estelle gnawed on her lip. "Nope, on account of I saw the bald man with Cherri Lucinda right when I hit the jackpot. I left the casino not more than five minutes later, and that's when that nasty man poked me with a gun and made me get into the elevator with him."

"Is there anything else you forgot to mention?"

"Don't get your nose out of joint. I did think to ask Cherri Lucinda about the bald man. She said he was nothing more than a customer who'd shown up at the club where she works."

"Yo!" called Baggins as he came down the hall. "I have been looking all over the casino, but not one tour member is down there. The show starts in ten minutes, and your tickets are paid for." He nodded at me. "You can have your mama's. C'Mon Tours wants everybody to be happy."

"Oh, Baggins, we *are* all happy," I said. "Cherri Lucinda and Rex are in this room. I can't promise they're in the mood for Elvisaromatica, but you can ask."

"Taylor's in there, too," contributed Estelle. "Of course the only thing that's gonna perk her up is Todd walking through the door."

"Where is he?" asked Baggins.

"Why don't you ask her?" I said as I steered him into the room.

The room was growing crowded. Taylor and Mrs. Jim Bob were off in the corner conversing; from their expressions, I had a feeling the perfidy of the male species was the subject. Cherri Lucinda and Rex had appropriated the two chairs. Mackenzie was seated on a bed, watching the others as if he anticipated a pack attack. Baggins opened his mouth, then closed it and moved to a neutral corner.

Nobody seemed to have much to say. I was about to suggest we turn on CNN when Japonica and Chief Sanderson came into the room.

"Medical examiner and paramedics are next door," Sanderson said gruffly. "This is a right dangerous place to stay. I'm thinking I'll get my mother-in-law a room when she comes this summer. Anybody have anything to say?"

"I do, Floyd," I said. "You had no way of knowing that all this goes back to what took place at a nightclub in Farberville earlier in the week. The name of the club is the Dew Drop Inn."

"You're making this up!" squeaked Cherri Lucinda. "The only thing that ever happens is when some drunk throws a frat boy through a window, and that's not more than two or three times a month."

"It was a tad more serious. A drug deal went haywire, and in the confusion someone absconded with fifty thousand dollars and a kilo of cocaine. Stormy, to be precise. She thought the Elvis Pilgrimage would be a safe way to get out of the state, but two of the unhappy dealers came after her. Several of the tour members spotted them, and Baggins here was gracious enough to spell out the itinerary for them."

"I did no such thing," Baggins said indignantly.

Estelle jabbed a finger in his direction. "I saw you talking to them, Hector Baggins. Don't go pretending they wanted your grandma's recipe for turnip greens. You were so scared you almost pissed your pants."

"Did not!" he snapped.

"Did, too!" she shot back.

I intervened before they degeneratated into spitting and hair-pulling. "Yes, you did. All they wanted was Stormy's bag, but she was hanging onto it like a cockle-burr. They had no luck Thursday night in Memphis, and they had no luck Friday night because C'Mon Tours never showed up at the motel in Tupelo. The two men arrived here today. One of them forced his way into this room and searched the bags. Someone tipped them off that Stormy had graciously offered to bring Estelle's and Ruby Bee's bags to their room, so eventually the same man created an opportunity to search their bags, too. It did not end well for him."

Cherri Lucinda waved her hand. "Okay, so what you're saying might explain why Stormy came along with us. But you're also saying this bald man and the other one weren't even here when Stormy was pushed off the balcony at dawn this morning. Did Jim Bob do it after all?"

"He most certainly did not!" snapped Mrs. Jim Bob. She narrowed her eyes. "Why does that concern you, missy? Have I seen you somewhere before?"

Japonica moved into the space between them. "Go ahead, Arly. This is better than a miniseries."

I shrugged. "No, Jim Bob didn't do it. The person who did it was desperate for money, and he had a good idea what he might find in Stormy's bag, assuming he could get it. Desperate for money because he's a compulsive gambler. How much did you lose last night, Rex?"

"A significant sum," he said crossly.

"I thought he was an Elvis scholar," said Taylor. "Besides, he's a college professor. He's most assuredly not the sort to be a compulsive gambler. They shoot craps in filthy basements and hang out at racetracks."

"Not always. Rex is so dedicated to gambling that he donned a disguise and infiltrated the tour simply to get into the casino. How long ago were you banned from every casino along this strip?"

"Who says I was?"

"I do," said Mackenzie. "The hairpiece had me fooled, but now that I have a good look at—"

"So what? You asses refused me credit just when I felt my luck change. I had to recoup my losses. I play a very sophisticated system that is inherently foolproof, but it takes time for the odds to shift in my favor."

Chief Sanderson glared at him until he looked away. "So he's a frustrated gambler. How does that get him in here—and out?"

I leaned against the edge of the dresser. "He ran out of cash long about dawn. He'd often met his bookie at the Dew Drop Inn, so he recognized Stormy—just as Cherri Lucinda recognized him that first day in the van."

"No, I didn't," said Cherri Lucinda. "The hairpiece had me fooled, too."

Estelle waggled a finger at her. "I saw you staring at him before we were halfway to the interstate."

"Well, I wasn't, so there's no point in arguing about it anymore."

"I think you should go on," Taylor added.

I agreed. "He learned about the missing money from the local news. Her behavior on the tour gave him a good idea where the money might be. He found a uniform in a linen closet, picked up a tray from room service set on the carpet by someone's door, and persuaded her to let him inside. She went ballistic and he ended up shoving her over the railing. Before he could leave, he heard Jim Bob and Cherri Lucinda come into the adjoining room. He stayed on the balcony for a few minutes. The scream from below must have been terrifying, but possibly not as much so as finding a dozen ladies in the hallway. Luckily, they were too distracted to notice him as he emerged, and assumed he had come from the service elevator to pick up a tray. Most of us would have leaped to that conclusion."

"It was an accident," Rex said. "She threatened to scream, so I did my best to keep my hand clamped on her mouth. She was a very strong young woman. I believe she intended to push me off the balcony, which means I acted in self-defense. It was very unfortunate. Had she simply given me the money—money that wasn't hers, in any case—none of this would have happened. I tried to tell her that we both would have been millionaires within a matter of hours. I have a foolproof system, you know, and my luck would have changed."

Nobody seemed impressed with his logic. After a

moment of silence, I said, "And now we're back to the bald man, garroted in the next room, and his colleague, shot earlier in this very room. Who tipped them off about the room numbers? Who was in the hotel when Stormy took three identical bags upstairs? Who could have supplied one of them with a hotel uniform?"

Mackenzie chuckled. "You just explained how Malanac found a uniform in a storage closet. For all I know, you have a uniform in your overnight bag."

"I don't have a list of room numbers," I said, "and maroon is not my color. Have you had transactions with these men in the past? Casinos have been known to launder drug money."

"Not here," he said in a surly voice.

"They piqued your interest with their questions about Stormy, didn't they? They expected your cooperation, but you decided you might just keep all the goodies for yourself. When the man with brown hair got too close, you barged into the room and shot him, claiming you were protecting your revered guests. Where did you come from, Mackenzie? Could it have been the next room? Did you find the bald man in the casino and tell him that you knew where the bag was?"

He eyed the distance to the door, but Chief Sanderson was blocking the potential path. "I'm not saying another word until I have a lawyer."

Japonica seemed to have forgiven me for past transgressions. "So where's the bag?"

"At the hospital," I said. "Mistakenly assuming it was Ruby Bee's, I took it to her earlier today. A few minutes ago I called Carlette and asked her to put it in a safe place overnight."

"Carlette? You told *her* where to find a bag with coke

and fifty thousand dollars? She just got out of prison three months ago for a drug conviction. She's probably three quarters of the way to Alabama by now." She brushed past her boss. "I'll go call the state police. Sweet Jesus, of all the people to tell . . ."

"Sorry," I called.

I'd never have nifty braids.

"Okay," boomed Brother Verber, "let's conga!"

The line formed behind him, with much snickering and good-natured pinching. Those sitting sedately at the bar stared as the line began to snake through the packed casino. The lyrics didn't make much sense, but it was impossible to ignore the ebullience of the performers.

" 'Violence and wickedness and extramarital affairs; with sluts that ain't your wife; yadeedahdeeyahdeedah and zionism; this is the sinful life! This is the sinful life!' "

Several men in gray suits grabbed their cell phones and commenced barking urgent demands. Unfortunately, the head of security was not in his office.

"B-twelve," Dahlia muttered over and over, as if this were a magic spell. "B-twelve."

Martha Hitebred sat down next to her, settled her purse on the floor, and began to get ready for the evening's entertainment. "Goodness gracious, Dahlia, you've got half the table covered."

"B-twelve."

"How much is the jackpot?"

Dahlia glowered at her. "Three thousand. Hush and let me concentrate. These cards are all that's left in the bank account."

The man calling the balls rattled off something that was not B-12. Dahlia pictured sweet Kevvie Junior and Rose Marie's little faces. She had to win for them so they'd have shoes in the winter and bicycles for Christmas (when the time came, anyway).

"B-twelve."

Her jaw dropped as she realized she herself had not said the magic words. She stared in disbelief at the board above the caller's head. B-12 gleamed like the star of Bethlehem.

"Bingo!" Dahlia screamed. "Bingo!"

"So," Ruby Bee said as she poured several teaspoons of sugar into a mug of coffee, "did you just run off and leave everybody in the lurch?"

"Hardly in the lurch," I said. "Japonica acknowledged that some weird local guy was responsible for the convenience-store robbery. The clerk recognized him despite the ski cap. When Jim Bob drags his sorry butt back, all the charges will be dropped and he'll be free to leave town. If he figures out that Mrs. Jim Bob is waiting, he may take his own sweet time. I would."

"Brother Verber ain't going to be in the mood to drive back anytime soon," Estelle said as she nibbled on a limp strip of bacon. "Mrs. Jim Bob went down the hall and banged on his door at seven this morning. When she came back, she said he was pea green and stank like a distillery. I don't think there were any converts in the casino last night." She put down the bacon. "I feel kinda bad about leaving Taylor. I talked to her in the lobby while I was waiting for you. She still hasn't laid eyes on Todd."

Ruby Bee sniffed. "I wouldn't feel so sorry for her,

Estelle. She tried to sound like she was high and mighty, but Cherri Lucinda told me that Taylor used to hang out at the Dew Drop Inn, trying to wheedle bikers into buying her beers. I wouldn't be surprised if this family farm consists of a couple of acres and a trailer."

"So that's who Cherri Lucinda was gaping at in the van," said Estelle. "Why didn't you tell me?"

"Hovering near death must have put it right out of my mind. I could almost hear the angels singing."

I put my arm around her and gave her a quick hug. "Don't ever scare me like that again," I said.

Estelle leaned across the table and caught Ruby Bee's hand. "Me neither. I was so worried I could scarcely eat a bite the entire time you were in the hospital. If something had happened to you, I don't believe I could have made myself go back to Maggody. It just wouldn't ever have been the same."

That was true, I thought as I gestured at the waitress to bring the check. "This one's on me," I said. "The fog should be clearing up soon, so we might as well get on the road."

Ruby Bee looked out the window. "I ain't so sure we shouldn't have another cup of coffee, Arly. We don't want to end up spinning our wheels in a muddy field. Another fifteen minutes . . ."

"What's wrong?" I said so shrilly that the other customers all turned to gape at me. "Is the pain back?"

She licked her lips, then turned to frown at me. "No, it's just that I thought for a second that I saw somebody out there. I couldn't make him out real well on account of the fog, but he looked . . . well, he looked sorta familiar. It couldn't have been . . . who I thought. I guess all that pain medicine has left me addled. The next thing

I know, I'll be seeing Raz Buchanon and his sow drive up and park next to that Cadillac."

"Let's hit the road for Maggody," I said brightly. "I could use some tranquillity and a grilled cheese sandwich."

"I swear, Arly Hanks," my mother said, "all you ever think about is food. What you need is to meet a nice young fellow and settle down."

I figured I'd hear about it all the way home.

There's More to Maggody Than Meets the Eye

Come visit the town of Maggody and its hilarious inhabitants on the Web.

www.Maggody.com

Raz Buchanon, Estelle Oppers, and Ruby Bee are waiting to show you around!

Visit the
Simon & Schuster Web site:

www.SimonSays.com

and sign up for our
mystery e-mail updates!

Keep up on the latest new releases,
author appearances, news, chats,
special offers, and more!
We'll deliver the information
right to your inbox—
if it's new, you'll know about it.

SIMON & SCHUSTER
A VIACOM COMPANY
www.SimonSays.com

2345

Praise for
Joan Hess

"Ms. Hess goes about things
with lively style."

—*New York Times
Book Review*

"Hess' low-key humor and bull's eye
dialogue are reason enough to read
anything she writes."

—*Publisher's Weekly*

"Hess is not only witty, but has a lot
of insight into human motivation."

—*Mystery News*

"[Hess'] well-paced and well-plotted
stories still delight."

—*Publisher's Weekly*